The Judge's House

House

And Other Weird Tales

Books by Bram Stoker

Novels

Crooken Sands
Dracula
Lady Athlyne
Miss Betty
The Jewel of Seven Stars
The Lady of the Shroud
The Lair of the White Worm (originally published
      in the United States as *The Garden of Evil*)
The Man from Shorrox's
The Man (also published as *The Gates of Life*)
The Mystery of the Sea
The Shoulder of Shasta
The Snake's Pass
The Watter's Mou

Collections

Dracula's Guest
Snowbound
Under the Sunset

Nonfiction

Sir Henry Irving and Miss Ellen Terry
A Glimpse of America
Famous Impostors
Personal Reminiscences of Henry Irving
The Duties of Clerks of Petty Sessions in Ireland

The Judge's House

And Other Weird Tales

BRAM STOKER

WILDSIDE PRESS
Doylestown, Pennsylvania

*The Judge's House
and Other Weird Tales*
A publication of
Wildside Press
P.O. Box 301
Holicong, PA 18928-0301

www.wildsidepress.com

Table of Contents

The Judge's House

When the time for his examination drew near Malcolm Malcolmson made up his mind to go somewhere to read by himself. He feared the attractions of the seaside, and also he feared completely rural isolation, for of old he knew its charms, and so he determined to find some unpretentious little town where there would be nothing to distract him. He refrained from asking suggestions from any of his friends, for he argued that each would recommend some place of which he had knowledge, and where he had already acquaintances. As Malcolmson wished to avoid friends he had no wish to encumber himself with the attention or friends' friends, and so he determined to look out for a place for himself. He packed a portmanteau with some clothes and all the books he required, and then took ticket for the first name on the local time-table which he did not know.

When at the end of three hours' journey he alighted at Benchurch, he felt satisfied that he had so far obliterated his tracks as to be sure of having a peaceful opportunity of pursuing his studies. He went straight to the one inn which the sleepy little place contained, and put up for the night. Benchurch was a market town, and once in three weeks was crowded to excess, but for the remainder of the twenty-one days it was as attractive as a desert. Malcolmson looked around the day after his arrival to try to find quarters more isolated than even so quiet an inn as "The Good Traveler" afforded. There was only one place which took his fancy, and it certainly satisfied his wildest ideas regarding quiet; in fact, quiet was not the proper word to apply to it – desolation was the only term conveying any suitable idea of its isolation. It was an old rambling, heavy-built house of the Jacobean style, with heavy gables and windows, unusually small, and set higher than was customary in such houses, and was surrounded with a high brick wall massively built. Indeed, on examination, it looked more like a fortified house than an ordinary dwelling. But all these things pleased Malcolmson. "Here," he thought, "is the very spot I have been looking for, and if I can only get opportunity of using it I shall be happy." His joy was increased when he realized beyond doubt that it was not at present inhabited.

From the post office he got the name of the agent, who was rarely surprised at the application to rent a part of the old house. Mr. Carnford, the local lawyer and agent, was a genial old gentleman, and frankly confessed his delight at anyone being willing to live in the house.

"To tell you the truth," said he, "I should be only too happy, on behalf of the owners, to let anyone have the house rent free for a term of years if only to accustom the people here to see it inhabited. It has been so long empty that some kind of absurd prejudice has grown up about it, and this can be best put down by its occupation — if only," he added with a sly glance at Malcomson, "by a scholar like yourself, who wants its quiet for a time."

Malcolmson thought it needless to ask the agent about the "absurd prejudice"; he knew he would get more information, if he should require it, on that subject from other quarters. He paid his three months' rent, got a receipt, and the name of an old woman who would probably undertake to "do" for him, and came away with the keys in his pocket. He then went to the landlady of the inn, who was a cheerful and most kindly person, and asked her advice as to such stores and provisions as he would be likely to require. She threw up her hands in amazement when he told her where he was going to settle himself.

"Not in the Judge's House!" she said, and grew pale as she spoke. He explained the locality of the house, saying that he did not know its name. When he had finished she answered:

"Aye, sure enough — sure enough the very place! It is the Judge's House sure enough." He asked her to tell him about the place, why so called, and what there was against it. She told him that it was so called locally because it had been many years before — how long she could not say, as she was herself from another part of the country, but she thought it must have been a hundred years or more — the abode of a judge who was held in great terror on account of his harsh sentences and his hostility to prisoners at Assizes. As to what there was against the house itself she could not tell. She had often asked, but no one could inform her; but there was a general feeling that there was something, and for her own part she would not take all the money in Drinkwater's Bank and stay in the house an hour by herself. Then she apologized to Malcolmson for her disturbing talk.

"It is too bad of me, sir, and you — and a young gentleman, too — if you will pardon me saying it, going to live there all alone. If you were my boy — and you'll excuse me for saying it — you wouldn't sleep there a night, not if I had to go there myself and pull the big alarm bell that's on the roof!" The good creature was so manifestly in earnest, and was so kindly in her intentions, that Malcolmson, although amused, was touched. He told her kindly how much he appreciated her interest in him, and added:

"But, my dear Mrs. Witham, indeed you need not be concerned about me! A man who is reading for the Mathematical Tripos has too much to think of to be disturbed by any of these mysterious 'somethings,' and his work is of too exact and prosaic a kind to allow of his having any corner in his mind for mysteries of any kind. Harmonical Progression, Permutations and Combinations, and Elliptic Functions have sufficient mysteries for me!" Mrs. Witham kindly undertook to see after his commissions, and he went himself to look for the old woman who had been recommended to him. When he returned to the Judge's House with her, after an interval of a couple of hours, he found Mrs. Witham herself waiting with several men and boys carrying parcels, and an upholsterer's man with a bed in a cart, for she said, though tables and chairs might be all very well, a bed that hadn't been aired for mayhap fifty years was not proper for young bones to lie on. She was evidently curious to see the inside of the house; and though manifestly so afraid of the 'somethings' that at the slightest sound she clutched on to Malcolmson, whom she never left for a moment, went over the whole place.

After his examination of the house, Malcolmson decided to take up his abode in the great dining room, which was big enough to serve for all his requirements; and Mrs. Witham, with the aid of the charwoman, Mrs. Dempster, proceeded to arrange matters. When the hampers were brought in and unpacked, Malcolmson saw that with much kind forethought she had sent from her own kitchen sufficient provisions to last for a few days. Before going she expressed all sorts of kind wishes; and at the door turned and said:

"And perhaps, sir, as the room is big and draughty it might be well to have one of those big screens put round your bed at night — though, truth to tell, I would die myself if I were to be so shut in with all kinds of — of 'things,' that put their heads round the sides, or over the top, and look on me!" The image which she had called up was too much for her nerves, and she fled incontinently.

Mrs. Dempster sniffed in a superior manner as the landlady disappeared, and remarked that for her own part she wasn't afraid of all the bogies in the kingdom.

"I'll tell you what it is, sir," she said; "bogies is all kinds and sorts of things — except bogies! Rats and mice, and beetles; and creaky doors, and loose slates, and broken panes, and stiff drawer handles, that stay out when you pull them and then fall down in the middle of the night. Look at the wainscot of the room! It is old — hundreds of years old! Do you think there's no rats and beetles there! And do you imagine, sir, that you won't see none of them! Rats is bogies, I tell you, and bogies is rats; and don't you get to think anything else!"

"Mrs. Dempster," said Malcolmson gravely, making her a polite bow, "you know more than a Senior Wrangler! And let me say, that, as a mark of esteem for your indubitable soundness of head and heart, I shall, when I go, give you possession of this house, and let you stay here by yourself for the last two months of my tenancy, for four weeks will serve my purpose."

"Thank you kindly, sir!" she answered, "but I couldn't sleep away from home a night. I am in Greenhow's Charity, and if I slept a night away from my rooms I should lose all I have got to live on. The rules is very strict; and there's too many watching for a vacancy for me to run any risks in the matter. Only for that, sir, I'd gladly come here and attend on you altogether during your stay."

"My good woman," said Malcolmson hastily, "I have come here on purpose to obtain solitude; and believe me that I am grateful to the late Greenhow for having so organized his admirable charity — whatever it is — that I am perforce denied the opportunity of suffering from such a form of temptation! Saint Anthony himself could not be more rigid on the point!"

The old woman laughed harshly. "Ah, you young gentlemen," she said, "you don't fear for naught; and belike you'll get all the solitude you want here." She set to work with her cleaning; and by nightfall, when Malcolmson returned from his walk — he always had one of his books to study as he walked — he found the room swept and tidied, a fire burning in the old hearth, the lamp lit, and the table spread for supper with Mrs. Witham's excellent fare. "This is comfort, indeed," he said, as he rubbed his hands.

When he had finished his supper, and lifted the tray to the other end of the great oak dining-table, he got out his books again, put fresh wood on the fire, trimmed his lamp, and set himself down to a spell of real hard work. He went on without pause till about eleven o'clock, when he knocked off for a bit to fix his fire and lamp, and to make himself a cup of tea. He had always been a tea-drinker, and during his college life had sat late at work and had taken tea late. The rest was a great luxury to him, and he enjoyed it with a sense of delicious, voluptuous ease. The renewed fire leaped and sparkled, and threw quaint shadows through the great old room; and as he sipped his hot tea he reveled in the sense of isolation from his kind. Then it was that he began to notice for the first time what a noise the rats were making.

"Surely," he thought, "they cannot have been at it all the time I was reading. Had they been. I must have noticed it!" Presently, when the noise increased, he satisfied himself that it was really new. It was evident that at first the rats had been frightened at the presence of a stranger, and the light of fire and lamp; but that as the time went on they had grown bolder and were now disporting themselves as was their wont.

How busy they were! and hark to the strange noises! Up and down behind the old wainscot, over the ceiling and under the floor they raced, and gnawed, and scratched! Malcolmson smiled to himself as he recalled to mind the saying of Mrs. Dempster, "Bogies is rats, and rats is bogies!" The tea began to have its effect of intellectual and nervous stimulus, he saw with joy another long spell of work to be done before the night was past, and in the sense of security which it gave him, he allowed himself the luxury of a good look round the room. He took his lamp in one hand, and went all around, wondering that so quaint and beautiful an old house had been so long neglected. The carving of the oak on the panels of the wainscot was fine, and on and round the doors and windows it was beautiful and of rare merit. There were some old pictures on the walls, but they were coated so thick with dust and dirt that he could not distinguish any detail of them, though he held his lamp as high as he could over his head. Here and there as he went round he saw some crack or hole blocked for a moment by the face of a rat with its bright eyes glittering in the light, but in an instant it was gone, and a squeak and a scamper followed.

The thing that most struck him, however, was the rope of the great alarm bell on the roof, which hung down in a corner of the room on the right-hand side of the fireplace. He pulled up close to the hearth a great high-backed carved oak chair, and sat down to his last cup of tea. When this was done he made up the fire, and went back to his work, sitting at the corner of the table, having the fire to his left. For a while the rats disturbed him somewhat with their perpetual scampering, but he got accustomed to the noise as one does to the ticking of a clock or to the roar of moving water; and he became so immersed in his work that everything in the world, except the problem which he was trying to solve, passed away from him.

He suddenly looked up, his problem was still unsolved, and there was in the air that sense of the hour before the dawn, which is so dread to doubtful life. The noise of the rats had ceased. Indeed it seemed to him that it must have ceased but lately and that it was the sudden cessation which had disturbed him. The fire had fallen low, but still it threw out a deep red glow. As he looked he started in spite of his sangfroid.

There on the great high-backed carved oak chair by the right side of the fireplace sat an enormous rat, steadily glaring at him with baleful eyes. He made a motion to it as though to hunt it away, but it did not stir. Then he made the motion of throwing something. Still it did not stir, but showed its great white teeth angrily, and its cruel eyes shone in the lamplight with an added vindictiveness.

Malcolmson felt amazed, and seizing the poker from the hearth ran at it to kill it. Before, however, he could strike it, the rat, with a squeak that sounded like the concentration of hate, jumped upon the floor, and, running up the rope of the alarm bell, disappeared in the darkness beyond the range of the green-shaded lamp. Instantly, strange to say, the noisy scampering of the rats in the wainscot began again.

By this time Malcolmson's mind was quite off the problem; and as a shrill cock-crow outside told him of the approach of morning, he went to bed and to sleep.

He slept so sound that he was not even waked by Mrs. Dempster coming in to make up his room. It was only when she had tidied up the place and got his breakfast ready and tapped on the screen which closed in his bed that he woke. He was a little tired still after his night's hard work, but a strong cup of tea soon freshened him up, and, taking his book, he went out for his morning walk, bringing with him a few sandwiches lest he should not care to return till dinner time. He found a quiet walk between high elms some way outside the town, and here he spent the greater part of the day studying his Laplace. On his return he looked in to see Mrs. Witham and to thank her for her kindness. When she saw him coming through the diamond-paned bay-window of her sanctum she came out to meet him and asked him in. She looked at him searchingly and shook her head as she said:

"You must not overdo it, sir. You are paler this morning than you should be. Too late hours and too hard work on the brain isn't good for any man! But tell me, sir, how did you pass the night? Well, I hope? But, my heart! sir, I was glad when Mrs. Dempster told me this morning that you were all right and sleeping sound when she went in."

"Oh, I was all right," he answered, smiling, "the 'some-things' didn't worry me, as yet. Only the rats; and they had a circus, I tell you, all over the place. There was one wicked looking old devil that sat up on my own chair by the fire, and wouldn't go till I took the poker to him, and then he ran up the rope of the alarm bell and got to somewhere up the wall or the ceiling — I couldn't see where, it was so dark."

"Mercy on us," said Mrs. Witham, "an old devil, and sitting on a chair by the fireside! Take care, sir! take care! There's many a true word spoken in jest."

"How do you mean? 'Pon my word I don't understand."

"An old devil! The old devil, perhaps. There! sir, you needn't laugh," for Malcolmson had broken into a hearty peal. "You young folks thinks it easy to laugh at things that makes older ones shudder. Never mind, sir! never mind! Please God, you'll laugh all the time. It's what I wish you myself!" and the good lady beamed all over in sympathy with his enjoyment, her fears gone for a moment.

"Oh, forgive me!" said Malcolmson presently. "Don't think me rude; but the idea was too much for me — that the old devil himself was on the chair last night!" And at the thought he laughed again. Then he went home to dinner.

This evening the scampering of the rats began earlier; indeed it had been going on before his arrival, and only ceased whilst his presence by its freshness disturbed them. After dinner he sat by the fire for a while and had a smoke; and then, having cleared his table, began to work as before. Tonight the rats disturbed him more than they had done on the previous night. How they scampered up and down and under and over! How they squeaked, and scratched, and gnawed! How they, getting bolder by degrees, came to the mouths of their holes and to the chinks and cracks and crannies in the wainscoting till their eyes shone like tiny lamps as the firelight rose and fell. But to him, now doubtless accustomed to them, their eyes were not wicked; only their playfulness touched him. Sometimes the boldest of them made sallies out on the floor or along the moldings of the wainscot. Now and again as they disturbed him Malcolmson made a sound to frighten them, smiting the table with his hand or giving a fierce "Hsh, hsh," so that they fled straightway to their holes.

And so the early part of the night wore on; and despite the noise Malcolmson got more and more immersed in his work.

All at once he stopped, as on the previous night, being overcome by a sudden sense of silence. There was not the faintest sound of gnaw, or scratch, or squeak. The silence was as of the grave. He remembered the odd occurrence of the previous night, and instinctively he looked at the chair standing close by the fireside. And then a very odd sensation thrilled through him.

There, on the great old high-backed carved oak chair beside the fireplace sat the same enormous rat, steadily glaring at him with baleful eyes.

Instinctively he took the nearest thing to his hand, a book of logarithms, and flung it at it. The book was badly aimed and the rat did not stir, so again the poker performance of the previous night was repeated; and again the rat, being closely pursued, fled up the rope of the alarm bell. Strangely too, the departure of this rat was instantly followed by the renewal of the noise made by the general rat community. On this occasion, as on the previous one, Malcolmson could not see at what part of the room the rat disappeared, for the green shade of his lamp left the upper part of the room in darkness, and the fire had burned low.

On looking at his watch he found it was close on midnight; and, not sorry for the divertissement, he made up his fire and made himself his nightly pot of tea. He had got through a good spell of work, and thought himself entitled to a cigarette; and so he sat on the great carved oak chair before the fire and enjoyed it. Whilst smoking he began to think that he would like to know where the rat disappeared to, for he had certain ideas for the morrow not entirely disconnected with a rat-trap. Accordingly he lit another lamp and placed it so that it would shine well into the right-hand corner of the wall by the fireplace. Then he got all the books he had with him, and placed them handy to throw at the vermin. Finally he lifted the rope of the alarm bell and placed the end of it on the table, fixing the extreme end under the lamp. As he handled it he could not help noticing how pliable it was, especially for so strong a rope, and one not in use. "You could hang a man with it," he thought to himself. When his preparations were made he looked around, and said complacently:

"There now, my friend, I think we shall learn something of you this time!" He began his work again, and though as before somewhat disturbed at first by the noise of the rats, soon lost himself in his propositions and problems.

Again he was called to his immediate surroundings suddenly. This time it might not have been the sudden silence only which took his attention; there was a slight movement of the rope, and the lamp moved. Without stirring, he looked to see if his pile of books was within range, and then cast his eye along the rope. As he looked he saw the great rat drop from the rope on the oak armchair and sit there glaring at him. He raised a book in his right hand, and taking careful aim, flung it at the rat. The latter, with a quick movement, sprang aside and dodged the missile. He then took another book, and a third, and flung them one after another at the rat, but each time unsuccessfully. At last, as he stood with a book poised in his hand to throw, the rat squeaked and seemed afraid. This made Malcolmson more than ever eager to strike, and the book flew and struck the rat a resounding blow. It gave a terrified squeak, and turning on its pursuer a look of terrible malevolence, ran up the chair-back and made a great jump to the rope of the alarm bell and ran up it like lightning. The lamp rocked under the sudden strain, but it was a heavy one and did not topple over. Malcolmson kept his eyes on the rat, and saw it by the light of the second lamp leap to a molding of the wainscot and disappear through a hole in one of the great pictures which hung on the wall, obscured and invisible through its coating of dirt and dust.

"I shall look up my friend's habitation in the morning," said the student, as he went over to collect his books. "The third picture from the fireplace; I shall not forget." He picked up the books one by one, commenting on them as he lifted them. "Conic Sections he does not mind, nor Cycloidal Oscillations, nor the Principia, nor Quaternions, nor Thermodynamics. Now for the book that fetched him!" Malcolmson took it up and looked at it. As he did so he started, and a sudden pallor overspread his face. He looked round uneasily and shivered slightly, as he murmured to himself:

"The Bible my mother gave me! What an odd coincidence." He sat down to work again, and the rats in the wainscot renewed their gambols. They did not disturb him, however; somehow their presence gave him a sense of companionship. But he could not attend to his work, and after striving to master the subject on which he was engaged gave it up in despair, and went to bed as the first streak of dawn stole in through the eastern window.

He slept heavily but uneasily, and dreamed much; and when Mrs. Dempster woke him late in the morning he seemed ill at ease, and for a few minutes did not seem to realize exactly where he was. His first request rather surprised the servant.

"Mrs. Dempster, when I am out today I wish you would get the steps and dust or wash those pictures — specially that one the third from the fireplace — I want to see what they are." Late in the afternoon Malcolmson worked at his books in the shaded walk, and the cheerfulness of the previous day came back to him as the day wore on, and he found that his reading was progressing well. He had worked out to a satisfactory conclusion all the problems which had as yet baffled him, and it was in a state of jubilation that he paid a visit to Mrs. Witham at "The Good Traveler." He found a stranger in the cozy sitting room with the landlady, who was introduced to him as Dr. Thornhill. She was not quite at ease, and this, combined with the Doctor's plunging at once into a series of questions, made Malcolmson come to the conclusion that his presence was not an accident, so without preliminary he said:

"Dr. Thornhill, I shall with pleasure answer you any question you may choose to ask me if you will answer me one question first."

The Doctor seemed surprised, but he smiled and answered at once. "Done! What is it?"

"Did Mrs. Witham ask you to come here and see me and advise me?"

Dr. Thornhill for a moment was taken aback, and Mrs.

Witham got fiery red and turned away; but the doctor was a frank and ready man, and he answered at once and openly:

"She did: but she didn't intend you to know it. I suppose it was my clumsy haste that made you suspect. She told me that she did not like the idea of your being in that house all by yourself, and that she thought you took too much strong tea. In fact, she wants me to advise you if possible to give up the tea and the very late hours. I was a keen student in my time, so I suppose I may take the liberty of a college man, and without offence, advise you not quite as a stranger."

Malcolmson with a bright smile held out his hand. "Shake! as they say in America," he said. "I must thank you for your kindness and Mrs. Witham too, and your kindness deserves a return on my part. I promise to take no more strong tea — no tea at all till you let me — and I shall go to bed tonight at one o'clock at latest. Will that do?"

"Capital," said the Doctor. "Now tell us all that you noticed in the old house," and so Malcolmson then and there told in minute detail all that had happened in the last two nights. He was interrupted every now and then by some exclamation from Mrs. Witham, till finally when he told of the episode of the Bible the landlady's pent-up emotions found vent in a shriek; and it was not till a stiff glass of brandy and water had been administered that she grew composed again. Dr. Thornhill listened with a face of growing gravity, and when the narrative was complete and Mrs. Witham had been restored he asked:

"The rat always went up the rope of the alarm bell?"

"Always."

"I suppose you know," said the Doctor after a pause, "what the rope is?"

"No!"

"It is," said the Doctor slowly, "the very rope which the hangman used for all the victims of the Judge's judicial rancor!" Here he was interrupted by another scream from Mrs. Witham, and steps had to be taken for her recovery. Malcolmson having looked at his watch, and found that it was close to his dinner hour, had gone home before her complete recovery.

When Mrs. Witham was herself again she almost assailed

the Doctor with angry questions as to what he meant by putting such horrible ideas into the poor young man's mind. "He has quite enough there already to upset him," she added. Dr. Thornhill replied:

"My dear madam, I had a distinct purpose in it! I wanted to draw his attention to the bell rope, and to fix it there. It may be that he is in a highly overwrought state, and has been studying too much, although I am bound to say that he seems as sound and healthy a young man, mentally and bodily, as ever I saw — but then the rats — and that suggestion of the devil." The doctor shook his head and went on. "I would have offered to go and stay the first night with him but that I felt sure it would have been a cause of offence. He may get in the night some strange fright or hallucination; and if he does I want him to pull that rope. All alone as he is it will give us warning, and we may reach him in time to be of service. I shall be sitting up pretty late tonight and shall keep my ears open. Do not be alarmed if Benchurch gets a surprise before morning."

"Oh, Doctor, what do you mean? What do you mean?"

"I mean this; that possibly — nay, more probably — we shall hear the great alarm bell from the Judge's House tonight," and the Doctor made about as effective an exit as could be thought of.

When Malcolmson arrived home he found that it was a little after his usual time, and Mrs. Dempster had gone away — the rules of Greenhow's Charity were not to be neglected. He was glad to see that the place was bright and tidy with a cheerful fire and a well-trimmed lamp. The evening was colder than might have been expected in April, and a heavy wind was blowing with such rapidly-increasing strength that there was every promise of a storm during the night. For a few minutes after his entrance the noise of the rats ceased; but so soon as they became accustomed to his presence they began again. He was glad to hear them, for he felt once more the feeling of companionship in their noise, and his mind ran back to the strange fact that they only ceased to manifest themselves when that other — the great rat with the baleful eyes — came upon the scene. The reading-lamp only was lit and its green shade kept the ceiling and the upper part of the room in darkness, so that the cheerful light from the hearth spreading over the floor and shining on the white cloth laid over the end of the table was warm and cheery. Malcolmson sat down to his dinner with a good appetite and a buoyant spirit. After his dinner and a cigarette he sat steadily down to work, determined not to let anything disturb him, for he remembered his promise to the doctor, and made up his mind to make the best of the time at his disposal.

For an hour or so he worked all right, and then his thoughts began to wander from his books. The actual circumstances around him, the calls on his physical attention, and his nervous susceptibility were not to be denied. By this time the wind had become a gale, and the gale a storm. The old house, solid though it was, seemed to shake to its foundations, and the storm roared and raged through its many chimneys and its queer old gables, producing strange, unearthly sounds in the empty rooms and corridors. Even the great alarm bell on the roof must have felt the force of the wind, for the rope rose and fell slightly, as though the bell were moved a little from time to time, and the limber rope fell on the oak floor with a hard and hollow sound.

As Malcolmson listened to it he bethought himself of the doctor's words, "It is the rope which the hangman used for the victims of the Judge's judicial rancor," and he went over to the corner of the fireplace and took it in his hand to look at it. There seemed a sort of deadly interest in it, and as he stood there he lost himself for a moment in speculation as to who these victims were, and the grim wish of the Judge to have such a ghastly relic ever under his eyes. As he stood there the swaying of the bell on the roof still lifted the rope now and again; but presently there came a new sensation — a sort of tremor in the rope, as though something was moving along it.

Looking up instinctively Malcolmson saw the great rat coming slowly down towards him, glaring at him steadily. He dropped the rope and started back with a muttered curse, and the rat turning ran up the rope again and disappeared, and at the same instant Malcolmson became conscious that the noise of the rats, which had ceased for a while, began again.

All this set him thinking, and it occurred to him that he had not investigated the lair of the rat or looked at the pictures, as he had intended. He lit the other lamp without the shade, and, holding it up, went and stood opposite the third picture from the fireplace on the right-hand side where he had seen the rat disappear on the previous night.

At the first glance he started back so suddenly that he almost dropped the lamp, and a deadly pallor overspread his face. His knees shook, and heavy drops of sweat came on his forehead, and he trembled like an aspen. But he was young and plucky, and pulled himself together, and after the pause of a few seconds stepped forward again, raised the lamp, and examined the picture which had been dusted and washed, and now stood out clearly.

It was of a judge dressed in his robes of scarlet and ermine. His face was strong and merciless, evil, crafty, and vindictive, with a sensual mouth, hooked nose of ruddy color, and shaped like the beak of a bird of prey. The rest of the face was of a cadaverous color. The eyes were of peculiar brilliance and with a terribly malignant expression. As he looked at them, Malcolmson grew cold, for he saw there the very counterpart of the eyes of the great rat. The lamp almost fell from his hand, he saw the rat with its baleful eyes peering out through the hole in the corner of the picture, and noted the sudden cessation of the noise of the other rats. However, he pulled himself together, and went on with his examination of the picture.

The Judge was seated in a great high-backed carved oak chair, on the right-hand side of a great stone fireplace where, in the corner, a rope hung down from the ceiling, its end lying coiled on the floor. With a feeling of something like horror, Malcolmson recognized the scene of the room as it stood, and gazed around him in an awe-struck manner as though he expected to find some strange presence behind him. Then he looked over to the corner of the fireplace – and with a loud cry he let the lamp fall from his hand.

There, in the Judge's armchair, with the rope hanging behind, sat the rat with the Judge's baleful eyes, now intensified and with a fiendish leer. Save for the howling of the storm without there was silence.

The fallen lamp recalled Malcolmson to himself. Fortunately it was of metal, and so the oil was not spilt. However, the practical need of attending to it settled at once his nervous apprehensions. When he had turned it out, he wiped his brow and thought for a moment.

"This will not do," he said to himself. "If I go on like this I shall become a crazy fool. This must stop! I promised the Doctor I would not take tea. Faith, he was pretty right! My nerves must have been getting into a queer state. Funny I did not notice it. I never felt better in my life. However, it is all right now, and I shall not be such a fool again."

Then he mixed himself a good stiff glass of brandy and water and resolutely sat down to his work.

It was nearly an hour when he looked up from his book, disturbed by the sudden stillness. Without, the wind howled and roared louder than ever, and the rain drove in sheets against the windows, beating like hail on the glass; but within there was no sound whatever save the echo of the wind as it roared in the great chimney, and now and then a hiss as a few raindrops found their way down the chimney in a lull of the storm. The fire had fallen low and had ceased to flame, though it threw out a red glow. Malcolmson listened attentively, and presently heard a thin, squeaking noise, very faint. It came from the corner of the room where the rope hung down, and he thought it was the creaking of the rope on the floor as the swaying of the bell raised and lowered it. Looking up, however, he saw in the dim light the great rat clinging to the rope and gnawing it. The rope was already nearly gnawed through — he could see the lighter color where the strands were laid bare. As he looked the job was completed, and the severed end of the rope fell clattering on the oaken floor, whilst for an instant the great rat remained like a knob or tassel at the end of the rope, which now began to sway to and fro. Malcolmson felt for a moment another pang of terror as he thought that now the possibility of calling the outer world to his assistance was cut off, but an intense anger took its place, and seizing the book he was reading he hurled it at the rat. The blow was well aimed, but before the missile could reach it the rat dropped off and struck the floor with a soft thud. Malcolmson instantly rushed over towards it, but it darted away and disappeared in the darkness of the shadows of the room. Malcolmson felt that his work was over for the night, and determined then and there to vary the monotony of the proceedings by a hunt for the rat, and took off the green shade of the lamp so as to insure a wider spreading light. As he did so the gloom of the upper part of the room was relieved, and in the new flood of light, great by comparison with the previous darkness, the pictures on the wall stood out boldly. From where he stood, Malcolmson saw right opposite to him the third picture on the wall from the right of the fireplace. He rubbed his eyes in surprise, and then a great fear began to come upon him.

In the center of the picture was a great irregular patch of brown canvas, as fresh as when it was stretched on the frame. The background was as before, with chair and chimney-corner and rope, but the figure of the Judge had disappeared.

Malcolmson, almost in a chill of horror, turned slowly round, and then he began to shake and tremble like a man in a palsy. His strength seemed to have left him, and he was incapable of action or movement, hardly even of thought. He could only see and hear.

There, on the great high-backed carved oak chair sat the Judge in his robes of scarlet and ermine, with his baleful eyes glaring vindictively, and a smile of triumph on the resolute, cruel mouth, as he lifted with his hands a black cap. Malcolmson felt as if the blood was running from his heart, as one does in moments of prolonged suspense. There was a singing in his ears. Without, he could hear the roar and howl of the tempest, and through it, swept on the storm, came the striking of midnight by the great chimes in the market place. He stood for a space of time that seemed to him endless, still as a statue and with wide-open, horror-struck eyes, breathless. As the clock struck, so the smile of triumph on the Judge's face intensified, and at the last stroke of midnight he placed the black cap on his head.

Slowly and deliberately the Judge rose from his chair and picked up the piece of the rope of the alarm bell which lay on the floor, drew it through his hands as if he enjoyed its touch, and then deliberately began to knot one end of it, fashioning it into a noose. This he tightened and tested with his foot, pulling hard at it till he was satisfied and then making a running noose of it, which he held in his hand. Then he began to move along the table on the opposite side to Malcolmson, keeping his eyes on him until he had passed him, when with a quick movement he stood in front of the door. Malcolmson then began to feel that he was trapped, and tried to think of what he should do. There was some fascination in the Judge's eyes, which he never took off him, and he had, perforce, to look. He saw the Judge approach — still keeping between him and the door — and raise the noose and throw it towards him as if to entangle him. With a great effort he made a quick movement to one side, and saw the rope fall beside him, and heard it strike the oaken floor. Again the Judge raised the noose and tried to ensnare him, ever keeping his baleful eyes fixed on him, and each time by a mighty effort the student just managed to evade it. So this went on for many times, the Judge seeming never discouraged nor discomposed at failure, but playing as a cat does with a mouse. At last in despair, which had reached its climax, Malcolmson cast a quick glance round him. The lamp seemed to have blazed up, and there was a fairly good light in the room. At the many rat-holes and in the chinks and crannies of the wainscot he saw the rats' eyes; and this aspect, that was purely physical, gave him a gleam of comfort. He looked around and saw that the rope of the great alarm bell was laden with rats. Every inch of it was covered with them, and more and more were pouring through the small circular hole in the ceiling whence it emerged, so that with their weight the bell was beginning to sway.

Hark! it had swayed till the clapper had touched the bell. The sound was but a tiny one, but the bell was only beginning to sway, and it would increase.

At the sound the Judge, who had been keeping his eyes fixed on Malcolmson, looked up, and a scowl of diabolical anger overspread his face. His eyes fairly glowed like hot coals, and he stamped his foot with a sound that seemed to make the house shake. A dreadful peal of thunder broke overhead as he raised the rope again, whilst the rats kept running up and down the rope as though working against time. This time, instead of throwing it, he drew close to his victim, and held open the noose as he approached. As he came closer there seemed something paralyzing in his very presence, and Malcolmson stood rigid as a corpse. He felt the Judge's icy fingers touch his throat as he adjusted the rope. The noose tightened — tightened. Then the Judge, taking the rigid form of the student in his arms, carried him over and placed him standing in the oak chair, and stepping up beside him, put his hand up and caught the end of the swaying rope of the alarm bell. As he raised his hand the rats fled squeaking, and disappeared through the hole in the ceiling. Taking the end of the noose which was round Malcolmson's neck he tied it to the hanging bell-rope, and then descending pulled away the chair.

*W*hen the alarm bell of the Judge's House began to sound a crowd soon assembled. Lights and torches of various kinds appeared, and soon a silent crowd was hurrying to the spot. They knocked loudly at the door, but there was no reply. Then they burst in the door, and poured into the great dining room, the doctor at the head.

There at the end of the rope of the great alarm bell hung the body of the student, and on the face of the Judge in the picture was a malignant smile.

Bridal of Dead*

*T*he time wore away, wondrous slowly in some ways, wonderfully quickly in others. Today, in the new-found joyous certainty of the return of my love, I should have liked to have had Margaret all to myself. But this day was not for love or for love-making. The shadow of fearful expectation was over it. The more I thought over the coming experiment, the more strange it all seemed; and the more foolish were we who were deliberately entering upon it. It was all so stupendous, so mysterious, so unnecessary! The issues were so vast; the danger so strange, so unknown. Even if it should be successful, what new difficulties would it not raise. What changes might happen, did men know that the portals of the House of Death were not in very truth eternally fixed; and that the Dead could come forth again! Could we realize what it was for us modern mortals to be arrayed against the Gods of Old, with their mysterious powers gotten from natural forces, or begotten of them when the world was young. When land and water were forming themselves from out the primeval slime. When the very air was purifying itself from elemental dross. When the "dragons of the prime" were changing their forms and their powers, made only to combat with geologic forces, to grow in accord with the new vegetable life which was springing up around them. When animals, when even man himself and man's advance were growths as natural as the planetary movements, growths as natural as the planetary movements, or the shining of the stars. Aye! and further back

---

* Also published as "Chapter XVI, Powers – Old and New" in the 1903 first edition of *The Jewel of the Seven Stars.*

still, when as yet the Spirit which moved on the face of the waters had not spoken the words commanding to come into existence Light and the Life which followed it.

Nay, even beyond this was a still more overwhelming conjecture. The whole possibility of the Great Experiment to which we were now pledged was based on the reality of the existence of the Old Forces which seemed to be coming in contact with the New Civilization. That there were, and are, such cosmic forces we cannot doubt, and that the Intelligence, which is behind them, was and is. Were those primal and elemental forces controlled at any time by other than that Final Cause which Christendom holds as its very essence? If there were truth at all in the belief of Ancient Egypt then their Gods had real existence, real power, real force. Godhead is not a quality subject to the ills of mortals: as in its essence it is creative and recreative, it cannot die. Any belief to the contrary would be antagonistic to reason; for it would hold that a part is greater than the whole. If then the Old Gods held their forces, wherein was the supremacy of the new? Of course, if the Old Gods had lost their power, or if they never had any, the Experiment could not succeed. But if it should indeed succeed, or if there were a possibility of success, then we should be face to face with an inference so overwhelming that one hardly dared to follow it to its conclusion. This would be: that the struggle between Life and Death would no longer be a matter of the earth, earthy; that the war of supra-elemental forces would be moved from the tangible world of facts to the Mid-Region, wherever it may be, which is the home of the Gods. Did such a region exist? What was it that Milton saw with his blind eyes in the rays of poetic light falling between him and Heaven? Whence came that stupendous vision of the Evangelist which has for eighteen centuries held spellbound the intelligence of Christendom? Was there room in the Universe for opposing Gods; or if such there were, would the stronger allow manifestations of power on the part of the opposing Force which would tend to the weakening of His own teaching and designs? Surely, surely if this supposition were correct there would be some strange and awful development — something unexpected and unpredictable — before the end should be allowed to come. . . !

The subject was too vast and, under the present conditions, too full of strange surmises. I dared not follow it! I set myself to wait in patience till the time should come.

Margaret remained divinely calm. I think I envied her, even whilst I admired and loved her for it. Mr. Trelawny was nervously anxious, as indeed were the other men. With him it took the form of movement; movement both of body and mind. In both respects he was restless, going from one place to another with or without a cause, or even a pretext; and changing from one subject of thought to another. Now and again he would show glimpses of the harrowing anxiety which filled him, by his manifest expectation of finding a similar condition in myself. He would be ever explaining things. And in his explanations I could see the way in which he was turning over in his mind all the phenomena; all the possible causes; all the possible results. Once, in the midst of a most learned dissertation on the growth of Egyptian Astrology, he broke out on a different subject, or rather a branch or corollary of the same:

"I do not see why starlight may not have some subtle quality of its own! We know that other lights have special forces. The Rontgen Ray is not the only discovery to be made in the world of light. Sunlight has its own forces, that are not given to other lights. It warms wine; it quickens fungoid growth. Men are often moonstruck. Why not, then, a more subtle, if less active or powerful, force in the light of the stars. It should be a pure light coming through such vastness of space, and may have a quality which a pure, unimpulsive force may have. The time may not be far off when Astrology shall be accepted on a scientific basis. In the recrudescence of the art, many new experiences will be brought to bear; many new phases of old wisdom will appear in the light of fresh discovery, and afford bases for new reasoning. Men may find that what seemed empiric deductions were in reality the results of a loftier intelligence and a learning greater than our own. We know already that the whole of the living world is full of microbes of varying powers and of methods of working quite antagonistic. We do not know yet whether they can lie latent until quickened by some ray of light as yet unidentified as a separate and peculiar force. As yet we know nothing of what

goes to create or evoke the active spark of life. We have no
knowledge of the methods of conception; of the laws which
govern molecular or fetal growth, of the final influences
which attend birth. Year by year, day by day, hour by hour,
we are learning; but the end is far, far off. It seems to me that
we are now in that stage of intellectual progress in which the
rough machinery for making discovery is being invented.
Later on, we shall have enough of first principles to help us
in the development of equipment for the true study of the
inwardness of things. Then we may perhaps arrive at the
perfection of means to an end which the scholars of Old Nile
achieved at a time when Methuselah was beginning to brag
about the number of his years, perhaps even when the great
grandchildren of Adam were coming to regard the old man
as what our Transatlantic friends call a 'back number.' Is it
possible, for instance, that the people who invented Astronomy did not finally use instruments of extraordinary preci-
sion; that applied optics was not a cult of some of the
specialists in the Colleges of the Theban priesthood. The
Egyptians were essentially specialists. It is true that, in so far
as we can judge, the range of their study was limited to
subjects connected with their aims of government on earth
by controlling all that bore on the life to follow it. But can
anyone imagine that by the eyes of men, unaided by lenses
of wondrous excellence, Astronomy was brought to such a
pitch that the true orientation of temples and pyramids and
tombs followed for four thousand years the wanderings of
the planetary systems in space. If an instance of their knowledge of microscopy is wanted let me hazard a conjecture. How
was it that in their hieroglyphic writing they took as the
symbol or determinative of 'flesh' the very form which the
science of today, relying on the revelations of a microscope
of a thousand powers, gives to protoplasm – that unit of
living organism which has been differentiated as Flagellula.
If they could make analysis like this, why may they not have
gone further? In that wonderful atmosphere of theirs, where
sunlight fierce and clear is perpetually co-existent with day,
where the dryness of earth and air gives perfect refraction,
why may they not have learned secrets of light hidden from
us in the density of our northern mists? May it not have been

possible that they learned to store light, just as we have learned to store electricity. Nay more, is it not even possible that they did so. They must have had some form of artificial light which they used in the construction and adornment of those vast caverns hewn in the solid rock which became whole cemeteries of the dead. Why, some of these caverns, with their labyrinthine windings and endless passages and chambers, all sculptured and graven and painted with an elaboration of detail which absolutely bewilders one, must have taken years and years to complete. And yet in them is no mark of smoke, such as lamps or torches would have left behind them. Again, if they knew how to store light, is it not possible that they had learned to understand and separate its component elements? And if these men of old arrived at such a point, may not we too in the fullness of time? We shall see! We shall see!

"There is another matter, too, on which recent discoveries in science throw a light. It is only a glimmer at present; a glimmer sufficient to illuminate probabilities, rather than actualities, or even possibilities. The discoveries of the Curies and Laborde, of Sir William Crooks and Becquerel, may have far-reaching results on Egyptian investigation. This new metal, radium — or rather this old metal of which our knowledge is new — may have been known to the ancients. Indeed it may have been used thousands of years ago in greater degree than seems possible today. As yet Egypt has not been named as a place where the discovery of pitchblende, in which only as far as is known yet radium is contained, may be made. And yet it is more than probable that radium exists in Egypt. That country has perhaps the greatest masses of granite to be found in the world; and pitchblende is found as a vein in granitic rocks. In no place, at no time, has granite ever been quarried in such proportions as in Egypt during the earlier dynasties. Who may say what great veins of pitchblende may not have been found in the gigantic operations of hewing out columns for the temples, or great stones for the pyramids. Why, veins of pitchblende, of a richness unknown in our recent mines in Cornwall, or Bohemia, or Saxony, or Hungary, or Turkey, or Colorado, may have been found by these old quarrymen of Aswan, or Turra, or Mokattam, or Elephantine.

"Beyond this again, it is possible that here and there

amongst these vast granite quarries may have been found not merely veins but masses or pockets of pitchblende. In such case the power at the disposal of those who knew how to use it must have been wonderful. The learning of Egypt was kept amongst its priests, and in their vast colleges must have been men of great learning; men who knew well how to exercise to the best advantage, and in the direction they wished, the terrific forces at their command. And if pitchblende did and does exist in Egypt, do you not think that much of it must have been freed by the gradual attrition and wearing down of the granitic rocks? Time and weather bring in time all rocks to dust; the very sands of the desert, which in centuries have buried in this very land some of the greatest monuments of man's achievement, are the evidences of the fact. If, then, radium is divisible into such minute particles as the scientists tell us, it too must have been freed in time from its granite prison and left to work in the air. One might almost hazard a suggestion that the taking the scarab as the symbol of life may not have been without an empiric basis. Might it not be possible that Coprophagi have power or instinct to seize upon the minute particles of heat-giving, light-giving — perhaps life-giving — radium, and enclosing them with their ova in those globes of matter which they roll so assiduously, and from which they take their early name, Pilulariae. In the billions of tons of the desert waste there is surely mingled some proportion of each of the earths and rocks and metals of their zone; and, each to each, nature forms her living entities to flourish on those without life.

"Travelers tell us that glass left in tropic deserts changes color, and darkens in the fierce sunlight, just as it does under the influence of the rays of radium. Does not this imply some sort of similarity between the two forces yet to be identified!"

These scientific, or quasi-scientific discussions soothed me. They took my mind from brooding on the mysteries of the occult, by attracting it to the wonders of nature.

The Crystal Cup

I. The Dream-Birth

*T*he blue waters touch the walls of the palace; I can hear their soft, lapping wash against the marble whenever I listen. Far out at sea I can see the waves glancing in the sunlight, ever-smiling, ever-glancing, ever-sunny. Happy waves! — happy in your gladness, thrice happy that ye are free!

I rise from my work and spring up the wall till I reach the embrasure. I grasp the corner of the stonework and draw myself up till I crouch in the wide window. Sea, sea, out away as far as my vision extends. There I gaze till my eyes grow dim; and in the dimness of my eyes my spirit finds its sight. My soul flies on the wings of memory away beyond the blue, smiling sea — away beyond the glancing waves and the gleaming sails, to the land I call my home. As the minutes roll by, my actual eyesight seems to be restored, and I look round me in my old birth-house. The rude simplicity of the dwelling comes back to me as something new. There I see my old books and manuscripts and pictures, and there, away on their old shelves, high up above the door, I see my first rude efforts in art.

How poor they seem to me now! And yet, were I free, I would not give the smallest of them for all I now possess. Possess? How I dream.

The dream calls me back to waking life. I spring down from my window-seat and work away frantically, for every line I draw on paper, every new form that springs on the plaster, brings me nearer freedom. I will make a vase whose beauty will put to shame the glorious works of Greece in her golden prime! Surely a love like mine and a hope like mine must in time make some form of beauty spring to life! When He beholds it he will exclaim with rapture, and will order my instant freedom. I can forget my hate, and the deep debt of revenge which I owe him when I think of liberty — even from his hands. Ah! then on the wings of the morning shall I fly beyond the sea to my home — her home — and clasp her to my arms, never more to be separated!

But, oh Spirit of Day! if she should be — No, no, I cannot think of it, or I shall go mad. Oh Time, Time! maker and destroyer of men's fortunes, why hasten so fast for others whilst thou laggest so slowly for me? Even now my home may have become desolate, and she — my bride of an hour — may sleep calmly in the cold earth. Oh this suspense will drive me mad! Work, work! Freedom is before me; Aurora is the reward of my labor!

So I rush to my work; but to my brain and hand, heated alike, no fire or no strength descends. Half mad with despair, I beat myself against the walls of my prison, and then climb into the embrasure, and once more gaze upon the ocean, but find there no hope. And so I stay till night, casting its pall of blackness over nature, puts the possibility of effort away from me for yet another day.

So my days go on, and grow to weeks and months. So will they grow to years, should life so long remain an unwelcome guest within me; for what is man without hope? and is not hope nigh dead within this weary breast?

*L*ast night, in my dreams, there came, like an inspiration from the Day-Spirit, a design for my vase.

All day my yearning for freedom — for Aurora, or news of her — had increased tenfold, and my heart and brain were on fire. Madly I beat myself, like a caged bird, against my prison-bars. Madly I leaped to my window-seat, and gazed with bursting eyeballs out on the free, open sea. And there I sat till my passion had worn itself out; and then I slept, and dreamed of thee, Aurora — of thee and freedom. In my ears

I heard again the old song we used to sing together, when as children we wandered on the beach; when, as lovers, we saw the sun sink in the ocean, and I would see its glory doubled as it shone in thine eyes, and was mellowed against thy cheek; and when, as my bride, you clung to me as my arms went round you on that desert tongue of land whence rushed that band of sea-robbers that tore me away. Oh! how my heart curses those men — not men, but fiends! But one solitary gleam of joy remains from that dread encounter, — that my struggle stayed those hell-hounds, and that, ere I was stricken down, this right hand sent one of them to his home. My spirit rises as I think of that blow that saved thee from a life worse than death. With the thought I feel my cheeks burning, and my forehead swelling with mighty veins. My eyes burn, and I rush wildly round my prison-house, "Oh! for one of my enemies, that I might dash out his brains against these marble walls, and trample his heart out as he lay before me!" These walls would spare him not. They are pitiless, alas! I know too well. "Oh, cruel mockery of kindness, to make a palace a prison, and to taunt a captive's aching heart with forms of beauty and sculptured marble!" Wondrous, indeed, are these sculptured walls! Men call them passing fair; but oh, Aurora! with thy beauty ever before my eyes, what form that men call lovely can be fair to me? Like him who gazes sun-wards, and then sees no light on earth, from the glory that dyes his iris, so thy beauty or its memory has turned the fairest things of earth to blackness and deformity.

In my dream last night, when in my ears came softly, like music stealing across the waters from afar, the old song we used to sing together, then to my brain, like a ray of light, came an idea whose grandeur for a moment struck me dumb. Before my eyes grew a vase of such beauty that I knew my hope was born to life, and that the Great Spirit had placed my foot on the ladder that leads from this my palace-dungeon to freedom and to thee. Today I have got a block of crystal — for only in such pellucid substance can I body forth my dream — and have commenced my work.

I found at first that my hand had lost its cunning, and I was beginning to despair, when, like the memory of a dream, there came back in my ears the strains of the old song. I sang it softly to myself, and as I did so I grew calmer; but oh! how differently the song sounded to me when thy voice, Aurora, rose not in unison with my own! But what avails pining? To work! To work! Every touch of my chisel will bring me nearer thee.

*M*y vase is daily growing nearer to completion. I sing as I work, and my constant song is the one I love so well. I can hear the echo of my voice in the vase; and as I end, the wailing song note is prolonged in sweet, sad music in the crystal cup. I listen, ear down, and sometimes I weep as I listen, so sadly comes the echo to my song. Imperfect though it be, my voice makes sweet music, and its echo in the cup guides my hand towards perfection as I work. Would that thy voice rose and fell with mine, Aurora, and then the world would behold a vase of such beauty as never before woke up the slumbering fires of mans love for what is fair; for if I do such work in sadness, imperfect as I am in my solitude and sorrow, what would I do in joy, perfect when with thee? I know that my work is good as an artist, and I feel that it is as a man; and the cup itself, as it daily grows in beauty, gives back a clearer echo. Oh! if I worked in joy how gladly would it give back our voices! Then would we hear an echo and music such as mortals seldom hear; but now the echo, like my song, seems imperfect. I grow daily weaker; but still I work on — work with my whole soul — for am I not working for freedom and for thee?

*M*y work is nearly done. Day by day, hour by hour, the vase grows more finished. Ever clearer comes the echo whilst I sing; ever softer, ever more sad and heart-rending comes the echo of the wail at the end of the song. Day by day I grow weaker and weaker; still I work on with all my soul. At night the thought comes to me, whilst I think of thee, that I will never see thee more — that I breathe out my life into the crystal cup, and that it will last there when I am gone.

So beautiful has it become, so much do I love it, that I could gladly die to be maker of such a work, were it not for thee — for my love for thee, and my hope of thee, and my fear for thee, and my anguish for thy grief when thou knowest I am gone.

My work requires but few more touches. My life is slowly ebbing away, and I feel that with my last touch my life will pass out forever into the cup. Till that touch is given I must not die — I will not die. My hate has passed away. So great are my wrongs that revenge of mine would be too small a compensation for my woe. I leave revenge to a juster and a mightier than I. Thee, oh Aurora, I will await in the land of flowers, where thou and I will wander, never more to part, never more! Ah, never more! Farewell, Aurora — Aurora — Aurora!

II. The Feast of Beauty

The Feast of Beauty approaches rapidly, yet hardly so fast as my royal master wishes. He seems to have no other thought than to have this feast greater and better than any ever held before. Five summers ago his Feast of Beauty was nobler than all held in his sires reign together; yet scarcely was it over, and the rewards given to the victors, when he conceived the giant project whose success is to be tested when the moon reaches her full. It was boldly chosen and boldly done; chosen and done as boldly as the project of a monarch should be. But still I cannot think that it will end well. This yearning after completeness must be unsatisfied in the end — this desire that makes a monarch fling his kingly justice to the winds, and strive to reach his Mecca over a desert of blighted hopes and lost lives. But hush! I must not dare to think ill of my master or his deeds; and besides, walls have ears. I must leave alone these dangerous topics, and confine my thoughts within proper bounds.

The moon is waxing quickly, and with its fullness comes the Feast of Beauty, whose success as a whole rests almost solely on my watchfulness and care; for if the ruler of the feast should fail in his duty, who could fill the void? Let me see what arts are represented, and what works compete. All the arts will have trophies: poetry in its various forms, and prose-writing; sculpture with carving in various metals, and glass, and wood, and ivory, and engraving gems, and setting jewels; painting on canvas, and glass, and wood, and stone and metal; music, vocal and instrumental; and dancing. If that woman will but sing, we will have a real triumph of music; but she appears sickly too. All our best artists either get ill or die, although we promise them freedom or rewards or both if they succeed.

Surely never yet was a Feast of Beauty so fair or so richly dowered as this which the full moon shall behold and hear; but ah! the crowning glory of the feast will be the crystal cup. Never yet have these eyes beheld such a form of beauty, such a wondrous mingling of substance and light. Surely some magic power must have helped to draw such loveliness from a cold block of crystal. I must be careful that no harm happens the vase. Today when I touched it, it gave forth such a ringing sound that my heart jumped with fear lest it should sustain any injury. Henceforth, till I deliver it up to my master, no hand but my own shall touch it lest any harm should happen to it.

Strange story has that cup. Born to life in the cell of a captive torn from his artist home beyond the sea, to enhance the splendor of a feast by his labor — seen at work by spies, and traced and followed till a chance — cruel chance for him — gave him into the hands of the emissaries of my master. He too, poor moth, fluttered about the flame: the name of freedom spurred him on to exertion till he wore away his life. The beauty of that cup was dearly bought for him. Many a man would forget his captivity whilst he worked at such a piece of loveliness; but he appeared to have some sorrow at his heart, some sorrow so great that it quenched his pride.

How he used to rave at first! How he used to rush about his chamber, and then climb into the embrasure of his window, and gaze out away over the sea! Poor captive! perhaps over the sea some one waited for his coming who was dearer to him than many cups, even many cups as beautiful as this, if such could be on earth. . . . Well, well, we must all die soon or late, and who dies first escapes the more sorrow, perhaps, who knows? How, when he had commenced the cup, he used to sing all day long, from the moment the sun shot its first fiery arrow into the retreating hosts of night-clouds, till the shades of evening advancing drove the lingering sunbeams into the west — and always the same song!

How he used to sing, all alone! Yet sometimes I could almost imagine I heard not one voice from his chamber, but two. . . . No more will it echo again from the wall of a dungeon, or from a hillside in free air. No more will his eyes behold the beauty of his crystal cup.

It was well he lived to finish it. Often and often have I trembled to think of his death, as I saw him day by day grow weaker as he worked at the unfinished vase. Must his eyes never more behold the beauty that was born of his soul? Oh, never more! Oh Death, grim King of Terrors, how mighty is thy scepter! All-powerful is the wave of thy hand that summons us in turn to thy kingdom away beyond the poles!

Would that thou, poor captive, hadst lived to behold thy triumph, for victory will be thine at the Feast of Beauty such as man never before achieved. Then thou mightst have heard the shout that hails the victor in the contest, and the plaudits that greet him as he passes out, a free man, through the palace gates. But now thy cup will come to light amid the smiles of beauty and rank and power, whilst thou liest there in thy lonely chamber, cold as the marble of its walls.

And, after all, the feast will be imperfect, since the victors cannot all be crowned. I must ask my master's direction as to how a blank place of a competitor, should he prove a victor, is to be filled up. So late? I must see him ere the noontide hour of rest be past.

Great Spirit! how I trembled as my master answered my question!

I found him in his chamber, as usual in the noontide. He was lying on his couch disrobed, half-sleeping; and the drowsy zephyr, scented with rich odors from the garden, wafted through the windows at either side by the fans, lulled him to complete repose. The darkened chamber was cool and silent. From the vestibule came the murmuring of many fountains, and the pleasant splash of falling waters. "Oh, happy," said I, in my heart, "oh, happy great King, that has such pleasures to enjoy!" The breeze from the fans swept over the strings of the Æolian harps, and a sweet, confused, happy melody arose like the murmuring of children's voices singing afar off in the valleys, and floating on the wind.

As I entered the chamber softly, with muffled foot-fall and pent-in breath, I felt a kind of awe stealing over me. To me who was born and have dwelt all my life within the precincts of the court — to me who talk daily with my royal master, and take his minutest directions as to the coming feast — to me who had all my life looked up to my king as to a spirit, and had venerated him as more than mortal — came a feeling of almost horror; for my master looked then, in his quiet chamber, half-sleeping amid the drowsy music of the harps and fountains, more like a common man than a God. As the thought came to me I shuddered in affright, for it seemed to me that I had been guilty of sacrilege. So much had my veneration for my royal master become a part of my nature, that but to think of him as another man seemed like the anarchy of my own soul.

I came beside the couch, and watched him in silence. He seemed to be half-listening to the fitful music; and as the melody swelled and died away his chest rose and fell as he breathed in unison with the sound.

After a moment or two he appeared to become conscious of the presence of some one in the room, although by no motion of his face could I see that he heard any sound, and his eyes were shut. He opened his eyes, and, seeing me, asked, "Was all right about the Feast of Beauty?" for that is the subject ever nearest to his thoughts. I answered that all was well, but that I had come to ask his royal pleasure as to how a vacant place amongst the competitors was to be filled up. He asked, "How vacant?" and on my telling him, "from death," he asked again, quickly, "Was the work finished?" When I told him that it was, he lay back again on his couch with a sigh of relief, for he had half arisen in his anxiety as he asked the question. Then he said, after a minute, "All the competitors must be present at the feast." "All?" said I. "All," he answered again, "alive or dead; for the old custom must be preserved, and the victors crowned." He stayed still for a minute more, and then said, slowly, "Victors or martyrs." And I could see that the kingly spirit was coming back to him.

Again he went on. "This will be my last Feast of Beauty; and all the captives shall be set free. Too much sorrow has sprung already from my ambition. Too much injustice has soiled the name of king."

He said no more, but lay still and closed his eyes. I could see by the working of his hands and the heaving of his chest that some violent emotion troubled him, and the thought arose, "He is a man, but he is yet a king; and, though a king as he is, still happiness is not for him. Great Spirit of Justice! thou metest out his pleasures and his woes to man, to king and slave alike! Thou lovest best to whom thou givest peace!"

Gradually my master grew more calm, and at length sunk into a gentle slumber; but even in his sleep he breathed in unison with the swelling murmur of the harps.

"To each is given," said I gently, "something in common with the world of actual things. Thy life, oh King, is bound by chains of sympathy to the voice of Truth, which is Music! Tremble, lest in the presence of a master-strain thou shouldst feel thy littleness, and die!" and I softly left the room.

III. The Story of the Moonbeam

Slowly I creep along the bosom of the waters.

Sometimes I look back as I rise upon a billow, and see behind me many of my kin sitting each upon a wave-summit as upon a throne. So I go on for long, a power that I wist not forcing me onward, without will or purpose of mine.

At length, as I rise upon a mimic wave, I see afar a hazy light that springs from a vast palace, through whose countless windows flame lamps and torches. But at the first view, as if my coming had been the signal, the lights disappear in an instant.

Impatiently I await what may happen; and as I rise with each heart-beat of the sea, I look forward to where the torches had gleamed. Can it be a deed of darkness that shuns the light?

*T*he time has come when I can behold the palace without waiting to mount upon the waves. It is built of white marble, and rises steep from the brine. Its sea-front is glorious with columns and statues; and from the portals the marble steps sweep down, broad and wide to the waters, and below them, down as deep as I can see.

No sound is heard, no light is seen. A solemn silence abounds, a perfect calm.

Slowly I climb the palace walls, my brethren following as soldiers up a breach. I slide along the roofs, and as I look behind me walls and roofs are glistening as with silver. At length I meet with something smooth and hard and translucent; but through it I pass and enter a vast hall, where for an instant I hang in mid-air and wonder.

My coming has been the signal for such a burst of harmony as brings back to my memory the music of the spheres as they rush through space; and in the full-swelling anthem of welcome I feel that I am indeed a sun-spirit, a child of light, and that this is homage to my master.

I look upon the face of a great monarch, who sits at the head of a banquet-table. He has turned his head upwards and backwards, and looks as if he had been awaiting my approach. He rises and fronts me with the ringing out of the welcome-song, and all the others in the great hall turn towards me as well. I can see their eyes gleaming. Down along the immense table, laden with plate and glass and flowers, they stand holding each a cup of ruby wine, with which they pledge the monarch when the song is ended, as they drink success to him and to the "Feast of Beauty."

I survey the hall. An immense chamber, with marble walls covered with bas-reliefs and frescoes and sculptured figures, and paneled by great columns that rise along the surface and support a dome-ceiling painted wondrously; in its center the glass lantern by which I entered.

On the walls are hung pictures of various forms and sizes, and down the center of the table stretches a raised platform on which are placed works of art of various kinds.

At one side of the hall is a dais on which sit persons of both sexes with noble faces and lordly brows, but all wearing the same expression — care tempered by hope. All these hold scrolls in their hands.

At the other side of the hall is a similar dais, on which sit others fairer to earthly view, less spiritual and more marked by surface-passion. They hold music-scores. All these look more joyous than those on the other platform, all save one, a woman, who sits with downcast face and dejected mien, as of one without hope. As my light falls at her feet she looks up, and I feel happy. The sympathy between us has called a faint gleam of hope to cheer that poor pale face.

Many are the forms of art that rise above the banquet-table, and all are lovely to behold. I look on all with pleasure one by one, till I see the last of them at the end of the table away from the monarch, and then all the others seem as nothing to me. What is this that makes other forms of beauty seem as naught when compared with it, when brought within the radius of its luster? A crystal cup, wrought with such wondrous skill that light seems to lose its individual glory as it shines upon it and is merged in its beauty. "Oh Universal Mother, let me enter there. Let my life be merged in its beauty, and no more will I regret my sun-strength hidden deep in the chasms of my moon-mother. Let me live there and perish there, and I will be joyous whilst it lasts, and content to pass into the great vortex of nothingness to be born again when the glory of the cup has fled."

Can it be that my wish is granted, that I have entered the cup and become a part of its beauty? "Great Mother, I thank thee."

Has the cup life? or is it merely its wondrous perfectness that makes it tremble, like a beating heart, in unison with the ebb and flow, the great wave-pulse of nature? To me it feels as if it had life.

I look through the crystal walls and see at the end of the table, isolated from all others, the figure of a man seated. Are those cords that bind his limbs? How suits that crown of laurel those wide, dim eyes, and that pallid hue? It is passing strange. This Feast of Beauty holds some dread secrets, and sees some wondrous sights.

I hear a voice of strange, rich sweetness, yet wavering — the voice of one almost a king by nature. He is standing up; I see him through my palace-wall. He calls a name and sits down again.

Again I hear a voice from the platform of scrolls, the Throne of Brows; and again I look and behold a man who stands trembling yet flushed, as though the morning light shone bright upon his soul. He reads in cadenced measure a song in praise of my moon-mother, the Feast of Beauty, and the king. As he speaks, he trembles no more, but seems inspired, and his voice rises to a tone of power and grandeur, and rings back from walls and dome. I hear his words distinctly, though saddened in tone, in the echo from my crystal home. He concludes and sits down, half-fainting, amid a whirlwind of applause, every note, every beat of which is echoed as the words had been.

Again the monarch rises and calls "Aurora," that she may sing for freedom. The name echoes in the cup with a sweet, sad sound. So sad, so despairing seems the echo, that the hall seems to darken and the scene to grow dim.

"Can a sun-spirit mourn, or a crystal vessel weep?"

She, the dejected one, rises from her seat on the Throne of Sound, and all eyes turn upon her save those of the pale one, laurel-crowned. Thrice she essays to begin, and thrice naught comes from her lips but a dry, husky sigh, till an old man who has been moving round the hall settling all things, cries out, in fear lest she should fail, "Freedom!"

The word is re-echoed from the cup. She hears the sound, turns towards it and begins.

Oh, the melody of that voice! And yet it is not perfect alone; for after the first note comes an echo from the cup that swells in unison with the voice, and the two sounds together, seem as if one strain came ringing sweet from the lips of the All-Father himself. So sweet it is, that all throughout the hall sit spellbound, and scarcely dare to breathe.

In the pause after the first verses of the song, I hear the voice of the old man speaking to a comrade, but his words are unheard by any other, "Look at the king. His spirit seems lost in a trance of melody. Ah! I fear me some evil: the nearer the music approaches to perfection the more rapt he becomes. I dread lest a perfect note shall prove his death-call." His voice dies away as the singer commences the last verse.

Sad and plaintive is the song; full of feeling and tender love, but love overshadowed by grief and despair. As it goes on the voice of the singer grows sweeter and more thrilling, more real; and the cup, my crystal time-home, vibrates more and more as it gives back the echo. The monarch looks like one entranced, and no movement is within the hall. . . . The song dies away in a wild wail that seems to tear the heart of the singer in twain; and the cup vibrates still more as it gives back the echo. As the note, long-swelling, reaches its highest, the cup, the Crystal Cup, my wondrous home, the gift of the All-Father, shivers into millions of atoms, and passes away.

Ere I am lost in the great vortex I see the singer throw up her arms and fall, freed at last, and the King sitting, glory-faced, but pallid with the hue of Death.

The Dualitists

or, the Death Doom of the Double Born

Chapter I.
Bis Dat Qui Non Cito Dat

(He gives twice who does not give quickly.)

*T*here was joy in the house of Bubb.

For ten long years had Ephraim and Sophonisba Bubb mourned in vain the loneliness of their life. Unavailingly had they gazed into the emporia of baby-linen, and fixed their searching glances on the basket-makers' warehouses where the cradles hung in tempting rows. In vain had they prayed, and sighed, and groaned, and wished, and waited, and wept, but never had even a ray of hope been held out by the family physician.

*B*ut now at last the wished-for moment had arrived. Month after month had flown by on leaden wings, and the destined days had slowly measured their course. The months had become weeks; the weeks had dwindled down to days; the days had been attenuated to hours; the hours had lapsed into minutes, the minutes had slowly died away, and but seconds remained.

Ephraim Bubb sat cowering on the stairs, and tried with high-strung ears to catch the strain of blissful music from the lips of his first-born. There was silence in the house — silence as of the deadly calm before the cyclone. Ah! Ephra Bubb, little thinkest thou that another moment may forever destroy the peaceful, happy course of thy life, and open to thy too craving eyes the portals of that wondrous land where Childhood reigns supreme, and where the tyrant infant with the wave of his tiny hand and the imperious treble of his tiny voice sentences his parent to the deadly vault beneath the castle moat. As the thought strikes thee thou becomest pale. How thou tremblest as thou findest thyself upon the brink of the abyss! Wouldst that thou could recall the past!

But hark! the die is cast for good or ill. The long years of praying and hoping have found an end at last. From the chamber within comes a sharp cry, which shortly after is repeated. Ah! Ephraim, that cry is the feeble effort of childish lips as yet unused to the rough, worldly form of speech to frame the word Father. In the glow of thy transport all doubts are forgotten; and when the doctor cometh forth as the harbinger of joy he findeth thee radiant with newfound delight.

"My dear sir, allow me to congratulate you — to offer twofold felicitations. Mr. Bubb, sir, you are the father of Twins!"

Chapter II. Halcyon Days

*T*he twins were the finest children that ever were seen — so at least said the cognoscenti, and the parents were not slow to believe. The nurse's opinion was in itself a proof.

It was not, ma'am, that they was fine for twins, but they was fine for singles, and she had ought to know, for she had nussed a many in her time, both twins and singles. All they wanted was to have their dear little legs cut off and little wings on their dear little shoulders, for to be put one on each side of a white marble tombstone, cut beautiful, sacred to the relic of Ephraim Bubb, that they might, sir, if so be that missus was to survive the father of two such lovely twins — although she would make bold to say, and no offence intended, that a handsome gentleman, though a trifle or two older than his good lady, though for the matter of that she heerd that gentlemen was never too old at all, and for her own part she liked them the better for it: not like bits of boys that didn't know their own minds — that a gentleman what was the father of two such 'eavenly twins (God bless them!) couldn't be called anything but a boy; though for the matter of that she never knowed in her experience — which it was much — of a boy as had such twins, or any twins at all so much for the matter of that.

The twins were the idols of their parents, and at the same time their pleasure and their pain. Did Zerubbabel cough, Ephraim would start from his balmy slumbers with an agonized cry of consternation, for visions of innumerable twins black in the face from croup haunted his nightly pillow. Did Zacariah rail at ethereal expansion, Sophonisba with pallid hue and disheveled locks would fly to the cradle of her offspring. Did pins torture or strings afflict, or flannel or flies tickle, or light dazzle, or darkness affright, or hunger or thirst assail the synchronous productions, the household of Bubb would be roused from quiet slumbers or the current of its manifold workings changed.

The twins grew apace; were weaned; teethed; and at length arrived at the stage of three years!

"They grew in beauty side by side,
They filled one home," etc.

Chapter III. Rumors of Wars

*H*arry Merford and Tommy Santon lived in the same range of villas as Ephraim Bubb. Harry's parents had taken up their abode in No. 25, No. 27 was happy in the perpetual sunshine of Tommy's smiles, and between these two residences Ephraim Bubb reared his blossoms, the number of his mansion being 26. Harry and Tommy had been accustomed from the earliest times to meet each other daily. Their primal method of communication had been by the housetops, till their respective sires had been obliged to pay compensation to Bubb for damages to his roof and dormer windows; and from that time they had been forbidden by the home authorities to meet, whilst their mutual neighbor had taken the precaution of having his garden walls pebble-dashed and topped with broken glass to prevent their incursions. Harry and Tommy, however, being gifted with daring souls, lofty ambitions, impetuous natures, and strong seats to their trousers, defied the rugged walls of Bubb and continued to meet in secret.

Compared with these two youths, Castor and Pollux, Damon and Pythias, Eloisa and Abelard are but tame examples of duality or constancy and friendship. All the poets from Hyginus to Schiller might sing of noble deeds done and desperate dangers held as naught for friendship's sake, but they would have been mute had they but known of the mutual affection of Harry and Tommy. Day by day, and often night by night, would these two brave the perils of nurse, and father, and mother, of whip and imprisonment, and hunger and thirst, and solitude and darkness to meet together. What they discussed in secret none other knew. What deeds of darkness were perpetrated in their symposia none could tell. Alone they met, alone they remained, and alone they departed to their several abodes. There was in the garden of Bubb a

summer house overgrown with trailing plants, and surrounded by young poplars which the fond father had planted
on his children's natal day, and whose rapid growth he had
proudly watched. These trees quite obscured the summer-
house, and here Harry and Tommy, knowing after a careful
observation that none ever entered the place, held their con-
claves. Time after time they met in full security and followed
their customary pursuit of pleasure. Let us raise the mysterious veil and see what was the great Unknown at whose shrine
they bent the knee.

Harry and Tommy had each been given as a Christmas box
a new knife; and for a long time – nearly a year – these knives,
similar in size and pattern, were their chief delights. With
them they cut and hacked in their respective homes all things
which would not be likely to be noticed; for the young
gentlemen were wary and had no wish that their moments of
pleasure should be atoned for by moments of pain. The
insides of drawers, and desks, and boxes, and underparts of
tables and chairs, the backs of picture frames, even the floors,
where corners of the carpets could surreptitiously be turned
up, all bore marks of their craftsmanship; and to compare
notes on these artistic triumphs was a source of joy. At length,
however, a critical time came, some new field of action should
be opened up, for the old appetites were sated, and the old
joys had begun to pall. It was absolutely necessary that the
existing schemes of destruction should be enlarged; and yet
this could hardly be done without a terrible risk of discovery,
for the limits of safety had long since been reached and
passed. But, be the risk great or small, some new ground
should be broken – some new joy found, for the old earth
was barren, and the craving for pleasure was growing fiercer
with each successive day.

The crisis had come: who could tell the issue?

Chapter IV. The Tucket Sounds

*T*hey met in the arbor, determined to discuss this grave question. The heart of each was big with revolution, the head of each was full of scheme and strategy, and the pocket of each was full of sweet-stuff, the sweeter for being stolen. After having dispatched the sweets, the conspirators proceeded to explain their respective views with regard to the enlargement of their artistic operations. Tommy unfolded with much pride a scheme which he had in contemplation of cutting a series of holes in the sounding board of the piano, so as to destroy its musical properties. Harry was in no wise behindhand in his ideas of reform. He had conceived the project of cutting the canvas at the back of his great grandfather's portrait, which his father held in high regard among his lares and penates, so that in time when the picture should be moved the skin of paint would be broken, the head fall bodily out from the frame.

At this point of the council a brilliant thought occurred to Tommy. "Why should not the enjoyment be doubled, and the musical instruments and family pictures of both establishments be sacrificed on the altar of pleasure?" This was agreed to nem. con.; and then the meeting adjourned for dinner. When they next met it was evident that there was a screw loose somewhere — that there was "something rotten in the state of Denmark." After a little fencing on both sides, it came out that all the schemes of domestic reform had been foiled by maternal vigilance, and that so sharp had been the reprimand consequent on a partial discovery of the schemes that they would have to be abandoned — till such time, at least, as increased physical strength would allow the reformers to laugh to scorn parental threats and injunctions.

Sadly the two forlorn youths took out their knives and regarded them; sadly, sadly they thought, as erst did Othello,

of all the fair chances of honor and triumph and glory gone
forever. They compared knives with almost the fondness of
doting parents. There they were – so equal in size and strength
and beauty – dimmed by no corrosive rust, tarnished by no
stain, and with unbroken edges of the keenness of Saladin's
sword.

So like were the knives that but for the initials scratched
in the handles neither boy could have been sure which was
his own. After a little while they began mutually to brag of
the superior excellence of their respective weapons. Tommy
insisted that his was the sharper, Harry asserted that his was
the stronger of the two. Hotter and hotter grew the war of
words. The tempers of Harry and Tommy got inflamed, and
their boyish bosoms glowed with manly thoughts of daring
and of hate. But there was abroad in that hour a spirit of a
bygone age – one that penetrated even to that dim arbor in
the grove of Bubb. The world – old scheme of ordeal was
whispered by the spirit in the ear of each, and suddenly the
tumult was allayed. With one impulse the boys suggested that
they should test the quality of their knives by the ordeal of
the Hack.

No sooner said than done. Harry held out his knife edge
uppermost; and Tommy, grasping his firmly by the handle,
brought down the edge of the blade crosswise on Harry's. The
process was then reversed, and Harry became in turn the
aggressor. Then they paused and eagerly looked for the result.
It was not hard to see; in each knife were two great dents of
equal depth; and so it was necessary to renew the contest, and
seek a further proof.

What needs it to relate seriatim the details of that direful
strife? The sun had long since gone down, and the moon with
fair, smiling face had long risen over the roof of Bubb, when,
wearied and jaded, Harry and Tommy sought their respective
homes. Alas! the splendor of the knives was gone forever.
Ichabod! – Ichabod! the glory had departed and naught
remained but two useless wrecks, with keen edges destroyed,
and now like unto nothing save the serried hills of Spain.

But though they mourned for their fondly cherished weapons, the hearts of the boys were glad; for the bygone day had
opened to their gaze a prospect of pleasure as boundless as

the limits of the world.

Chapter V. The First Crusade

*F*rom that day a new era dawned in the lives of Harry and Tommy. So long as the resources of the parental establishments could hold out so long would their new amusement continue. Subtly they obtained surreptitious possession of articles of family cutlery not in general use, and brought them one by one to their rendezvous. These came fair and spotless from the sanctity of the butlers' pantry. Alas! they returned not as they came.

But in course of time the stock of available cutlery became exhausted, and again the inventive faculties of the youths were called into requisition. They reasoned thus: "The knife game, it is true, is played out, but the excitement of the Hack is not to be dispensed with. Let us carry, then, this Great Idea into new worlds; let us still live in the sunshine of pleasure; let us continue to hack, but with objects other than knives."

It was done. Not knives now engaged the attention of the ambitious youths. Spoons and forks were daily flattened and beaten out of shape; pepper castor met pepper castor in combat, and both were borne dying from the field; candlesticks met in fray to part no more on this side of the grave; even epergnes were used as weapons in the crusade of Hack.

At last all the resources of the butler's pantry became exhausted, and then began a system of miscellaneous destruction that proved in a little time ruinous to the furniture of the respective homes of Harry and Tommy. Mrs. Santon and Mrs. Merford began to notice that the wear and tear in their households became excessive. Day after day some new domestic calamity seemed to have occurred. Today a valuable edition of some book whose luxurious binding made it an object for public display would appear to have suffered some dire misfortune, for the edges were frayed and broken and the back loose if not altogether displaced; tomorrow the same awful fate would seem to have followed some miniature frame; the day following the legs of some chair or spider-table would show signs of extraordinary hardship. Even in the nursery the sounds of lamentation were heard. It was a thing of daily occurrence for the little girls to state that when going to bed at night they had laid their dear dollies in their beds with tender care, but that when again seeking them in the period of recess they had found them with all their beauty gone, with legs and arms amputated and faces beaten from all semblance of human form.

Then articles of crockery began to be missed. The thief could in no case be discovered, and the wages of the servants, from constant stoppages, began to be nominal rather than real. Mrs. Merford and Mrs. Santon mourned their losses, but Harry and Tommy gloated day after day over their spoils, which lay in an ever-increasing heap in the hidden grove of Bubb. To such an extent had the fondness of the Hack now grown that with both youths it was an infatuation — a madness — a frenzy.

At length one awful day arrived. The butlers of the houses of Merford and Santon, harassed by constant losses and complaints, and finding that their breakage account was in excess of their wages, determined to seek some sphere of occupation where, if they did not meet with a suitable reward or recognition of their services, they would, at least, not lose whatever fortune and reputation they had already acquired. Accordingly, before rendering up their keys and the goods entrusted to their charge, they proceeded to take a preliminary stock of their own accounts, to make sure of their accredited accuracy. Dire indeed was their distress when they knew to the full the havoc which had been wrought; terrible their anguish of the present, bitter their thoughts of the future. Their hearts, bowed down with weight of woe, failed them quite; reeled the strong brains that had erst overcome foes of deadlier spirit than grief; and fell their stalwart forms prone on the floors of their respective sancta sanctorum.

Late in the day when their services were required they were sought for in bower and hall, and at length discovered where they lay.

But alas for justice! They were accused of being drunk and for having, whilst in that degraded condition, deliberately injured all the property on which they could lay hands. Were not the evidences of their guilt patent to all in the hecatombs of the destroyed? Then they were charged with all the evils wrought in the houses, and on their indignant denial Harry and Tommy, each in his own home, according to their concerted scheme of action, stepped forward and relieved their minds of the deadly weight that had for long in secret borne them down. The story of each ran that time after time he had seen the butler, when he thought that nobody was looking, knocking knives together in the pantry, chairs and books and pictures in the drawing room and study, dolls in the nursery, and plates in the kitchen. Then, indeed, was the master of each household stern and uncompromising in his demands for justice. Each butler was committed to the charge of myrmidons of the law under the double charge of drunkenness and willful destruction of property.

*S*oftly and sweetly slept Harry and Tommy in their little beds that night. Angels seemed to whisper to them, for they smiled as though lost in pleasant dreams. The rewards given by proud and grateful parents lay in their pockets, and in their hearts the happy consciousness of having done their duty.

Truly sweet should be the slumbers of the just.

Chapter VI.
"Let the Dead Past Bury Its Dead"

*I*t might be supposed that now the operations of Harry and Tommy would be obliged to be abandoned.

Not so, however. The minds of these youths were of no

common order, nor were their souls of such weak nature as to yield at the first summons of necessity. Like Nelson, they knew not fear; like Napoleon, they held "impossible" to be the adjective of fools; and they reveled in the glorious truth that in the lexicon of youth is no such word as "fail." Therefore on the day following the eclaircissement of the butlers' misdeeds, they met in the arbor to plan a new campaign.

In the hour when all seemed blackest to them, and when the narrowing walls of possibility hedged them in on every side, thus ran the deliberations of these dauntless youths: —

"We have played out the meaner things that are inanimate and inert; why not then trench on the domains of life? The dead have lapsed into the regions of the forgotten past — let the living look to themselves."

That night they met when all households had retired to balmy sleep, and naught but the amorous wailings of nocturnal cats told of the existence of life and sentience. Each bore into the arbor in his arms a pet rabbit and a piece of sticking-plaster. Then, in the peaceful, quiet moonlight, commenced a work of mystery, blood, and gloom. The proceedings began by the fixing of a piece of sticking-plaster over the mouth of each rabbit to prevent it making a noise, if so inclined. Then Tommy held up his rabbit by its scutty tail, and it hung wriggling, a white mass in the moonlight. Slowly Harry raised his rabbit holding it in the same manner, and when level with his head brought it down on Tommy's client.

But the chances had been miscalculated. The boys held firmly to the tails, but the chief portions of the rabbits fell to earth. Ere the doomed beasts could escape, however, the operators had pounced upon them, and this time holding them by the hind legs renewed the trial.

Deep into the night the game was kept up, and the Eastern sky began to show signs of approaching day as each boy bore triumphantly the dead course of his favorite bunny and placed it within its sometime hutch.

Next night the same game was renewed with a new rabbit on each side, and for more than a week — so long as the hutches supplied the wherewithal — the battle was sustained. True that there were sad hearts and red eyes in the juveniles of Santon and Merford as one by one the beloved pets were found dead, but Harry and Tommy, with the hearts of heroes steeled to suffering and deaf to the pitiful cries of childhood, still fought the good fight on to the bitter end.

When the supply of rabbits was exhausted, other munition was not wanting, and for some days the war was continued with white mice, dormice, hedgehogs, guinea pigs, pigeons, lambs, canaries, parakeets, linnets, squirrels, parrots, marmots, poodles, ravens, tortoises, terriers, and cats. Of these, as might be expected, the most difficult to manipulate were the terriers and the cats, and of these two classes the proportion of the difficulties in the way of terrier-hacking was, when compared with those of cat-hacking, about that which the simple Lac of the British Pharmacopoeia bears to water in the compound which dairymen palm off upon a too confiding public as milk. More than once when engaged in the rapturous delights of cat-hacking had Harry and Tommy wished that the silent tomb could open its ponderous and massy jaws and engulf them, for the feline victims were not patient in their death agonies, and often broke the bonds in which the security of the artists rested, and turned fiercely on their executioners.

At last, however, all the animals available were sacrificed; but the passion for hacking still remained. How was it all to end?

Chapter VII.
A Cloud with Golden Lining

*T*ommy and Harry sat in the arbor dejected and disconsolate. They wept like two Alexanders because there were no more worlds to conquer. At last the conviction had been forced upon them that the resources available for hacking were exhausted. That very morning they had had a desperate battle, and their attire showed the ravages of direful war. Their hats were battered into shapeless masses, their shoes were soleless and heelless and had the uppers broken, the ends of their braces, their sleeves, and their trousers were frayed, and had they indulged in the manly luxury of coat tails these too would have gone.

Truly, hacking had become an absorbing passion with them. Long and fiercely had they been swept onward on the wings of the demon of strife, and powerless at the best of times had been the promptings of good; but now, heated with combat, maddened by the equal success of arms, and with the lust for victory still unsated, they longed more fiercely than ever for some new pleasure: like tigers that have tasted blood they thirsted for a larger and more potent libation.

As they sat, with their souls in a tumult of desire and despair, some evil genius guided into the garden the twin blossoms of the tree of Bubb. Hand in hand Zacariah and Zerubbabel advanced from the back door; they had escaped from their nurses, and with the exploring instinct of human-ity, advanced boldly into the great world – the terra incognita, the Ultima Thule of the paternal domain.

In the course of time they approached the hedge of poplars, from behind which the anxious eyes of Harry and Tommy looked for their approach, for the boys knew that where the twins were the nurses were accustomed to be gathered to-gether, and they feared discovery if their retreat should be cut off.

It was a touching sight, these lovely babes, alike in form, feature, size, expression, and dress; in fact, so like each other that one "might not have told either from which." When the startling similarity was recognized by Harry and Tommy, each suddenly turned, and, grasping the other by the shoulder, spoke in a keen whisper:

"Hack! They are exactly equal! This is the very apotheosis of our art!"

With excited faces and trembling hands they laid their plans to lure the unsuspecting babes within the precincts of their charnel house, and they were so successful in their efforts that in a little time the twins had toddled behind the hedge and were lost to the sight of the parental mansion.

Harry and Tommy were not famed for gentleness within

the immediate precincts of their respective homes, but it would have delighted the heart of any philanthropist to see the kindly manner in which they arranged for the pleasures of the helpless babes. With smiling faces and playful words and gentle wiles they led them within the arbor, and then, under pretence of giving them some of those sudden jumps in which infants rejoice, they raised them from the ground. Tommy held Zacariah across his arm with his baby moon-face smiling up at the cobwebs on the arbor roof, and Harry, with a mighty effort, raised the cherubic Zerubbabel aloft.

Each nerved himself for a great endeavor, Harry to give, Tommy to endure a shock, and then the form of Zerubbabel was seen whirling through the air round Harry's glowing and determined face. There was a sickening crash and the arm of Tommy yielded visibly.

The pasty face of Zerubbabel had fallen fair on that of Zacariah, for Tommy and Harry were by this time artists of too great experience to miss so simple a mark. The puttylike noses collapsed, the puttylike cheeks became for a moment flattened, and when in an instant more they parted, the faces of both were dabbled in gore. Immediately the firmament was rent with a series of such yells as might have awakened the dead. Forthwith from the house of Bubb came the echoes in parental cries and footsteps. As the sounds of scurrying feet rang through the mansion, Harry cried to Tommy:

"They will be on us soon. Let us cut to the roof of the stable and draw up the ladder."

Tommy answered by a nod, and the two boys, regardless of consequences, and bearing each a twin, ascended to the roof of the stable by means of a ladder which usually stood against the wall, and which they pulled up after them.

As Ephraim Bubb issued from his house in pursuit of his lost darlings, the sight which met his gaze froze his very soul. There, on the coping of the stable roof, stood Harry and Tommy renewing their game. They seemed like two young demons forging some diabolical implement, for each in turn the twins were lifted high in air and let fall with stunning force on the supine form of its fellow. How Ephraim felt none but a tender and imaginative father can conceive. It would be enough to wring the heart of even a callous parent to see his children, the darlings of his old age — his own beloved twins — being sacrificed to the brutal pleasure of unregenerate youths, without being made unconsciously and helplessly guilty of the crime of fratricide.

Loudly did Ephraim and also Sophonisba, who, with disheveled locks, had now appeared upon the scene, bewail their unhappy lot and shriek in vain for aid; but by rare ill chance no eyes save their own saw the work of butchery or heard the shrieks of anguish and despair. Wildly did Ephraim, mounting on the shoulders of his spouse, strive, but in vain, to scale the stable wall.

Baffled in every effort, he rushed into the house and appeared in a moment bearing in his hands a double-barreled gun, into which he poured the contents of a shot pouch as he ran. He came anigh the stable and hailed the murderous youths:

"Drop them twins and come down here or I'll shoot you like a brace of dogs."

"Never!" exclaimed the heroic two with one impulse, and continued their awful pastime with a zest tenfold as they knew that the agonized eyes of parents wept at the cause of their joy.

"Then die!" shrieked Ephraim, as he fired both barrels, right-left, at the hackers.

But, alas! love for his darlings shook the hand that never shook before. As the smoke cleared off and Ephraim recovered from the kick of his gun, he heard a loud twofold laugh of triumph and saw Harry and Tommy, all unhurt, waving in the air the trunks of the twins — the fond father had blown the heads completely off his own offspring.

Tommy and Harry shrieked aloud in glee, and after playing catch with the bodies for some time, seen only by the agonized eyes of the infanticide and his wife, flung them high in the air. Ephraim leaped forward to catch what had once been Zacariah, and Sophonisba grabbed wildly for the loved remains of her Zerubbabel.

But the weight of the bodies and the height from which they fell were not reckoned by either parent, and from being ignorant of a simple dynamical formula each tried to effect an object which calm, common sense, united with scientific knowledge, would have told them was impossible. The masses fell, and Ephraim and Sophonisba were stricken dead by the falling twins, who were thus posthumously guilty of the crime of parricide.

An intelligent coroner's jury found the parents guilty of the crimes of infanticide and suicide, on the evidence of Harry and Tommy, who swore, reluctantly, that the inhuman monsters, maddened by drink, had killed their offspring by shooting them into the air out of a cannon — since stolen — whence like curses they had fallen on their own heads; and that then they had slain themselves *suis manibus* with their own hands.

Accordingly Ephraim and Sophonisba were denied the solace of Christian burial, and were committed to the earth with "maimed rites," and had stakes driven through their middles to pin them down in their unhallowed graves till the Crack of Doom.

Harry and Tommy were each rewarded with National honors and were knighted, even at their tender years.

Fortune seemed to smile upon them all the long after years, and they lived to a ripe old age, hale of body, and respected and beloved of all.

Often in the golden summer eves, when all nature seemed at rest, when the oldest cask was opened and the largest lamp was lit, when the chestnuts glowed in the embers and the kid turned on the spit, when their great-grandchildren pretended to mend fictional armor and to trim an imaginary helmet's plume, when the shuttles of the good wives of their grandchildren went flashing each through its proper loom, with shouting and with laughter they were accustomed to tell the tale of THE DUALISTS; OR, THE DEATH-DOOM OF THE DOUBLE-BORN.

The Fate of Fenella*

*L*ord Francis Onslow lifted his cap. The action was an instinctive one, for he was face to face with a lady; but he was half dazed with the unexpected meeting, and could not collect his thoughts. He only remembered that when he had last seen his wife she was opening the door of her chamber to De Murger. For weeks he had been schooling himself for such a meeting, for he knew that on his return such might at any time occur; but now, when the moment had come, and unexpectedly, the old pain of his shame overwhelmed him anew. His face grew white — white till it seemed to Fenella that it was of the pallor of death. She knew that she had been so far guilty of what had happened that the murder had been the outcome of her previous acts. She knew also that her husband was ignorant of his part in the deed — and her horror of the man, blood-guilty in such a way, was fined down by the sense of her own partial guilt. The trial, with all its consequent pain to a proud and sensitive woman, had softened her, and she grasped at any hope. The sight of Frank, his gaunt cheeks, which told their tale of suffering, and now the deadly pallor, awoke all the protective feeling which is a part of a woman's love. It was with her whole soul in her voice that she said again:

"Frank!" His voice was stern as well as sad as he answered

---

* "The Fate of Fenella" was published in 1892 as a serial novel in *Cassell's Magazine* with a different author writing each of the twenty-four chapters. Chapter ten of the series was written by Bram Stoker. The story was also published as "A Deed of Vengeance?"

her:

"What is it?" Her heart went cold, but she persevered.

"Frank, I must have a word with you — I must. For God's sake, for Ronny's sake, do not deny me." She did not know that as yet Frank Onslow was in ignorance of De Murger's death; and when his answer came it seemed more hard than even he intended:

"Do you wish to speak of that night?" In a faint voice she answered:

"I do." Then looking in his eyes and seeing the hard look becoming harder still — for a man is seldom generous with a woman where his honor is concerned, she added:

"O Heaven! Frank! You do not think me guilty! No, no, not you! not you! That would be too cruel!"

Frank Onslow paused and said:

"Fenella, God help me! but I do," and he turned away his head. His wife, of course, thought that he alluded to the murder, and not to her sin against him as he saw it, and with a low moan she turned away and hid her face in her hands. Then with an effort she drew herself up, and without a word or a single movement to show that she even recognized his presence, she passed on up the street.

Frank Onslow stood for a few moments watching her retreating figure, and then went across the street and turned the next corner on his way to the post office, for which he had been inquiring when he met his wife. At the door he was stopped by a cheery voice and an outstretched hand:

"Onslow!"

"Castleton! The two men shook hands warmly.

"I see you did not get my telegram," said Lord Castleton. "It is waiting for you at the post office."

"What telegram?"

"To tell you that I was on my way here from London. I went in your interest, old fellow. I thought you would like full particulars — the newspapers are so vague."

"What papers? My interest? Tell me all. I am ignorant of all that has passed for the last six weeks." A vague, shadowy fear began to creep over his spirits. Castleton's voice was full of sympathy as he answered:

"Then you have not heard of — but stay. It is a long story.

Come back to the yacht. I was just going to join you there. We shall be all alone, and I can tell you all. I have the newspapers here for you." He motioned to a roll under his arm.

The two went down to the harbor, and finding the sailor waiting with the boat at the steps, were rowed to the yacht and got on board. Here the two men were all alone. Then, with a preliminary clearing of his voice, Castleton began his story:

"Frank Onslow — better get the worst over at once — just after you went away from Harrogate your wife was tried for murder and acquitted."

"My God! Fenella tried for murder? Whose murder?"

"That scoundrel De Murger. It seems he went into her room in the night and attempted violence, so she stabbed him —"

Castleton stopped in amazement, for a look of radiance came over Frank Onslow's face, as he murmured "Thank God!" Recalled to himself by Castleton's silence, for he was too amazed to go on, Frank said. "I have a reason, old fellow; I shall tell it to you later, but go on. Tell me all the facts, or let me read the papers. Remember I am as yet quite ignorant of it all and I am full of anxiety!"

Without a word Castleton handed him the papers, and, lighting a fresh cigar, sat down with his back to him, and presently yielded to the sun and fresh air and fell into a doze.

Frank Onslow took the papers, and read carefully from end to end the account of the trial of his wife for the murder of De Murger. When he had finished he sat with the folded paper in his hand, and his eyes had the same faraway look in them which they had had on that fatal night. The hypnotic trance was on him again.

Presently he rose, and with stealthy steps approached his sleeping friend. Murmuring "Why did I not kill him?" he struck with the folded paper, as though with a dagger, the form before him. Castleton, who had sunk into a pleasant sleep and whose fat face was wreathed with a smile, was annoyed at the rude awakening. "What the devil!" he began angrily, and then stopped as his eyes met the face of his friend and he realized that he was in some sort of trance. He grew very pale as he saw Frank Onslow stab, and stab, and stab again. There was a certain grotesqueness in the affair — the man in such terrible earnest, in his mind committing murder, while his real weapon was but a folded paper. As he stabbed he hissed, "Why did I not kill him? Why did I not kill him?" Then he went through a series of movements as though he were softly pulling an imaginary door shut behind him, and so back to his own chair, where he sat down hiding his face in his hands.

Castleton sat looking at him in amazement, and then murmured to himself:

"They thought it was someone stronger than Fenella whose grasp made those marks on the dead man's throat." He suddenly looked round to see that no one but himself had observed what had happened, and then, being satisfied on this point, murmured again:

"A noble woman, by Jove! A noble woman!" He called out:

"Frank — Frank Onslow! Wake up, man." Onslow raised his head as a man does when suddenly awakened, and smiled as he said:

"What is it, old man? Have I been asleep?" It was quite evident that he had no recollection of what had just passed. Castleton came and sat down beside him, and his kindly face was grave as he asked:

"You have read the papers?"

"I have."

"Now tell me — you offered to do so — why you said 'Thank God!' when I told you that your wife had killed De Murger?"

Frank Onslow paused. Although the memory of what he had thought to be his shame had been with him daily and nightly until he had become familiarized with it, it was another thing to speak of it, even to such a friend as Castleton. Even now, when it was apparent from the issue of the trial that his wife had avenged so dreadfully the attempt upon her honor, he felt it hard to speak on the subject. Castleton saw the doubt and struggle in his mind which was reflected in his face, and said earnestly, as he laid his hand upon his shoulder:

"Do not hesitate to tell me, Frank. I do not ask out of mere curiosity. I am perhaps a better friend than you think in helping to clear up a certain doubt which I see before me. I think you know I am a friend."

"One of the best a man ever had!" said Frank impulsively, as he took the other's hand. Then turning away his head, he said slowly:

"You were surprised because I was glad Fenella killed that scoundrel. I can tell you, Castleton, but I would not tell anyone else. It was because I saw him enter her room, and, God forgive me! I thought at the time that it was by her wish. That is why I came away from Harrogate that night. That is what kept me away. How could I go back and face my friends with such a shame fresh upon me? It was your lending me your yacht, old man, that made life possible. When I was by myself through the wildness of the Bay of Biscay and among the great billows of the Atlantic I began to be able to bear. I had steeled myself, I thought, and when I heard that so far from my wife being guilty of such a shame, she actually killed the man that attempted her honor, is it any wonder that I felt joyful?"

After a pause Castleton asked:

"How did you come to see — to see it. Why did you take no step to prevent it? Forgive me, old fellow, but I want to understand."

Frank Onslow went to the rail, and leaned over. When he came back Castleton saw that his eyes were wet. With what cheerfulness he could assume, he answered:

"On that very night I had made up my mind to try to win back my wife's love. I wrote a letter to her, a letter in which I poured out my whole soul, and I left my room to put it under her door, so that she would get it in the morning. But" — here he paused, and then said, slowly, "but when in the corridor, I saw her door open, and at the same moment De Murger appeared."

"Did she seem surprised?"

"Not at first. But a moment after a look of amazement crossed her face, and she stepped back into the room, he following her." As he said this he put his head between his hands and groaned.

"And then?" added his friend.

"And then I hardly know what happened. My mind seems

full of a dim memory of a blank existence, and then a series of wild whirling thoughts, something like that last moment after death in Wiertz's picture. I think I must have slept, for it was two o'clock when I saw Fenella, and the clock was striking five when I crossed the bridge after I had left the hotel.

"And the letter? What became of it?"

Frank started. "The letter? I never thought of it. Stay! I must have left it on the table in my room. I remember seeing it there a little while before I came away."

"How was it addressed? Do not think me inquisitive, but I cannot help thinking that that letter may yet be of some great importance."

Frank smiled, a sad smile enough, as he answered: "By the pet name I had for Fenella — Mrs. Right. I used to chaff her because she always defended her position when we argued, and so, when I wanted to tease her, I called her Mrs. Right."

"Was it written on hotel paper?"

"No. I was going to write on some, but I thought it would be better to use the sort we had when — when we were first married. There were a few sheets in my writing case, so I took one."

"That was headed somewhere in Surrey, was it not?"

"Yes; Chiddingford, near Haslemere. It was a pretty place, too, called The Grange. Fenella fell in love with it, and made me buy it right away."

"Is anyone living there now?"

"It is let to someone. I don't think that I heard the name. The agent knows. When the trouble came I told him to do what he could with it, and not to bother me with it anymore. After a while he wrote and asked if I would mind it being let to a foreigner? I told him he might let it to a devil so long as he did not worry me."

Lord Castleton paused awhile, and asked the next question in a hesitating way. He felt embarrassed, and showed it:

"Tell me one thing more, old fellow — if — if you don't mind."

"My dear Castleton, I'll tell you anything you like."

"How did you sign the letter?" Onslow's face looked sad as he answered:

"I signed it by another old pet name we both understood. We had pet names – people always have when they are first married," he added with embarrassment.

"Of course," murmured the sympathetic Castleton.

"One such name lasted a long time. An old friend of my father's came to see us, and in a playful moment he said I was a 'sad dog'. Fenella took it up and used to call me 'Doggie,' and I often signed myself 'Frank Doggie' – as men usually do."

"Of course," again murmured Castleton, as if such a signature was a customary thing. Then he added, "And on this occasion?"

"On this occasion I used the name that seemed full of happiest memories. 'Frank Doggie' may seem idiotic to an outsider, but to Fenella and myself it might mean much."

The two men sat silent awhile, and then Castleton asked softly:

"I suppose it may be taken for granted that Lady Francis never got the letter?"

"I take it, it is so; but it is no matter now, I refused to speak with her just before I met you. I did not know then what I know now – and she will never speak to me again." He sighed as he spoke, and turned away. Then he went to the rail of the yacht and leaned over with his head down, looking into the still blue water beneath him.

"Poor old Frank!" said Castleton to himself. "I can't but think that this matter may come right yet. I must find out what became of that letter, in case Lady Francis never got it. It would prove to her that Frank –"

His train of thought suddenly stopped. A new idea seemed to strike him so forcibly that it quite upset him. Onslow, who had come over from the rail, noticed it. "I say, Castleton, what is wrong with you? You have got quite white about the gills."

"Nothing – nothing," he answered hastily, "I am subject to it. They call it heart. Pardon me for a bit, I'll go to my bunk and lie down," and he went below.

In truth, he was overwhelmed by the thought which had just struck him. If his surmise were true, that Onslow, in a hypnotic trance, as he had almost proved by its recurrence, had killed De Murger, where, then, was Fenella's heroism after all? True that she had taken the blame on herself; but might it not have been that she was morally guilty all the same? Why, then, had she taken the blame? Was it not because she feared that her husband might have refused to screen her shame; or because she feared that if any less heroic aspect of the tragedy was presented to the public, her own fair fame might suffer in greater degree? Could it indeed be that Fenella Onslow was not a heroine, but only a calculating woman of exceeding smartness? Then, again, if Frank Onslow believed that his wife had avenged her honor, was it wise to disturb such belief? He might think, if once the suggestion were made to him, that his honor was preserved only by his own unconscious act.

Was it then wise to disturb existing relations between the husband and wife, sad though they were? Did they come together again, they might in mutual confidence arrive at a real knowledge of the facts, and then — and then, what would be the result? And besides, might there not be some danger in any suggestion made as to his suspicion of who struck the blow? It was true that Lady Francis had been acquitted of the crime, although she confessed to the killing; but her husband might still be tried — and if tried? What then would be the result of the discovery of the missing letter on which he had been building such hopes?

The problem was too much for Lord Castleton. His life had been too sunny and easy-going to allow of familiarity with great emotions, and such a problem as this was to him overwhelming. The issue was too big for him; and revolving in his own mind all that belonged to it, he glided into sleep.

The Specter of Doom*

*T*ime goes on in the Country Under the Sunset much as it does here.

Many years passed away; and they wrought much change. And now we find a time when the people that lived in good King Mago's time would hardly have known their beautiful Land if they had seen it again.

It had sadly changed indeed. No longer was there the same love or the same reverence towards the king – no longer was there perfect peace. People had become more selfish and more greedy, and had tried to grasp all they could for themselves. There were some very rich and there were many poor. Most of the beautiful gardens were laid waste. Houses had grown up close round the palace; and in some of these dwelt many persons who could only afford to pay for part of a house.

All the beautiful Country was sadly changed, and changed was the life of the dwellers in it. The people had almost forgotten Prince Zaphir, who was dead many, many years ago; and no more roses were spread on the pathways. Those who lived now in the Country Under the Sunset laughed at the idea of more Giants, and they did not fear them because they did not see them. Some of them said,

"Tush! what can there be to fear? Even if there over were giants there are none now."

And so the people sang and danced and feasted as before, and thought only of themselves. The Spirits that guarded the Land were very, very sad. Their great white shadowy wings drooped as they stood at their posts at the Portals of the Land.

---

* Also published as "The Invisible Giant"

They hid their faces, and their eyes were dim with continuous weeping, so that they heeded not if any evil thing went by them. They tried to make the people think of their evil-doing; but they could not leave their posts, and the people heard their moaning in the night season and said,

"Listen to the sighing of the breeze; how sweet it is!"

So is it ever with us also, that when we hear the wind sighing and moaning and sobbing round our houses in the lonely nights, we do not think our Angels may be sorrowing for our misdeeds, but only that there is a storm coming. The Angels wept evermore, and they felt the sorrow of dumbness — for though they could speak, those they spoke to would not hear.

Whilst the people laughed at the idea of Giants, there was one old man who shook his head, and made answer to them, when he heard them, and said:

"Death has many children, and there are Giants in the marshes still. You may not see them, perhaps — but they are there, and the only bulwark of safety is in a land of patient, faithful hearts."

The name of this good old man was Knoal, and he lived in a house built of great blocks of stone, in the middle of a wild place far from the city.

In the city there were many great old houses, storey upon storey high; and in these houses lived many poor people. The higher you went up the great steep stairs the poorer were the people that lived there, so that in the garrets were some so poor that when the morning came they did not know whether they should have anything to eat the whole long day. This was very, very sad, and gentle children would have wept if they had seen their pain.

In one of these garrets there lived all alone a little maiden called Zaya. She was an orphan, for her father had died many years before, and her poor mother, who had toiled long and wearily for her dear little daughter — her only child — had died also not long since.

Poor little Zaya had wept so bitterly when she saw her dear mother lying dead, and she had been so sad and sorry for a long time, that she quite forgot that she had no means of living. However, the poor people who lived in the house had given her part of their own food, so that she did not starve.

Then after awhile she had tried to work for herself and earn her own living. Her mother had taught her to make flowers out of paper; so that she made a lot of flowers, and when she had a full basket she took them into the street and sold them. She made flowers of many kinds, roses and lilies, and violets, and snowdrops, and primroses, and mignonette, and many beautiful sweet flowers that only grow in the Country Under the Sunset. Some of them she could make without any pattern, but others she could not, so when she wanted a pattern she took her basket of paper and scissors, and paste, and brushes, and all the things she used, and went into the garden which a kind lady owned, where there grew many beautiful flowers. There she sat down and worked away, looking at the flowers she wanted.

Sometimes she was very sad, and her tears fell thick and fast as she thought of her dear dead mother. Often she seemed to feel that her mother was looking down at her, and to see her tender smile in the sunshine on the water; then her heart was glad, and she sang so sweetly that the birds came around her and stopped their own singing to listen to her.

She and the birds grew great friends, and sometimes when she had sung a song they would all cry out together, as they sat round her in a ring, in a few notes that seemed to say quite plainly:

"Sing to us again. Sing to us again."

So she would sing again. Then she would ask them to sing, and they would sing till there was quite a concert. After a while the birds knew her so well that they would come into her room, and they even built their nests there, and they followed her wherever she went. The people used to say:

"Look at the girl with the birds; she must be half a bird herself, for see how the birds know and love her." From so many people coming to say things like this, some silly people actually believed that she was partly a bird, and they shook their heads when wise people laughed at them, and said:

"Indeed she must be; listen to her singing; her voice is sweeter even than the birds."

So a nickname was applied to her, and naughty boys called it after her in the street, and the nickname was "Big Bird." But Zaya did not mind the name; and although often naughty boys said it to her, meaning to cause her pain, she did not dislike it, but the contrary, for she so gloried in the love and trust of her little sweet-voiced pets that she wished to be thought like them.

Indeed it would be well for some naughty little boys and girls if they were as good and harmless as the little birds that work all day long for their helpless baby birds, building nests and bringing food, and sitting so patiently hatching their little speckled eggs.

One evening Zaya sat alone in her garret very sad and lonely. It was a lovely summer's evening, and she sat in the window looking out over the city. She could see over the many streets towards the great cathedral whose spire towered aloft into the sky higher by far even than the great tower of the king's palace. There was hardly a breath of wind, and the smoke went up straight from the chimneys, getting further and fainter till it was lost altogether.

Zaya was very sad. For the first time for many days her birds were all away from her at once, and she did not know where they had gone. It seemed to her as if they had deserted her, and she was so lonely, poor little maid, that she wept bitter tears. She was thinking of the story which long ago her dead mother had told her, how Prince Zaphir had slain the Giant, and she wondered what the prince was like, and thought how happy the people must have been when Zaphir and Bluebell were king and queen. Then she wondered if there were any hungry children in those good days, and if, indeed, as the people said, there were no more Giants. So she went on with her work before the open window.

Presently she looked up from her work and gazed across the city. There she saw a terrible thing — something so terrible that she gave a low cry of fear and wonder, and leaned out of the window, shading her eyes with her hands to see more clearly.

In the sky beyond the city she saw a vast shadowy Form with its arms raised. It was shrouded in a great misty robe that covered it, fading away into air so that she could only see the face and the grim, spectral hands.

The Form was so mighty that the city below it seemed like a child's toy. It was still far off the city.

The little maid's heart seemed to stand still with fear as she thought to herself, "The Giants, then, are not dead. This is another of them."

Quickly she ran down the high stairs and out into the street. There she saw some people, and cried to them,

"Look! look! the Giant, the Giant!" and pointed towards the Form which she still saw moving onwards to the city.

The people looked up, but they could not see anything, and they laughed and said,

"The child is mad."

Then poor little Zaya was more than ever frightened, and ran down the street crying out still,

"Look, look! the Giant, the Giant!" But no one heeded her, and all said, "The child is mad," and they went on their own ways.

Then the naughty boys came around her and cried out,

"Big Bird has lost her mates. She sees a bigger bird in the sky, and she wants it." And they made rhymes about her, and sang them as they danced round.

Zaya ran away from them; and she hurried right through the city, and out into the country beyond it, for she still saw the great Form before her in the air.

As she went on, and got nearer and nearer to the Giant, it grew a little darker. She could see only the clouds; but still there was visible the form of a Giant hanging dimly in the air.

A cold mist closed around her as the Giant appeared to come onwards towards her. Then she thought of all the poor people in the city, and she hoped that the Giant would spare them, and she knelt down before him and lifted up her hands appealingly, and cried aloud:

"Oh, great Giant! spare them, spare them!"

But the Giant moved onwards still as though he never heard. She cried aloud all the more,

"Oh, great Giant! spare them, spare them!" And she bowed her head and wept, and the Giant still, though very slowly, moved onward towards the city.

There was an old man not far off standing at the door of a small house built of great stones, but the little maid saw him not. His face wore a look of fear and wonder, and when he saw the child kneel and raise her hands, he drew nigh and listened to her voice. When he heard her say, "Oh, great Giant!" he murmured to himself,

"It is then even as I feared. There are more Giants, and truly this is another." He looked upwards, but he saw nothing, and he murmured again,

"I see not, yet this child can see; and yet I feared, for something told me that there was danger. Truly knowledge is blinder than innocence."

The little maid, still not knowing there was any human being near her, cried out again, with a great cry of anguish:

"Oh, do not, do not, great Giant, do them harm. If someone must suffer, let it be me. Take me, I am willing to die, but spare them. Spare them, great Giant and do with me even as thou wilt." But the giant heeded not.

And Knoal — for he was the old man — felt his eyes fill with tears, and he said to himself,

"Oh, noble child, how brave she is, she would sacrifice herself!" And coming closer to her, he put his hand upon her head.

Zaya, who was again bowing her head, started and looked round when she felt the touch. However, when she saw that it was Knoal, she was comforted, for she knew how wise and good he was, and felt that if any person could help her, he could. So she clung to him, and hid her face in his breast; and he stroked her hair and comforted her. But still he could see nothing.

The cold mist swept by, and when Zaya looked up, she saw that the Giant had passed by, and was moving onward to the city.

"Come with me, my child," said the old man; and the two arose, and went into the dwelling built of great stones.

When Zaya entered, she started, for lo! the inside was as a Tomb. The old man felt her shudder, for he still held her close to him, and he said,

"Weep not, little one, and fear not. This place reminds me and all who enter it, that to the tomb we must all come at the last. Fear it not, for it has grown to be a cheerful home to me."

Then the little maid was comforted, and began to examine

all around her more closely. She saw all sorts of curious instruments, and many strange and many common herbs and simples hung to dry in bunches on the walls. The old man watched her in silence till her fear was gone, and then he said:

"My child, saw you the features of the Giant as he passed?"

She answered, "Yes."

"Can you describe his face and form to me?" he asked again.

Whereupon she began to tell him all that she had seen. How the Giant was so great that all the sky seemed filled. How the great arms were outspread, veiled in his robe, till far away the shroud was lost in air. How the face was as that of a strong man, pitiless, yet without malice; and that the eyes were blind.

The old man shuddered as he heard, for he knew that the Giant was a very terrible one; and his heart wept for the doomed city where so many would perish in the midst of their sin.

They determined to go forth and warn again the doomed people; and making no delay, the old man and the little maid hurried towards the city.

As they left the small house, Zaya saw the Giant before them, moving towards the city. They hurried on; and when they had passed through the cold mist, Zaya looked back and saw the Giant behind them.

Presently they came to the city.

It was a strange sight to see that old man and that little maid flying to tell people of the terrible Plague that was coming upon them. The old man's long white beard and hair and the child's golden locks were swept behind them in the wind, so quick they came. The faces of both were white as death. Behind them, seen only to the eyes of the pure-hearted little maid when she looked back, came ever onward at slow pace the spectral Giant that hung a dark shadow in the evening air.

But those in the city never saw the Giant; and when the old man and the little maid warned them, still they heeded not, but scoffed and jeered at them, and said,

"Tush! there are no Giants now"; and they went on their way, laughing and jeering.

Then the old man came and stood on a raised place amongst them, on the lowest step of the great fountain with the little maid by his side, and he spake thus:

"Oh, people, dwellers in this Land, be warned in time. This pure-hearted child, round whose sweet innocence even the little birds that fear men and women gather in peace, has this night seen in the sky the form of a Giant that advances ever onward menacingly to our city. Believe, oh, believe; and be warned, whilst ye may. To myself even as to you the sky is a blank; and yet see that I believe. For listen to me: all unknowing that another Giant had invaded our land, I sat pensive in my dwelling; and, without cause or motive, there came into my heart a sudden fear for the safety of our city. I arose and looked north and south and east and west, and on high and below, but never a sign of danger could I see. So I said to myself, 'Mine eyes are dim with a hundred years of watching and waiting, and so I cannot see.' And yet, oh people, dwellers in this land, though that century has dimmed mine outer eyes, still it has quickened mine inner eyes — the eyes of my soul. Again I went forth, and lo! this little maid knelt and implored a Giant, unseen by me, to spare the city; but he heard her not, or, if he heard, answered her not, and she fell prone. So hither we come to warn you. Yonder, says the maid, he passes onward to the city. Oh, be warned; be warned in time."

Still the people heeded not; but they scoffed and jeered the more, and said,

"Lo, the maid and the old man both are mad"; and they passed onwards to their homes — to dancing and feasting as before.

Then the naughty boys came and mocked them, and said that Zaya had lost her birds, and gone mad; and they made songs, and sang them as they danced round.

Zaya was so sorely grieved for the poor people that she heeded not the cruel boys. Seeing that she did not heed them, some of them got still more rude and wicked; they went a little way off, and threw things at them, and mocked them all the more.

Then, sad of heart, the old man arose, and took the little maid by the hand, and brought her away into the wilderness;

and lodged her with him in the house built with great stones. That night Zaya slept with the sweet smell of the drying herbs all around her; and the old man held her hand that she might have no fear.

In the morning Zaya arose betimes, and awoke the old man, who had fallen asleep in his chair.

She went to the doorway and looked out, and then a thrill of gladness came upon her heart; for outside the door, as though waiting to see her, sat all her little birds, and many, many more. When the birds saw the little maid they sang a few loud joyous notes, and flew about foolishly for very joy — some of them fluttering their wings and looking so funny that she could not help laughing a little.

When Knoal and Zaya had eaten their frugal breakfast and given to their little feathered friends, they set out with sorrowful hearts to visit the city, and to try once more to warn the people. The birds flew around them as they went, and to cheer them sang as joyously as they could, although their little hearts were heavy.

As they walked they saw before them the great shadowy Giant; and he had now advanced to the very confines of the city.

Once again they warned the people, and great crowds came around them, but only mocked them more than ever; and naughty boys threw stones and sticks at the little birds and killed some of them. Poor Zaya wept bitterly, and Knoal's heart was very sad. After a time, when they had moved from the fountain, Zaya looked up and started with joyous surprise, for the great shadowy Giant was nowhere to be seen. She cried out in joy, and the people laughed and said,

"Cunning child! she sees that we will not believe her, and she pretends that the Giant has gone."

They surrounded her, jeering, and some of them said,

"Let us put her under the fountain and duck her, as a lesson to liars who would frighten us." Then they approached her with menaces. She clung close to Knoal, who had looked terribly grave when she had said she did not see the Giant any longer, and who was now as if in a dream, thinking. But at her touch he seemed to wake up; and he spoke sternly to the people, and rebuked them. But they cried out on him also, and said that as he had aided Zaya in her lie he should be ducked also, and they advanced to lay hands on them both.

The hand of one who was a ringleader was already out-stretched, when he gave a low cry, and pressed his hand to his side; and, whilst the others turned to look at him in wonder, he cried out in great pain, and screamed horribly. Even whilst the people looked, his face grew blacker and blacker, and he fell down before them, and writhed a while in pain, and then died.

All the people screamed out in terror, and ran away, crying aloud:

"The Giant! the Giant! he is indeed amongst us!" They feared all the more that they could not see him.

But before they could leave the marketplace, in the center of which was the fountain, many fell dead and their corpses lay.

There in the center knelt the old man and the little maid, praying; and the birds sat perched around the fountain, mute and still, and there was no sound heard save the cries of the people far off. Then their wailing sounded louder and louder, for the Giant — Plague — was amongst and around them, and there was no escaping, for it was now too late to fly.

Alas! in the Country Under the Sunset there was much weeping that day; and when the night came there was little sleep, for there was fear in some hearts and pain in others. None were still except the dead, who lay stark about the city, so still and lifeless that even the cold light of the moon and the shadows of the drifting clouds moving over them could not make them seem as though they lived.

And for many a long day there was pain and grief and death in the Country Under the Sunset.

Knoal and Zaya did all they could to help the poor people, but it was hard indeed to aid them, for the unseen Giant was amongst them, wandering through the city to and fro, so that none could tell where he would lay his ice-cold hand.

Some people fled away out of the city; but it was little use, for go how they would and fly never so fast they were still within the grasp of the unseen Giant. Ever and anon he turned their warm hearts to ice with his breath and his touch, and they fell dead.

Some, like those within the city, were spared, and of these some perished of hunger, and the rest crept sadly back to the city and lived or died amongst their friends. And it was all, oh! so sad, for there was nothing but grief and fear and weeping from morn till night.

Now, see how Zaya's little bird friends helped her in her need.

They seemed to see the coming of the Giant when no one — not even the little maid herself — could see anything, and they managed to tell her when there was danger just as well as though they could talk.

At first Knoal and she went home every evening to the house built of great stones to sleep, and came again to the city in the morning, and stayed with the poor sick people, comforting them and feeding them, and giving them medicine which Knoal, from his great wisdom, knew would do them good. Thus they saved many precious human lives, and those who were rescued were very thankful, and henceforth ever after lived holier and more unselfish lives.

After a few days, however, they found that the poor sick people needed help even more at night than in the day, and so they came and lived in the city altogether, helping the stricken folk day and night.

At the earliest dawn Zaya would go forth to breathe the morning air; and there, just waked from sleep, would be her feathered friends waiting for her. They sang glad songs of joy, and came and perched on her shoulders and her head, and kissed her. Then, if she went to go towards any place where, during the night, the Plague had laid his deadly hand, they would flutter before her, and try to impede her, and scream out in their own tongue,

"Go back! go back!"

They pecked of her bread and drank of her cup before she touched them; and when there was danger — for the cold hand of the Giant was placed everywhere — they would cry,

"No, no!" and she would not touch the food, or let anyone else do so. Often it happened that, even whilst it pecked at the bread or drank of the cup, a poor little bird would fall down and flutter its wings and die; but all they that died, did so with a chirp of joy, looking at their little mistress, for whom they had gladly perished. Whenever the little birds found that the bread and the cup were pure and free from danger, they would look up at Zaya jauntily, and flap their wings and try to crow, and seemed so saucy that the poor sad little maiden would smile.

There was one old bird that always took a second, and often a great many pecks at the bread when it was good, so that he got quite a hearty meal; and sometimes he would go on feeding till Zaya would Shake her finger at him and say,

"Greedy!" and he would hop away as if he had done nothing.

There was one other dear little bird — a robin, with a breast as red as the sunset — that loved Zaya more than one can think. When he tried the food and found that it was safe to eat, he would take a tiny piece in his bill, and fly up and put it in her mouth.

Every little bird that drank from Zaya's cup and found it good raised its head to say grace; and ever since then the little birds do the same, and they never forget to say their grace — as some thankless children do.

Thus Knoal and Zaya lived, although many around them died, and the Giant still remained in the city. So many people died that one began to wonder that so many were left; for it was only when the town began to get thinned that people thought of the vast numbers that had lived in it.

Poor little Zaya had got so pale and thin that she looked a shadow, and Knoal's form was bent more with the sufferings of a few weeks than it had been by his century of age. But although the two were weary and worn, they still kept on their good work of aiding the sick.

Many of the little birds were dead.

One morning the old man was very weak — so weak that he could hardly stand. Zaya got frightened about him, and said,

"Are you ill, father?" for she always called him father now.

He answered her in a voice alas! hoarse and low, but very, very tender:

"My child, I fear the end is coming: take me home, that there I may die."

At his words Zaya gave a low cry and fell on her knees

beside him, and buried her head in his bosom and wept bitterly, whilst she hugged him close. But she had little time for weeping, for the old man struggled up to his feet, and, seeing that he wanted aid, she dried her tears and helped him.

The old man took his staff, and with Zaya helping to support him, got as far as the fountain in the midst of the marketplace; and there, on the lowest step, he sank down as though exhausted. Zaya felt him grow cold as ice, and she knew that the chilly hand of the Giant had been laid upon him.

Then, without knowing why, she looked up to where she had last seen the Giant as Knoal and she had stood beside the fountain. And lo! as she looked, holding Knoal's hand, she saw the shadowy form of the terrible Giant who had been so long invisible growing more and more clearly out of the clouds.

His face was stern as ever, and his eyes were still blind.

Zaya cried to the Giant, still holding Knoal tightly by the hand:

"Not him, not him! Oh, mighty Giant! not him! not him!" and she bowed her head and wept.

There was such. anguish in her hart that to the blind eyes of the shadowy Giant came tears that fell like dew on the forehead of the old man. Knoal spake to Zaya:

"Grieve not, my child. I am glad that you see the Giant again, for I have hope that he will leave our city free from woe. I am the last victim, and I gladly die."

Then Zaya knelt to the Giant, and said:

"Spare him! oh! spare him and take me! but spare him! spare him!"

The old man raised himself upon his elbow as he lay, and spake to her:

"Grieve not, my little one, and repine not. Sooth I know that you would gladly give your life for mine. But we must give for the good of others that which is dearer to us than our lives. Bless you, my little one, and be good. Farewell! farewell!"

As he spake the last word he grew cold as death, and his spirit passed away.

Zaya knelt down and prayed; and when she looked up she

saw the shadowy Giant moving away.

The Giant turned as he passed on, and Zaya saw that his blind eyes looked towards her as though he were trying to see. He raised the great shadowy arms, draped still in his shroud of mist, as though blessing her; and she thought that the wind that came by her moaning bore the echo of the words:

"Innocence and devotion save the land."

*P*resently she saw far off the great shadowy Giant Plague moving away to the border of the Land, and passing between the Guardian Spirits out through the Portal into the deserts beyond — forever.

The Seer

I had just arrived at Cruden Bay on my annual visit, and after a late breakfast was sitting on the low wall which was a continuation of the escarpment of the bridge over the Water of Cruden. Opposite to me, across the road and standing under the only little clump of trees in the place was a tall, gaunt old woman, who kept looking at me intently. As I sat, a little group, consisting of a man and two women, went by. I found my eyes follow them, for it seemed to me after they had passed me that the two women walked together and the man alone in front carrying on his shoulder a little black box — a coffin. I shuddered as I thought, but a moment later I saw all three abreast as they had been. The old woman was now looking at me with eyes that blazed. She came across the road and said to me without preface:

"What saw ye then, that yer e'en looked so awed?" I did not like to tell her so I did not answer. Her great eyes were fixed keenly upon me, seeming to look me through and through. I felt that I grew quite red, whereupon she said, apparently to herself: "I thocht so! Even I did not see that which he saw."

"How do you mean?" I queried. She answered ambiguously:

"Wait! Ye shall perhaps know before this hour tomorrow!"

Her answer interested me and I tried to get her to say more; but she would not. She moved away with a grand stately movement that seemed to become her great gaunt form.

After dinner whilst I was sitting in front of the hotel, there was a great commotion in the village; much running to and fro of men and women with sad mien. On questioning them I found that a child had been drowned in the little harbor below. Just then a woman and a man, the same that had passed the bridge earlier in the day, ran by with wild looks. One of the bystanders looked after them pityingly as he said:

"Puir souls. It's a sad home-comin' for them the nicht."

"Who are they?" I asked. The man took off his cap reverently as he answered:

"The father and mother of the child that was drowned!" As he spoke I looked round as though someone had called me.

There stood the gaunt woman with a look of triumph on her face.

*T*he curved shore of Cruden Bay, Aberdeenshire, is backed by a waste of sandhills in whose hollows seagrass and moss and wild violets, together with the pretty "grass of Parnassus" form a green carpet. The surface of the hills is held together by bent-grass and is eternally shifting as the wind takes the fine sand and drifts it to and fro. All behind is green, from the meadows that mark the southern edge of the bay to the swelling uplands that stretch away and away far in the distance, till the blue mist of the mountains at Braemar sets a kind of barrier. In the center of the bay the highest point of the land that runs downward to the sea looks like a miniature hill known as the Hawklaw; from this point onward to the extreme south the land runs high with a gentle trend downwards.

Cruden sands are wide and firm and the sea runs out a considerable distance. When there is a storm with the wind on shore the whole bay is a mass of leaping waves and broken water that threatens every instant to annihilate the stake-nets which stretch out here and there along the shore. More than a few vessels have been lost on these wide stretching sands, and it was perhaps the roaring of the shallow seas and the terror which they inspired which sent the crews to the spirit room and the bodies of those of them which came to shore later on, to the churchyard on the hill.

If Cruden Bay is to be taken figuratively as a mouth, with the sand hills for soft palate, and the green Hawklaw as the tongue, the rocks which mark the extremities are its teeth. To the north the rocks of red granite rise jagged and broken. To the south, a mile and a half away as the crow flies, Nature seems to have manifested its wildest forces. It is here, where the little promontory called Whinnyfold juts out, that the two great geological features of the Aberdeen coast meet. The red sienite of the north joins the black gneiss of the south. That union must have been originally a wild one; there are evidences of an upheaval which must have shaken the earth to its center. Here and there are great masses of either species of rock hurled upwards in every conceivable variety of form, sometimes fused or pressed together so that it is impossible to say exactly where gneiss ends or sienite begins; but broadly speaking here is an irregular line of separation. This line runs seawards to the east and its strength is shown in its outcrop. For half a mile or more the rocks rise through the sea singly or in broken masses ending in a dangerous cluster known as "The Skares" and which has had for centuries its full toll of wreck and disaster. Did the sea hold its dead where they fell, its floor around the Skares would be whitened with their bones, and new islands could build themselves with the piling wreckage. At times one may see here the ocean in her fiercest mood; for it is when the tempest drives from the southeast that the sea is fretted amongst the rugged rocks and sends its spume landwards. The rocks that at calmer times rise dark from the briny deep are lost to sight for moments in the grand onrush of the waves. The seagulls which usually whiten them, now flutter around screaming, and the sound of their shrieks comes in on the gale almost in a continuous note, for the single cries are merged in the multitudinous roar of sea and air.

The village, squatted beside the emboucher of the Water of Cruden at the northern side of the bay is simple enough; a few rows of fishermen's cottages, two or three great red-tiled drying-sheds nestled in the sand-heap behind the fishers' houses. For the rest of the place as it was when first I saw it, a little lockout beside a tall flagstaff on the northern cliff, a few scattered farms over the inland prospect, one little hotel down on the western bank of the Water of Cruden with a fringe of willows protecting its sunk garden which was always full of fruits and flowers.

From the most southern part of the beach of Cruden Bay to Whinnyfold village the distance is but a few hundred yards; first a steep pull up the face of the rock; and then an even way, beside part of which runs a tiny stream. To the left of this path, going towards Whinnyfold, the ground rises in a bold slope and then falls again all round, forming a sort of wide miniature hill of some eighteen or twenty acres. Of this the southern side is sheer, the black rock dipping into the waters of the little bay of Whinnyfold, in the center of which is a picturesque island of rock shelving steeply from the water on the northern side, as is the tendency of all the gneiss and granite in this part. But to east and north there are irregular bays or openings, so that the furthest points of the promotory stretch out like fingers. At the tips of these are reefs of sunken rock falling down to deep water and whose existence can only be suspected in bad weather when the rush of the current beneath sends up swirling eddies or curling masses of foam. These little bays are mostly curved and are green where falling earth or drifting sand have hidden the outmost side of the rocks and given a foothold to the seagrass and clover. Here have been at some time or other great caves, now either fallen in or silted up with sand, or obliterated with the earth brought down in the rush of surface-water in times of long rain. In one of these bays, Broad Haven, facing right out to the Skares, stands an isolated pillar of rock called locally the "Puir mon" through whose base, time and weather have worn a hole through which one may walk dry shod.

Through the masses of rocks that run down to the sea from the sides and shores of all these bays are here and there natural channels with straight edges as though cut on purpose for the taking in of the cobbles belonging to the fisher folk of Whinnyfold.

When first I saw the place I fell in love with it. Had it been possible I should have spent my summer there, in a house of my own, but the want of any place in which to live forbade such an opportunity. So I stayed in the little hotel, the Kilmarnock Arms.

The next year I came again, and the next, and the next. And then I arranged to take a feu at Whinnyfold and to build a house overlooking the Skares for myself. The details of this kept me constantly going to Whinnyfold, and my house to be was always in my thoughts.

Hitherto my life had been an uneventful one. At school I was, though secretly ambitious, dull as to results. At College I was better off, for my big body and athletic powers gave me a certain position in which I had to overcome my natural shyness. When I was about eight and twenty I found myself nominally a barrister, with no knowledge whatever of the practice of law and but little less of the theory, and with a commission in the Devil's Own — the irrelevant name given to the Inns of Court Volunteers. I had few relatives, but a comfortable, though not great, fortune; and I had been round the world, dilettante fashion.

*A*ll that night I thought of the dead child and of the peculiar vision which had come to me. Sleeping or waking it was all the same; my mind could not leave the parents in procession as seen in imagination, or their distracted mien in reality. Mingled with them was the great-eyed, aquiline-featured, gaunt old woman who had taken such an interest in the affair; and in my part of it. I asked the landlord if he knew her, since from his position as postmaster he knew almost everyone for miles around. He told me that she was a stranger to the place. Then he added:

"I can't imagine what brings her here. She has come over from Peterhead two or three times lately; but she doesn't seem to have anything at all to do. She has nothing to sell and she buys nothing. She's not a tripper, and she's not a beggar, and she's not a thief, and she's not a worker of any sort. She's a queer-looking lot anyhow. I fancy from her speech that she's from the west; probably from some of the far-out islands. I can tell that she has the Gaelic from the way she speaks."

Later on in the day, when I was walking on the shore near the Hawklaw, she came up to speak to me. The shore was quite lonely, for in those days it was rare to see anyone on the beach except when the salmon fishers drew their nets at the ebbing tide. I was walking towards Whinnyfold when she came upon me silently from behind. She must have been hidden among the bent-grass of the sandhills for had she been anywhere in view I must have seen her on that desolate shore. She was evidently a most imperious person; she at once addressed me in a tone and manner which made me feel as though I were in some way an inferior, and in somehow to blame:

"What for did ye no tell me what ye saw yesterday?" Instinctively I answered:

"I don't know why. Perhaps because it seemed so ridiculous." Her stern features hardened into scorn as she replied:

"Are Death and the Doom then so redeekulous that they pleasure ye intil silence?" I somehow felt that this was a little too much and was about to make a sharp answer, when suddenly it struck me as a remarkable thing that she knew already. Filled with surprise I straightway asked her:

"Why, how on earth do you know? I told no one." I stopped for I felt all at sea; there was some mystery here which I could not fathom. She seemed to read my mind like an open book, for she went on looking at me as she spoke, searchingly and with an odd smile.

"Eh! laddie, do ye no ken that ye hae een that can see? Do ye no understand that ye hae een that can speak? Is it that one with the Gift o' Second Sight has no an understandin' o' it. Why, yer face when ye saw the mark o' the Doom, was like a printed book to een like mine."

"Do you mean to tell me," I asked, "that you could tell what I saw, simply by looking at my face?"

"Na! na! laddie. Not all that, though a Seer am I; but I knew that you had seen the Doom! It's no that varied that there need be any mistake. After all Death is only one, in whatever way we may speak!" After a pause of thought I asked her:

"If you have the power of Second Sight why did you not see the vision, or whatever it was, yourself?"

"Eh! laddie," she answered, shaking her head, "'Tis little ye ken o' the wark o' the Fates! Learn ye then that the Voice speaks only as it listeth into chosen ears, and the Vision comes to chosen een. None can will to hear or to see, to pleasure theirsels."

"Then," I said, and I felt that there was a measure of triumph in my tone, "if to none but the chosen is given to know, how comes it that you, who seem not to have been chosen on this occasion at all events, know all the same?" She answered with a touch of impatience:

"Do ye ken, young sir, that even mortal een have power to see much, if there be behind them the thocht, an' the knowledge and the experience to guide them aright. How, think ye, is it that some can see much, and learn much as they gang; while others go blind as the mowdiwart, at the end o' the journey as before it?"

"Then perhaps you will tell me how much you saw, and how you saw it?"

"Ah! to them that have seen the Doom there needs but sma' guidance to their thochts. Too lang, an' too often hae I mysen seen the death-sark an' the watch-candle an' the dead-hole, not to know when they are seen tae ither een. Na, na! laddie, what I kent o' yer seein' was no by the Gift but only by the use o' my proper een. I kent not the muckle o' what ye saw. Not whether it was ane or ither o' the garnishins o' the dead; but weel I kent that it was o' death."

"Then," I said interrogatively, "Second Sight is altogether a matter of chance?"

"Chance! chance!" she repeated with scorn. "Na! young sir; when the Voice has spoken there is no more chance than that the nicht will follow the day."

"You mistake me," I said, feeling somewhat superior now that I had caught her in an error, "I did not for a moment mean that the Doom — whatever it is — is not a true forerunner. What I meant was that it seems to be a matter of chance in whose ear the Voice — whatever it is — speaks; when once it has been ordained that it is to sound in the ear of some one." Again she answered with scorn:

"Na, na! there is no chance o' ocht about the Doom. Them that send forth the Voice and the Seein' know well to whom it is sent and why. Can ye no comprehend that it is for no bairn-play that such goes forth. When the Voice speaks, it is mainly followed by tears an' woe an' lamentation! Nae! nor is it only one bit manifestation that stands by its lanes, remote and isolate from all ither. Truly 'tis but a pairt o' the great scheme o' things; an' be sure that who so is chosen to see or to hear is chosen weel, an' must hae their pairt in what is to be, on to the verra end."

"Am I to take it," I asked, "that Second Sight is but a little bit of some great purpose which has to be wrought out by means of many kinds; and that who so sees the Vision or hears the Voice is but the blind unconscious instrument of Fate?"

"Aye! laddie. Weel eneuch the Fates know their wishes an' their wark, no to need the help or the thocht of any human-blind or seein', sane or silly, conscious or unconscious."

All through her speaking I had been struck by the old woman's use of the word "Fate," and more especially when she used it in the plural. It was evident that, Christian though she might be — and in the West they are generally devout observants of the duties of their creed — her belief in this respect came from some of the old pagan mythologies. I should have liked to question her on this point; but I feared to shut her lips against me. Instead I asked her:

"Tell me, will you, if you don't mind, of some case you have known yourself of Second Sight?"

"Tis no for them to brag or boast to whom has been given to see the wark o' the hand o' Fate. But sine ye are yerself a Seer an' would learn, then I may speak. I hae seen the sea ruffle wi'oot cause in the verra spot where later a boat was to gang doon, I hae heard on a lone moor the hammerin' o' the coffin-wright when one passed me who was soon to dee. I hae seen the death-sarli fold round the speerit o' a drowned one, in baith ma sleepin' an' ma wakin' dreams. I hae heard the settin' doom o' the spaiks, an' I hae seen the weepers on a' the crood that walked. Aye, an' in money anither way hae I seen an' heard the Coming o' the Doom."

"But did all the seeings and hearings come true?" I asked. "Did it ever happen that you heard queer sounds or saw strange sights and that yet nothing came of them? I gather that you do not always know to whom something is going to happen; but only that death is coming to some one!" She was not displeased at my questioning but replied at once:

"Na doot! but there are times when what is seen or heard has no manifest following. But think ye, young sir, how mony a corp, still waited for, lies in the depths o' the sea; how mony lie oot on the hillsides, or are fallen in deep places where their bones whiten unkent. Nay! more, to how many has Death come in a way that men think the wark o' nature when his hastening has come frae the hand of man, untold." This was a difficult matter to answer so I changed or rather varied the subject.

"How long must elapse before the warning comes true?"

"Ye know yersel', for but yestreen ye hae seen, how the Death can follow hard upon the Doom; but there be times, nay mostly are they so, when days or weeks pass away ere the Doom is fulfilled."

"Is this so?" I asked, "when you know the person regarding whom the Doom is spoken." She answered with an air of certainty which somehow carried conviction, secretly, with it.

"Even so! I know one who walks the airth now in all the pride o' his strength. But the Doom has been spoken of him. I saw him with these verra een lie prone on rocks, wi' the water runnin' down from his hair. An' again I heard the minute bells as he went by me on a road where is no bell for a score o' miles. Aye, an' yet again I saw him in the kirk itsel' wi' corbies flyin' round him, an' mair gatherin' from afar!"

Here was indeed a case where Second Sight might be tested; so I asked her at once, though to do so I had to overcome a strange sort of repugnance:

"Could this be proved? Would it not be a splendid case to make known; so that if the death happened it would prove beyond all doubt the existence of such a thing as Second Sight." My suggestion was not well received. She answered with slow scorn:

"Beyon' all doot! Doot! Wha is there that doots the bein' o' the Doom? Learn ye too, young sir, that the Doom an' all thereby is no for traffickin' wi' them that only cares for curiosity and publeecity. The Voice and the Vision o' the Seer is no for fine madams and idle gentles to while away their time in play-toy make-believe!" I climbed down at once.

"Pardon me!" I said, "I spoke without thinking. I should not have said so — to you at any rate." She accepted my apology with a sort of regal inclination; but the moment after she showed by her words she was after all but a woman!

"I will tell ye; that so in the full time ye may hae no doot yersel'. For ye are a Seer and as Them that has the power hae gien ye the Gift it is no for the like o' me to cumber the road o' their doin'. Know ye then, and remember weel, how it was told ye by Gormala MacNiel that Lauchlane Macleod o' the Outer Isles hae been Called; tho' as yet the Voice has no sounded in his ears but only in mine. But ye will see the time —"

She stopped suddenly as though some thought had struck her, and then went on impressively:

"When I saw him lie prone on the rocks there was ane that bent ower him that I kent not in the nicht wha it was, though the licht o' the moon was around him. We shall see! We shall see!"

Without a word more she turned and left me. She would not listen to my calling after her; but with long strides passed up the beach and was lost among the sandhills.

The Man from Shorrox'

*T*hroth, yer 'ann'rs, I'll tell ye wid pleasure; though, trooth to tell, it's only poor wurrk telling the same shtory over an' over agin. But I niver object to tell it to rale gintlemin, like yer 'ann'rs, what don't forget that a poor man has a mouth on to him as much as Creeshus himself has.

The place was a market town in Kilkenny — or maybe King's County or Queen's County. At all evints, it was wan of them counties what Cromwell — bad cess to him! — gev his name to. An' the house was called after him that was the Lord Liftinint an' invinted the polis — God forgive him! It was kep' be a man iv the name iv Misther Mickey Byrne an' his good lady — at laste it was till wan dark night whin the bhoys mistuk him for another gindeman, an unknown man, what had bought a contagious property — mind ye the impidence iv him. Mickey was comin' back from the Curragh Races wid his skin that tight wid the full of the whiskey inside of him that he couldn't open his eyes to see what was goin' on, or his mouth to set the bhoys right afther he had got the first tap on the head wid wan of the blackthorns what they done such jobs wid. The poor bhoys was that full of sorra for their mishap whin they brung him home to his widdy that the crather hadn't the hearrt to be too sevare on thim. At the first iv course she was wroth, bein' only a woman afther all, an' weemun not bein' gave to rayson like nun is. Millia murdher! but for a bit she was like a madwoman, and was nigh to have cut the heads from affav thim wid the mate chopper, till, seein' thim so white and quite, she all at wance flung down the chopper an' knelt down be the corp.

"Lave me to me dead," she sez. "Oh mm! it's no use more people nor is needful bein' made unhappy over this night's terrible wurrk. Mick Byrne would have no man worse for him whin he was living, and he'll have harm to none for his death! Now go; an', oh bhoys, be dacent and quite, an' don't thry a poor widdied sowl too hard!"

Well, afther that she made no change in things ginerally, but kep' on the hotel jist the same; an' whin some iv her friends wanted her to get help, she only sez: "Mick an' me run this house well enough; an' whin I'm thinkin' of takun' help I'll tell yez. I'll go on be meself, as I mane to, till Mick an' me comes together agun."

An', sure enough, the ould place wint on jist the same, though, more betoken, there wasn't Mick wid his shillelagh to kape the pace whin things got pretty hot on fair nights, an' in the gran' ould election times, when heads was bruk like eggs — glory be to God!

My! but she was the fine woman, was the Widdy Byrne! A gran' crathur intirely: a fine upshtandin' woman, nigh as tall as a modheratesized man, wid a forrm on her that'd warrm yer hearrt to look at, it sthood out that way in the right places. She had shkin like satin, wid a warrm flush in it, like the sun shinun' on a crock iv yestherday's crame; an' her cheeks an' her neck was that firrm that ye couldn't take a pinch iv thim — though sorra wan iver dar'd to thry, the worse luck! But her hair! Begor, that was the finishing touch that set all the min crazy. It was jist wan mass iv red, like the heart iv a burnun' furze-bush whin the smoke goes from aff iv it. Musha! but it'd make the blood come up in yer eyes to see the glint iv that hair wid the light shinun' on it. There was niver a man, what was a man at all at all, iver kem in be the door that he didn't want to put his two arrms round the widdy an' giv' her a hug immadiate. They was fine min too, some iv thim — and warrm men — big graziers from Kildare, and the like, that counted their cattle be scores, an' used to come ridin' in to market on huntin' horses what they'd refuse hundlireds iv pounds for from officers in the Curragh an' the quality. Begor, but some iv thim an' the dhrovers was rare

miii in a fight. More nor wance I seen them, forty, maybe
half a hundred, strong, clear the marketplace at Banagher or
Athy. Well do I remimber the way the big, red, hairy wrists
iv thim'd go up in the air, an' down'd come the springy
ground-ash saplins what they carried for switches. The whole
lot iv thim wanted to come coortun' the widdy; but sorra wan
iv her'd look at thim. She'd flirt an' be coy an' taze thim and
make thim mad for love iv her, as weemin likes to do. Thank
God for the same! for mayhap we min wouldn't love thim as
we do only for their thricky ways; an' thin what'd become iv
the counthry wid nothin' in it at all except single min an'
ould maids jist dyin', and growin' crabbed for want iv chuid-
her to kiss an' tache an' shpank an' make love to? Shure, yer
'ann'rs, 'tis childher as makes the hearrt iv man green, jist as
it is fresh wather that makes the grass grow. Divil a shtep
nearer would the widdy iver let mortial man come. "No,"
she'd say; "whin I see a man fit to fill Mick's place, I'll let yez
know iv it; thank ye kindly'; an' wid that she'd shake her head
till the beautiful red hair iv it'd be like shparks iv fire — an'
the mm more mad for her nor iver.

But, mind ye, she wasn't no shpoil-shport; Mick's wife
knew more nor that, an' his widdy didn't forgit the thrick iv
it. She'd lade the laugh herself if 'twas anything a dacent
woman could shmile at; an' if it wasn't, she'd send the girrls
aff to their beds, an' tell the min they might go on talkin'
that way, for there was only herself to be insulted; an' that'd
shut thim up pretty quick I'm tellin' yez. But av any iv thim'd
thry to git affectionate, as min do whin they've had all they
can carry, well, thin she had a playful way iv dalin' wid thim
what'd always turn the laugh agin' thim. She used to say that
she lamed the beginnun' iv it at the school an' the rest iv it
from Mick. She always kep by her on the counther iv the bar
wan iv thim rattan canes wid the curly ends, what the soldiers
carries whin they can't barry a whip, an' are goin' out wid
their cap on three hairs, an' thim new oiled, to scorch the
girrls. An' thin whin any iv the shuitors'd get too affectionate
she'd lift the cane an' swish them wid it, her laughin' out iv
her like mad all the time. At first wan or two iv the min'd
say that a kiss at the widdy was worth a clip iv a cane; an' wan
iv thim, a warrm horse-fanner from Poul-a-Phoka, said he'd

complate the job av she was to cut him into ribbons. But she
was a handy woman wid the cane — which was shtrange
enough, for she had no childer to be practisin' on — an' whin
she threw what was left iv him back over the bar, wid his face
like a gridiron, the other min what was laughin' along wid
her tuk the lesson to hearrt. Whiniver afther that she laid her
hand on the cane, no matther how quietly, there'd be no more
talk iv thryin' for kissin' in that quarther.

Well, at the time I'm comm' to there was great divarshuns
intirely goin' on in the town. The fair was on the morra, an'
there was a power iv people in the town; an' cattle, an' geese,
an' turkeys, an' butther, an' pigs, an' vegetables, an' all kinds
iv divilment, includin' a berryin' — the same bein' an ould
attorney-man, savin' yer prisince; a lone man widout friends,
lyin' out there in the gran' room iv the hotel what they call
the "Queen's Room." Well, I needn't tell yer 'ann'rs that the
place was pretty full that night. Musha, but it's the fleas
thimselves what had the bad time iv it, wid thim crowded out
on the outside, an' shakin', an' thrimblin' wid the cowld. The
widdy, av coorse, was in the bar passin' the time iv the day
wid all that kem in, an' keepin' her eyes afore an' ahint her
to hould the girrls up to their wurrk an' not to be thriflin'
wid the mm. My! but there was a power iv min at the bar that
night; warrm farmers from four counties, an' graziers wid
their ground-ash plants an' big frieze coats, an' plinty iv
commercials, too. In the middle iv it all, up the shtreet at a
hand gallop comes an Athy carriage wid two horses, an' pulls
up at the door wid the horses shmokin'. An' begor', the man
in it was smokin' too, a big cygar nigh as long as yer arrm.
He jumps out an' walks up as bould as brass to the bar, jist
as if there was niver a livin' sowl but himself in the place. He
chucks the widdy undher the chin at wanst, an', taking aff
his hat, sez:

"I want the best room in the house. I travel for Shorrox',
the greatest long-cotton firrm in the whole worrld, an' I want
to open up a new line here! The best is what I want, an' that's
not good enough for me!"

Well, gintlemun, ivery wan in the place was spacheless at
his impidence; an', begor! that was the only time in her life
I'm tould whin the widdy was tuk back. But, glory be, it didn't

take long for her to recover herself, an' sez she quitely: "I don't doubt ye, sur! The best can't be too good for a gintleman what makes himself so aisy at home!" an' she shmiled at him till her teeth shone like jools.

God knows, gintlemin, what does be in weemin's minds whin they're dalin' wid a man! Maybe it was that Widdy Byrne only wanted to kape the pace wid all thim min crowdin' roun' her, an' thim clutchin' on tight to their shticks an' aiger for a fight wid any man on her account. Or maybe it was that she forgive him his impidence; for well I know that it's not the most modest man, nor him what kapes his distance, that the girrls, much less the widdies, like the best. But anyhow she spake out iv her to the man from Manchesther: "I'm sorry, sur, that I can't give ye the best room — what we call the best — for it is engaged already."

"Then turn him out!" sez he.

"I can't," she says — "at laste not till tomorra; an' ye can have the room thin iv ye like."

There was a kind iv a sort iv a shnicker among some iv the min, thim knowin' iv the corp, an' the Manchesther man tuk it that they was laughin' at him; so he sez: "I'll shleep in that room tonight; the other gintleman can put up wid me iv I can wid him. Unless," sez he, oglin' the widdy, "I can have the place iv the masther iv the house, if there's a priest or a parson handy in this town — an' sober," sez he.

Well, tho' the widdy got as red as a Claddagh cloak, she jist laughed an' turned aside, sayin': "Throth, sur, but it's poor Mick's place ye might have, an' welkim, this night."

"An' where might that be now, ma'am?" sez he, lanin' over the bar; an' him would have chucked her under the chin agun, only that she moved her head away that quick.

"In the churchyard!" she sez. "Ye might take Mick's place there, av ye like, an' I'll not be wan to say ye no."

At that the min round all laughed, an' the man from Manchesther got mad, an' shpoke out, rough enough too it seemed: "Oh, he's all right where he is. I daresay he's quiter times where he is than whin he had my luk out. Him an' the Devil can toss for choice in bein' lonely or bein' quite."

Wid that the widdy blazes up all iv a suddunt, like a live sod shtuck in the thatch, an' sez she:

"Who are ye that dares to shpake ill iv the dead, an' to couple his name wid the Divil, an' to his widdy's very face? It's aisy seen that poor Mick is gone!" an' wid that she threw her apron over her head an' sot down an' rocked herself to and fro, as widdies do whin the fit is on thim iv missin' the dead.

There was more nor wan man there what'd like to have shtud opposite the Manchesther man wid a bit iv a black-thorn in his hand; but they knew the widdy too well to dar to intherfere till they were let. At length wan iv thim — Mr. Hogan, from nigh Portarlington, a warrm man, that'd put down a thousand pounds iv dhry money any day in the week-kem over to the bar an' tuk aff his hat, an' sez he: "Mrs. Byrne, ma'am, as a friend of poor dear ould Mick, I'd be glad to take his quarrel on meself on his account, an' more than proud to take it on his widdy's, if, ma'am, ye'll only honor me be saying the wurrd."

Wid that she tuk down the apron from aff iv her head an' wiped away the tears in her jools iv eyes wid the corner iv it.

"Thank ye kindly," sez she; "but, guntlemin, Mick an' me run this hotel long together, an' I've run it alone since thin, an' I mane to go on runnin' it be meself, even if new min from Manchesther itself does be bringin' us new ways. As to you, sur," sez she, turnin' to him, "it's powerful afraid I am that there isn't accommodation here for a guntlemin what's so requireful. An' so I think I'll be askin' ye to find con-vanience in some other hotel in the town."

Wid that he turned on her an' sez, "I'm here now, an' I offer to pay me charges. Be the law ye can't refuse to resave me or refuse me lodgmint, especially whin I'm on the primises."

So the Widdy Byrne drewed herself up, an' sez she, "Sur, ye ask yer legal rights; ye shall have them. Tell me what it is ye require."

Sez he sthraight out: "I want the best room."

"I've tould you already," sez she, "there's a gintleman in it."

"Well," sez he, "what other room have ye vacant?"

"Sorra wan at all," sez she. "Every room in the house is tuk. Perhaps, sur, ye don't think or remimber that there's a fair on tomorra."

She shpoke so polite that ivery man in the place knew there
was somethin' comin' — later on. The Manchesther man felt
that the laugh was on him; but he didn't want for impidence,
so he up, an' sez he: "Thin, if I have to share wid another, I'll
share wid the best! It's the Queen's Room I'll be shleepin' in
this night."

Well, the min shtandin' by wasn't too well plazed wid what
was going on; for the man from Manchesther he was plumin'
himself for all the world like a cock on a dunghill. He laned
agin over the bar an' began makin' love to the widdy hot an'
fast. He was a fine, shtout — made man, wid a bull neck on
to him an' short hair, like wan iv thim "two-to-wan-bar-wans"
what I've seen at Punchestown an' Fairy House an' the Galway
races. But he seemed to have no manners at all in his coortin',
but done it as quick an' businesslike as takun' his commercial
ordhers. It was like this: "I want to make love; you want to
be made love to, bein' a woman. Hould up yer head!"

We all could see the widdy was boilin' mad; but, to do him
fair, the man from Manchesther didn't seem to care what any
wan thought. But we all seen what he didn't see at first, that
the widdy began widout thinkin' to handle the rattan cane
on the bar. Well, prisintly he began agun to ask about his
room, an' what kind iv a man it was that was to share it wid
him.

So sez the widdy, "A man wid less wickedness in him nor
you have, an' less impidence."

"I hope he's a quite man," sez he.

So the widdy began to laugh, an' sez she: "I'll warrant he's
quite enough."

"Does he shnore? I hate a man — or a woman ayther —
what shnores."

"Throth," sez she, "there's no shnore in him"; an' she
laughed agin.

Some iv the min round what knew iv the ould attorney-
man — saving yer prisince — began to laugh too; and this
made the Manchesther man suspicious. When the likes iv
him gets suspicious he gets rale nasty; so he sez, wid a shneer:
"You seem to be pretty well up in his habits, ma'am!"

The widdy looked round at the graziers, what was clutchin'

their ash plants hard, an' there was a laughin' divil in her eye that kep' thim quite; an' thin she turned round to the man, and sez she: "Oh, I know that much, anyhow, wid wan thing an' another, begor!" But she looked more enticin' nor iver at that moment. For sure the man from Manchesther thought so, for he laned nigh his whole body over the counther, an' whispered somethin' at her, puttin' out his hand as he did so, an' layin' it on her neck to dhraw her to him. The widdy seemed to know what was comm', an' had her hand on the rattan; so whin he was draggin' her to him an' puttin' out his lips to kiss her — an' her first as red as a turkey-cock an' thin as pale as a sheet — she ups wid the cane and gev him wan skelp across the face wid it, shpringin' back as she done so. Oh jool! but that was a skelp! A big wale iv blood riz up as quick as the blow was shtruck, jist as I've seen on the pigs' backs whin they do be prayin' aloud not to be tuk where they're wanted.

"Hands off, Misther Impidence!" sez she. The man from Manchesther was that mad that he ups wid the tumbler formnst him an' was goin' to throw it at her, whin there kem an odd sound from the graziers — a sort of "Ach!" as whin a man is workin' a sledge, an' I seen the ground-ash plants an' the big fists what held thim, and the big hairy wrists go up in the air. Begor, but polis thimselves wid bayonets wouldn't care to face thim like that! In the half of two twos the man from Manchesther would have been cut in ribbons, but there came a cry from the widdy what made the glasses ring: "Shtop! I'm not goin' to have any fightin' here; an' besides, there's bounds to the bad manners iv even a man from Shorrox'. He wouldn't dar to shtrike me — though I have no head! Maybe I hit a thought too hard; but I had rayson to remimber that somethin' was due on Mick's account too. I'm sorry, sur," sez she to the man, quite polite, "that I had to defind meself; but whin a gintleman claims the law to come into a house, an' thin assaults th' owner iv it, though she has no head, it's more restrainful he should be intirely!"

"Hear, hear!" cried some iv the mm, an' wan iv thim sez "Amen," sez he, an' they all begin to laugh. The Manchesther man he didn't know what to do; for begor he didn't like the look of thim ash plants up in the air, an' yit he was not wan to like the laugh agin' him or to take it aisy. So he turns to the widdy an' he lifts his hat an' sez he wid mock politeness: "I must complimint ye, ma'am, upon the shtrength iv yer arrm, as upon the mildness iv yer disposition. Throth, an' I'm thinkin' that it's misther Mick that has the best iv it, wid his body lyin' paceful in the churchyard, anyhow; though the poor sowl doesn't seem to have much good in changin' wan devil for another!" An' he looked at her rale spiteful.

Well, for a minit her eyes blazed, but thin she shmiled at him, an' made a low curtsey, an' sez she — oh! mind ye, she was a gran' woman at givin' back as good as she got — "Thank ye kindly, sur, for yer polite remarks about me arrm. Sure me poor dear Mick often said the same; only he said more an' wid shuparior knowledge! 'Molly', sez he — 'I'd mislike the shtrength iv yer arrm whin ye shtrike, only that I forgive ye for it whin it comes to the huggin'!' But as to poor Mick's prisint condition I'm not goin' to argue wid ye, though I can't say that I forgive ye for the way you've shpoke iv him that's gone. Bedad, it's fond iv the dead y'are, for ye seem onable to kape thim out iv yer mouth. Maybe ye'll be more respectful to thim before ye die!"

"I don't want no sarmons!" sez he, wery savage. "Am I to have me room tonight, or am I not?"

"Did I undherstand ye to say," sez she, "that ye wanted a share iv the Queen's Room?"

"I did! an' I demand it."

"Very well, sur," sez she very quitely, "ye shall have it!" Jist thin the supper war ready, and most iv the mm at the bar thronged into the coffee-room, an' among thim the man from Manchesther, what wint bang up to the top iv the table an sot down as though he owned the place, an' him niver in the house before.

A few iv the bhoys shtayed a minit to say another word to the widdy, an' as soon as they was alone Misther Hogan up, an' sez he: "Oh, darlint! but it's a jool iv a woman y' are! Do ye raly mane to put him in the room wid the corp?"

"He said he insisted on being in that room!" she says, quite sarious; an' thin givin' a look undher her lashes at the bhoys as made thim lep, sez she: "Oh! min, an ye love me give him his shkin that full that he'll tumble into his bed this night wid his sinses obscurifled. Dhrink toasts till he misremimbers where he is! Whist! Go, quick, so that he won't suspect nothin'!"

That was a warrm night, I'm telling ye! The man from Shorrox' had wine galore wid his mate; an' afther, whin the plates an' dishes was tuk away an' the nuts was brought in, Hogan got up an' proposed his health, an' wished him prosperity in his new line. Iv coorse he had to dhrink that; an' thin others got up, an' there was more toasts dhrunk than there was min in the room, till the man, him not bein' used to whiskey-punch, began to git onsartin in his shpache. So they gev him more toasts — "Ireland as a nation," an' "Home Rule," an' "The ruimory iv Dan O'Connell," an' "Bad luck to Boney," an' "God save the Queen," an' "More power to Manchesther," an' other things what they thought would plaze him, him bein' English. Long hours before it was time for the house to shut, he was as dhrunk as a whole row of fiddlers, an' kep shakin' hands wid ivery man an' promisin' thim to open a new line in Home Rule, an' sich nonsinse. So they tuk him up to the door iv the Queen's Room an' left him there.

He managed to undhress himself all except his hat, and got into bed wid the corp iv th' ould attorney-man, an' thin an' there fell asleep widout noticin' him.

Well, prisintly he woke wid a cowld feelin' all over him. He had lit no candle, an' there was only the light from the passage comm' in through the glass over the door. He felt himself nigh fallin' out iv the bed wid him almost on the edge, an' the cowld shtrange gindeman lyin' shlap on the broad iv his back in the middle. He had enough iv the dhrink in him to be quarrelsome.

"I'll throuble ye," sez he, "to kape over yer own side iv the bed — or I'll soon let ye know the rayson why." An' wid that he give him a shove. But iv coorse the ould attorney-man tuk no notice whatsumiver.

"Y'are not that warrm that one'd like to lie contagious to ye," sez he. "Move over, I say, to yer own side!" But divil a shtir iv the corp.

Well, thin he began to get fightin' angry, an' to kick an' shove the corp; but not gittin' any answer at all, he turned round an' hit him a clip on the side iv the head.

"Gitup," he sez, "iv ye're a man at all, an' put up yer dooks."

Then he got more madder shrill, for the dhrink was shtir-rin' in him, an' he kicked an' shoved an' grabbed him be the leg an' the arrm to move him.

"Begor!" sez he, "but ye're the cowldest chap I iver kem anigh iv. Musha! but yer hairs is like icicles."

Thin he tuk him be the head, an' shuk him an' brung him to the bedside, an' kicked him clane out on to the flure on the far side iv the bed.

"Lie there," he sez, "ye ould blast furnace! Ye can warrm yerself up on the flure till tomorra."

Be this time the power iv the dhrink he had tuk got ahoult iv him agin, an' he fell back in the middle iv the bed, wid his head on the pilla an' his toes up, an' wint aff ashleep, like a cat in the frost.

By-an'-by, whin the house was about shuttin' up, the watcher from th' undhertaker's kem to sit be the corp till the mornin', an' th' attorney him bein' a Protestan' there was no candles. Whin the house was quite, wan iv the girris, what was coortin' wid the watcher, shtole into the room.

"Are ye there, Michael?" sez she.

"Yis, me darlint!" he sez, comm' to her; an' there they shtood be the door, wid the lamp in the passage shinin' on the red heads iv the two iv thim.

"I've come," sez Katty, "to kape ye company for a bit, Michael; for it's crool lonesome worrk sittin' there alone all night. But I mustn't shtay long, for they're all goin' to bed soon, when the dishes is washed up."

"Give us a kiss," sez Michael.

"Oh, Michael!" sez she: "kissin' in the prisince iv a corp! It's ashamed iv ye I am."

"Sorra cause, Katty. Sure, it's more respectful than any other way. Isn't it next to kissin' in the chapel? — an' ye do that whin ye're bein' married. If ye kiss me now, begor but I don't know as it's mortial nigh a weddin' it is! Anyhow, give us a kiss, an' we'll talk iv the rights an' wrongs iv it afther-wards."

Well, somehow, yer 'ann'rs, that kiss was bein' gave — an' a kiss in the prisince iv a corp is a sarious thing an' takes a long time. Thim two was payin' such attintion to what was going on betune thim that they didn't heed nothin', whin suddint Katty stops, and sez: "Whist! what is that?"

Michael felt creepy too, for there was a quare sound comm' from the bed. So they grabbed one another as they shtud in the doorway an looked at the bed almost afraid to breathe till the hair on both iv thim began to shtand up in horror; for the corp rose up in the bed, an' they seen it pointin' at thim, an' heard a hoarse voice say, "It's in hell I am — Divils around me! Don't I see thim burnin' wid their heads like flames? an' it's burnin' lam too — burnin', burnin', burnin'! Me throat is on fire, an' me face is burnin'! Wather! wather! Give me wather, if only a dhrop on me tongue's tip!"

Well, thin Katty let one screetch out iv her, like to wake the dead, an' tore down the passage till she kem to the shtairs, and tuk a flyin' lep down an' fell in a dead faint on the mat below; and Michael yelled "murdher" wid all his might.

It wasn't long till there was a crowd in that room, I tell ye; an' a mighty shtrange thing it was that sorra wan iv the graziers had even tuk his coat from aff iv him to go to bed, or laid by his shtick. An' the widdy too, she was as nate an' tidy as iver, though seemin' surprised out iv a sound shleep, an' her clothes onto her, all savin' a white bedgown, an' a candle in her hand. There was some others what had been in bed, min an' wimin wid their bare feet an' slippers on to some iv thim, wid their bracers down their backs, an' their petti-coats flung on anyhow. An' some iv thim in big nightcaps, an' some wid their hair all screwed up in knots wid little wisps iv paper, like farden screws iv Limerick twist or Lundy Foot snuff. Musha! but it was the ould weemin what was afraid iv things what didn't alarrm the young wans at all. Divil resave me! but the sole thing they seemed to dhread was the min — dead or alive it was all wan to thim — an' 'twas ghosts an' corpses an' mayhap divils that the rest was afeard iv.

Well, whin the Manchesther man seen thim all come tumblin' into the room he began to git his wits about him; for the dhrink was wearin' aff, an' he was thryin' to remimber where he was. So whin he seen the widdy he put his hand up to his face where the red welt was, an' at wance seemed to undhershtand, for he got mad agin an' roared out: "What does this mane? Why this invasion iv me chamber? Clear out the whole kit, or I'll let yez know!"

Wid that he was goin' to jump out of bed, but the moment they seen his toes the ould weemin let a screech out iv thim, an' clung to the mm an' implored thim to save thim from murdher — an' worse. An' there was the Widdy Byrne laughin' like mad; an' Misther Hogan shtepped out, an' sez he: "Do jump out, Misther Shorrox! The boys has their switches, an' it's a mighty handy costume ye're in for a leatherin'!"

So wid that he jumped back into bed an' covered the clothes over him.

"In the name of God," sez he, "what does it all mane?"

"It manes this," sez Hogan, goin' round the bed an' drag-gin' up the corp an' layin' it on the bed beside him. "Begorra! but it's cantankerous kind iv a scut y'are. First nothin' will do ye but sharin' a room wid a corp; an' thin ye want the whole place to yerself."

"Take it away! Take it away," he yells out.

"Begorra," sez Mister Hogan, "I'll do no such thing. The gintleman ordhered the room first, an' it's he has the right to ordher you to be brung out!"

"Did he shnore much, sur?" says the widdy; an' wid that she burst out laughin' an' cryin' all at wanst. "That'll tache ye to shpake ill iv the dead agin!" An' she flung her petticoat over her head an' run out iv the room.

Well, we turned the min all back to their own rooms; for the most part iv thim had plenty iv dhrink on board, an' we feared for a row. Now that the fun was over, we didn't want any unplisintness to follow. So two iv the graziers wint into wan bed, an' we put the man from Manchesther in th' other room, an' gev him a screechin' tumbler iv punch to put the heartt in him agin.

I thought the widdy had gone to her bed; but whin I wint to put out the lights I seen one in the little room behind the bar, an' I shtepped quite, not to dishturb her, and peeped in. There she was on a low shtool rockin' herself to an' fro, an' goin' on wid her laughin' an' cryin' both together, while she tapped wid her fut on the flume. She was talkin' to herself in a kind iv a whisper, an' I heerd her say: "Oh, but it's the crool woman I am to have such a thing done in me house — an' that poor sowl, wid none to weep for him, knocked about that a way for shport iv dhrunken min — while me poor dear darlin' himself is in the cowid clay! — But oh! Mick, Mick, if ye were only here! Wouldn't it be you — you wid the fun iv ye an' yer merry hearrt — that'd be plazed wid the doin's iv this night!"

The Red Stockade

A Story Told
by the Old Coast Guard

W e was on the southern part of the China station, when the "George Ranger" was ordered to the Straits of Malacca, to put down the pirates that had been showing themselves of late. It was in the forties, when ships was ships, not iron-kettles full of wheels, and other devilments, and there was a chance of hand-to-hand fighting — not being blown up in an iron cellar by you don't know who. Ships was ships in them days!

There had been a lot of throat-cutting and scuttling, for them devils stopped at nothing. Some of us had been through the straits before, when we was in the "Polly Phemus," seventy-four, going to the China station, and although we had never come to quarters with the Malays, we had seen some of their work, and knew what kind they was. So, when we had left Singapore in the "George Ranger," for that was our saucy, little thirty-eight-gun frigate, — the place wasn't in them days what it is now, — many and many's the yarn was told in the fo'c'sle, and on the watches, of what the yellow devils could do, and had done. Some of us took it one way, and some another, but all, save a few, wanted to get into hand-grips with the pirates, for all their kreeses, and their stinkpots, and the devil's engines what they used. There was some that didn't mind cold steel of an ordinary kind, and would have faced cutlasses and boarding-pikes, any day, for a holiday, but that didn't like the idea of those knives like crooked flames, and that sliced a man in two, and hacked through the bowels of him. Naturally, we didn't take much stock of this kind; and many's the joke we had on them, and some of them cruel enough jokes, too.

You may be sure there was good stories, with plenty of cutting, and blood, and tortures in them, told in their watches, and nigh the whole ship's crew was busy, day and night, remembering and inventing things that'd make them gasp and grow white. I think that, somehow, the captain and the officers must have known what was goin' on, for there came tales from the ward-room that was worse nor any of ours. The midshipmen used to delight in them, like the ship's boys did, and one of them, that had a kreese, used to bring it out when he could, and show how the pirates used it when they cut the hearts out of men and women, and ripped them up to the chins. It was a bit cruel, at times, on them poor, white-livered chaps, — a man can't help his liver, I suppose, — but, anyhow, there's no place for them in a warship, for they're apt to do more harm by living where there's men of all sorts, than they can do by dying. So there wasn't any mercy for them, and the captain was worse on them than any. Captain Wynyard was him that commanded the corvette "Sentinel" on the China station, and was promoted to the "George Ranger" for cutting up a fleet of junks that was hammering at the "Rajah," from Canton, racing for Southampton with the first of the season's tea. He was a man, if you like, a bulldog full of hellfire, when he was on for fighting; he wouldn't have a white liver at any price. "God hates a coward," he said once, "and under Her Britannic Majesty I'm here to carry out God's will. Trice him up, and give him a dozen!" At least, that's the story they tell of him when he was round Shanghai, and one of his men had held back when the time came for boarding a fire-junk that was coming down the tide. And with that he went in, and steered her off with his own hands.

Well, the captain knew what work there was before us, and that it weren't no time for kid gloves and hair-oil, much less a bokey in your buttonhole and a top-hat, and he didn't mean that there should be any funk on his ship. So you take your davy that it wasn't his fault if things was made too pleasant aboard for men what feared fallin' into the clutches of the Malays.

Now and then he went out of his way to be nasty over such folk, and, boy or man, he never checked his tongue on a hard word when anyone's face was pale before him. There was one old chap on board that we called "Old Land's End," for he came from that part, and that had a boy of his on the "Billy Ruffian," when he sailed on her, and after got lost, one night, in cutting out a Greek sloop at Navarino, in 1827. We used to chaff him when there was trouble with any of the boys, for he used to say that his boy might have been in that trouble, too. And now, when the chaff was on about bein' afeered of the Malay's, we used to rub it into the old man; but he would flame up, and answer us that his boy died in his duty, and that he couldn't be afeered of naught.

One night there was a row on among the midshipmen, for they said that one of them, Tempest by name, owned up to being afraid of being kreesed. He was a rare bright little chap of about thirteen, that was always in fun and trouble of some kind; but he was soft-hearted, and sometimes the other lads would tease him. He would own up truthfully to anything he thought, or felt, and now they had drawn him to own something that none of them would — no matter how true it might be. Well, they had a rare fight, for the boy was never backward with his fists, and by accident it came to the notice of the captain. He insisted on being told what it was all about, and when young Tempest spoke out, and told him, he stamped on the deck, and called out:

"I'll have no cowards in this ship," and was going on, when the boy cut in:

"I'm no coward, sir; I'm a gentleman!"

"Did you say you were afraid? Answer me — yes, or no?"

"Yes, sir, I did, and it was true! I said I feared the Malay kreeses; but I did not mean to shirk them, for all that. Henry of Navarre was afraid, but, all the same, he —"

"Henry of Navarre be damned," shouted the captain, "and you, too! You said you were afraid, and that, let me tell you, is what we call a coward in the Queen's navy. And if you are one, you can, at least, have the grace to keep it to yourself!

No answer to me! To the masthead for the remainder of the day! I want my crew to know what to avoid, and to know it when they see it!" and he walked away, while the lad, without a word, ran up the maintop.

Some way, the men didn't say much about this. The only one that said anything to the point was Old Land's End, and says he:

"That may be a coward, but I'd chance it that he was a boy of mine."

As we went up the straits and got the sun on us, and the damp heat of that kettle of a place, — Lor' bless ye! ye steam there, all day and all night like a copper at the galley, — we began to look around for the pirates, and there wasn't a man that got drowsy on the watch. We coasted along as we went up north, and took a look into the creeks and rivers as we went. It was up these that the Malays hid themselves; for the fevers and such that swept off their betters like flies, didn't seem to have any effect on them. There was pretty bad bits, I tell you, up some of them rivers through the mango groves, where the marshes spread away, mile after mile, as far as you could see, and where everything that is noxious, both beast, and bird, and fish, and crawling thing, and insect, and tree, and bush, and flower, and creeper, is most at home.

But the pirate ships kept ahead of us; or, if they came south again, passed us by in the night, and so we ran up till about the middle of the peninsula, where the worst of the piracies had happened. There we got up as well as we could to look like a ship in distress; and, sure enough, we deceived the beggars, for two of them came out one early dawn and began to attack us. They was ugly looking craft, too — long, low hull and lateen — sails, and a double crew twice told in every one of them.

But if the crafts was ugly the men was worse, for uglier devils I never saw. Swarthy, yellow chaps, some of them, and some with shaven crowns and white eyeballs, and others as black as your shoe, with one or two white men, more shame, among them, but all carrying kreeses as long as your arm, and pistols in their belts.

They didn't get much change from us, I tell you. We let them get close, and then gave them a broadside that swept their decks like a hail-storm; but we was unlucky that we didn't grapple them, for they managed to shift off and ran for it. Our boats was out quick, but we daren't follow them where they ran into a wide creek, with mango swamps on each side as far as the eye could reach. The boat came back after a bit and reported that they had run up the river which was deep enough but with a winding channel between great mud-banks, where alligators lay in hundreds. There seemed some sort of fort where the river narrowed, and the pirates ran in behind it and disappeared up the bend of the river.

Then the preparations began. We knew that we had got two craft, at any rate, caged in the river, and there was every chance that we had found their lair. Our captain wasn't one that let things go asleep, and by daylight the next morning we was ready for an attack. The pinnace and four other boats started out under the first lieutenant to prospect, and the rest that was left on board waited, as well as they could, till we came back.

That was an awful day. I was in the second boat, and we all kept well together when we began to get into the narrows of the mouth of the river. When we started, we went in a couple of hours after the flood-tide, and so all we saw when the light came seemed fresh and watery. But as the tide ran out, and the big black mud-banks began to show their heads above everywhere, it wasn't nice, I can tell you. It was hardly possible for us to tell the channels, for everywhere the tide raced quick, and it was only when the boat began to touch the black slime that you knew that you was on a bank. Twice our boat was almost caught this way, but by good luck we pulled and pushed off in time into the ebbing tide; and hardly a boat but touched somewhere. One that was a bit out from the rest of us got stuck at last in a nasty cut between two mud-banks, and as the water ran away the boat turned over on the slope, despite all her crew could do, and we saw the poor fellows thrown out into the slime. More than one of them began to swim toward us, but behind each came a rush of something dark, and though we shouted and made what noise we could, and fired many shots, the alligators was too close, and with shriek after shriek they went down to the bottom of the filth and slime. Oh, man! it was a dreadful sight, and none the better that it was new to nigh all of us. How it would have taken us if we had time to think about it, I hardly know, but I doubt that more than a few would have grown cold over it; but just then there flew amongst us a hail of small shot from a fleet of boats that had stolen down on us. They drove out from behind a big mud-bank that rose steeper than the others and that seemed solider, too, for the gravel of it showed, as the scour of the tide washed the mud away. We was not sorry, I tell you, to have men to fight with, instead of alligators and mud-banks, in an ebbing tide, in a strange tropical river.

We gave chase at once, and the pinnace fired the twelve-pounder which she carried in the bows, in among the huddle of the boats, and the yells arose as the rush of the alligators turned to where the Malay heads bobbed up and down in the drift of the tide. Then the pirates turned and ran, and we after them as hard as we could pull, till round a sharp bend of the river we came to a narrow place, where one side was steep for a bit and then tailed away to a wilderness of marsh, worse than we had seen. The other side was crowned by a sort of fort, built on the top of a high bank, but guarded by a stockade and a mud-bank which lay at its base. From this there came a rain of bullets, and we saw some guns turned toward us. We was hardly strong enough to attack such a position without reconnoitering, and so we drew away; but not quite quick enough, for before we could get out of range of their guns a round shot carried away the whole of the starboard oars of one of our boats.

It was a dreary pull to the ship, and the tide was agin us, for we all got thinking of what we had to tell, — one boat and crew lost entirely, and a set of oars shot away, — and no work done.

The captain was furious; and, in the ward-room, and in the fo'c'sle that night, there was nothing that wasn't flavored with anger and curses. Even the boys, of all sorts, from the cabin-boys to the midshipmen, was wanting to get at the Malays. However, sharp was the order; and by daylight three boats was up at the stockaded fort, making an accurate survey. I was again in one of the boats; and, in spite of what the captain had said to make us all so angry, — and he had a tongue like vitriol, I tell you, — we all felt pretty down and cold when we got again amongst those terrible mud-banks and saw the slime that shone on them bubble up, when the gray of the morning let us see anything

We found that the fort was one that we would have to take if we wanted to follow the pirates up the river, for it barred the way without a chance. There was a gut of the river between the two great ridges of gravel, and this was the only channel where there was a chance of passing. But it had been staked on both sides, so that only the center was left free. Why, from the fort they could have stoned anyone in the boats passing there, only that there wasn't any stone, that we could see, in their whole blasted country!

When we got back, with two cases of sunstroke among us, and reported, the captain ordered preparations for an attack on the fort, and the next morning the ball began. It was ugly work. We got close up to the fort, but, as the tide ran out, we had to sheer away somewhat so as not to get stranded. The whole place swarmed with those grinning devils. They evidently had some way of getting to and from their boats behind the stockade. They did not fire a shot at us, — not at first, — and that was the most aggravating thing that you can imagine. They seemed to know something that we did not, and they only just waited. As the tide sank lower and lower, and the mud-banks grew steeper, and the sun on them began to fizzle, a steam arose that nigh turned our stomachs. Why, the sight of them alone would make your heart sink!

The slime shimmered in all kinds of colors, like the water when there's tarring work on hand, and the whole place seemed alive with all that was horrible. The alligators kept off the boats and the banks close to us, but the thick water was full of eels and water-snakes, and the mud was alive with water-worms and leeches, and horrible, gaudy-colored crabs. The very air was filled with pests, — flies of all kinds, and a sort of big-striped insect that they call the "tiger mosquito," which comes out in the daytime and bites you like red-hot pincers. It was bad enough, I tell you, for us men with hair on our faces, but some of the boys got very white and pale, and they was all pretty silent for a while. All at once the crowd of Malays behind the stockade began to roll their eyes and wave their kreeses and to shout. We knew that there was some cause for it, but couldn't make it out, and this exasperated us more than ever. Then the captain sings out to us to attack the stockade; so out we all jumped into the mud. We knew it couldn't be very deep just there, on account of the gravel beneath. We was knee-deep in a moment, but we struggled, and slipped, and fell over each other; and, when we got to the top of that bank, we was the queerest, filthiest-looking crowd you ever see. But the mud hadn't took the heart out of us, and the Malays, with their necks craned over the stockade, and with the nearest thing to a laugh or a smile that the devil lets them have, drew back and fell, one on another, when they heard our cheer.

Between them and us there was a bit of a dip where the water had been running in the ebb-tide, but which seemed now as dry as the rest, and the foremost of our men charged down the slope, and then we knew why they had kept silent and waited! We was in a regular trap. The first ranks disappeared at once in the mud and ooze in the hollow, and those next were up to their armpits before they could stop. Then those Malay devils opened on us, and while we tried to pull our chaps out, they mowed us down with every kind of small arm they had — and they had a queer assortment, I tell you.

It was all we could do to get back over the slope and to the boats again, — what was left of us, — and, as we hadn't hands enough left even to row with full strength, we had to make for the ship as fast as we could, for their boats began to pass out in a cloud through the narrow by the stockade. But before we went we saw them dragging the live and dead out of the mud with hooks on the end of long bamboos; and there was terrible shrieks from some poor fellows when the kreeses gashed through them. We daren't wait; but we saw enough to make us swear revenge. When we saw them devils stick the bleeding heads of our comrades on the spikes of the stockade, there was nigh a mutiny because the captain wouldn't let us go back and have another try for it. He was cool enough now; and those of us that knew him and understood what was in his mind, when the smile on him showed the white teeth in the corners of his mouth, felt that it was no good day's work that the pirates had done for themselves.

When we got back to the ship and told our tale, it wasn't long till the men was all on fire; and nigh every man took a turn with the grindstone at his cutlass, till they was all like razors. The captain mustered everyone on board, and detailed every man to his work in the boats, ready for the next time; and we knew that, by daylight, we were to have another slap at the pirates. We got six-pounders and twelve-pounders in most of the boats, for we was to give them a dose of big shot before we came to close quarters.

When we got up near the stockade, the tide had turned, and we thought it better to wait till dawn, for it was bad work among the mud-banks at the ebb in the dark. So we hung on a while, and then when the sky began to lighten, we made for the fort. When we got nigh enough to see it, there wasn't a man of us who didn't want to have some bloody revenge, for there, on the spikes of the stockade, were the heads of all the poor fellows that we had lost the day before, with a cloud of mosquitoes and flies already beginning to buzz around them in the dawn. But beyond that again, they had painted the outside of the stockade with blood, so that the whole place was a crimson mass. You could smell it as the sun came up!

Well, that day was a hard one. We opened fire with our guns, and the Malays returned it, with all they had got. A fleet of boats came out from beyond the fort, and for a while we had to turn our attention to these. The small guns served us well, and we made a rare havoc among the boats, for our shot went crashing through them, and quite a half of them were sunk. The water was full of bobbing heads; but the tide carried them away from us, and their cries and shrieks came from beyond the fort and then died away. The other boats recognized their danger, and turned and ran in through the narrow, and let us alone for hours after. Then we went at the fort again. We turned our guns at the piles of the stockade, and, of course, every shot told, — but their fire was at too close quarters, and with their rifles and matchlocks, and the rest, they picked us off too fast, and we had to sheer off where our heavy metal could tell without our being within their range. Before we sheered off, we could see that the hole we had knocked in the stockade was only in the outer work, and that the real fort was within. We had to go down the river, as we couldn't go far enough across without danger from the banks, and this only gave us a side view, and, do what we would, we couldn't make an impression, — at least any that we could see.

That was a long and awful day! The sun was blazing on us like a furnace, and we was nigh mad with heat, and flies, and drouth, and anger. It was that hot that if you touched metal it fairly burned you. When the tide was near the flood, the captain ordered up the boats in the wide water now opposite the fort; and there, for a while, we got a fair chance, till, when the ebb began, we should have to sheer off again. By this time our shot was nearly run out, and we thought that we should have to give over; but all at once came order to prepare for attack, and in a few minutes we was working for dear life across the river, straight for the stockade. The men set up a cheer, and the pirates showed over the top of the stockade and waved their kreeses, and more than one of them sliced off pieces of the heads on the spikes, and jeered at us, as much as to say that they would do the same for us in our turn! When we got close up, every one of them had disappeared, and there was a silence of the grave. We knew that there was something up, but what the move was we could not tell, till from behind the fort came rushing again a fleet of boats. We turned on them, and, like we did before, we made mincemeat of them. This time the tide made for us, and the bobbing heads went by us in dozens. Now and then there was a wild yell, as an alligator pulled some one down into the mud. This went on for a little, and we had beaten them off enough to be able to get our grappling — irons ready for climbing the stockade, when the second lieutenant, who was in the outer boat, called out:

"Back with the boats! Back, quick, the tide is falling!" and with one impulse we began to shove off. Then, in an instant, the place became alive again with the Malays, and they began firing on us so quickly that before we could get out into the whirl of tide there was many a dead man in our boats.

There was no use trying to do anymore that day, and after we had done what could be done for the wounded, and patched up our boats, for there was plenty of shot-holes to plug, we pulled back to the ship. The alligators had had a good day, and as we went along, and the mud-banks grew higher and higher with the falling of the tide, we could see them lie out lazily, as if they had been gorged. Aye! And there was enough left for the ground-sharks out in the offing; for the men on board told us that every while on the ebb something would go along, bobbing up and down in the swell, till presently there would be a swift ripple of a fin, and then there was no more pirate.

Well! when we got aboard, the rest was mighty anxious to know what had been done; and when we began, with the heads on spikes of the red stockade, the men ground their teeth, and Old Land's End up, and says he:

"The Red Stockade! We'll not forget the name! It'll be our turn next, and then we'll paint it inside this time." And so it was that we came to know the place by that name. That night the captain was like a man that would do murder. His face was like steel, and his eyes was as red as flames. He didn't seem to have a thought for anyone; and everything he did was as hard as though his heart were brass. He ordered all that was needful to be done for the wounded, but he added to the doctor: "And, mind you, get them well as soon as you can. We're too shorthanded already!"

Up to now, we all had known him treat men as men, but now he only thought of us as machines for fighting! True enough, he thought the same of himself. Twice that very night he cut up rough in a new way. Of course, the men was talking of the attack, and there was lots of brag and chaff, for all they was so grim earnest, and some of the old fooling went on about blood and tortures. The captain came on deck, and as he walked along, he saw one of the men that didn't like the kreeses, and he didn't evidently like the looks of him, for he turned on his heel and said savagely:

"Send the doctor here!" So the doctor came, and the captain he says to him, cold as ice, and as polite as you please:

"Dr. Fairbrother, there is a sick man here! look at his pale face. Something wrong with his liver, I suppose. It's the only thing that makes a seaman's face white when there's fighting ahead. Take him down to sick bay, and do something for him. I'd like to cut the accursed white liver out of him altogether!" and with that he went down to his cabin.

Well if we was hot for fighting before, we was boiling after that, and we all came to know that the next attack on the Red Stockade would be the last, one way or the other! We had to wait two more days before that could come off, for the boats and tackle had to be made ready, and there wasn't going to be any mistakes made this time.

It was just after midnight when we began to get ready. Every man was to his post. The moon was up, and it was lighter nor a London day, and the captain stood by and saw every man to his place, and nothing escaped him. By and by, as No. 6 boat was filling, and before the officer in charge of it got in, came the midshipman, young Tempest, and when the captain saw him he called him up and hissed out before all the crew:

"Why are you so white? What's wrong with you, anyway? Is your liver out of order, too?"

True enough, the boy was white, but at the flaming insult the blood rushed to his face and we could see it red in the starlight. Then in another moment it passed away and left him paler than ever, and he said with a gentle voice, though standing as straight as a ramrod:

"I can't help the blood in my face, sir. If I'm a coward because I'm pale, perhaps you are right. But I shall do my duty all the same!" and with that he pulled himself up, touched his cap, and went down into the boat.

Old Land's End was behind me in the boat with him, number five to my six, and he whispered to me through his shut teeth:

"Too rough that! He might have thought a bit that he's only a child. And he came all the same, even if he was afeer'd!"

We stole away with muffled oars, and dropped silently into the river on the floodtide. If any man had had any doubts as to whether we was in earnest at other times, he had none then, anyhow. It was a pretty grim time, I tell you, for the most of us felt that whether we won or not this time, there would be many empty hammocks that night in the "George Ranger;" but we meant to win even if we went into the maws of the sharks and crocodiles for it. When we came up close on the flood we lost no time but went slap at the fort. At first, of course, we had crawled up the river in silence, and I think that we took the beggars by surprise, for we was there before the time they expected us. Howsomever, they turned out quick enough and there was soon music on both sides of the stockade. We didn't want to take any chance on the mud-banks this time, so we ran in close under the stockade at once and hooked on. We found that they had repaired the breach we had made the last time. They fought like devils, for they knew that we could beat them hand to hand, if we could once get in, and they sent round the boats to take us on the flank, as they had done each time before. But this time we wasn't to be drawn away from our attack, and we let our boats outside tackle them, while we minded our own business closer home.

It was a long fight and a bloody one. They was sheltered inside, and they knew that time was with them, for when the tide should have fallen, if we hadn't got in we should have our old trouble with the mud-banks all over again. But we knew it, too, and we didn't lose no time. Still, men is only men, after all, and we couldn't fly up over a stockade out of a boat, and them as did get up was sliced about dreadful, — they are handy workmen with their kreeses, and no doubt! We was so hot on the job we had on hand that we never took no note of time at all, and all at once we found the boat fixed tight under us.

The tide had fallen and left us on the bank under the Red Stockade, and the best half of the boats was cut off from us. We had some thirty men left, and we knew we had to fight whether we liked it or not. It didn't much matter, anyhow, for we was game to go through with it. The captain, when he seen the state of things, gave his orders to take the boats out into mid-stream, and shell and shot the fort, whilst we was to do what we could to get in. It was no use trying to bridge over the slobs, for the masts of an old seventy-four wouldn't have done it. We was in a tight place, then, I can tell you, between two fires, for the guns in the boats couldn't fire high enough to clear us every time, without going over the fort altogether, and more than one of our own shots did some of us a harm. The cutter came into the game, and began sending the war-rockets from the tubes. The pirates didn't like that, I tell you, and more betoken, no more did we, for we got as much of them as they did, till the captain saw the harm to us, and bade them cease. But he knew his business, and he kept all the fire of the guns on the one side of the stockade, till he knocked a hole that we could get in by. When this was done, the Malays left the outer wall and went within the fort proper. This gave us some protection, since they couldn't fire right down on us, and our guns kept the boats away that would have taken us from the riverside. But it was hot work, and we began dropping away with stray shots, and with the stinkpots and hand-grenades that they kept hurling over the stockade on to us.

So the time came when we found that we must make a dash for the fort, or get picked out, one by one, where we stood. By this time some of our boats was making for the opening, and there seemed less life behind the stockade; some of them was up to some move, and was sheering off to make up some other devilment. Still, they had their guns in the fort, and there was danger to our boats if they tried to cross the opening between the piles. One did, and went down with a hole in her within a minute. So we made a burst inside the stockade, and found ourselves in a narrow place between the two walls of piles. Anyhow, the place was drier, and we felt a relief in getting out of up to our knees in steaming mud. There was no time to lose, and the second lieutenant, Webster by name, told us to try to scale the stockade in front.

It wasn't high, but it was slimy below and greasy above, and do what we would, we couldn't get no nigher. A shot from a pistol wiped out the lieutenant, and for a moment we thought we was without a leader. Young Tempest was with us, silent all the time, with his face as white as a ghost, though he done his best, like the rest of us. Suddenly he called out:

"Here, lads! take and throw me in. I'm light enough to do it, and I know that when I'm in you'll all follow."

Ne'er a man stirred. Then the lad stamped his foot and called again, and I remember his young, high voice now:

"Seamen to your duty! I command here!"

At the word we all stood at attention, just as if we was at quarters. Then Jack Pring, that we called the Giant, for he was six feet four and as strong as a bullock, spoke out:

"It's no duty, sir, to fling an officer into hell!" The lad

looked at him and nodded.

"Volunteers for dangerous duty!" he called, and every man of the crowd stepped out.

"All right, boys!" says he. "Now take me up and throw me in. We'll get down that flag, anyhow," and he pointed to the black flag that the pirates flew on the flagstaff in the fort. Then he took the small flag of the float and put it on his breast, and says he: "This'll suit better."

"Won't I do, sir?" said Jack, and the lad laughed a laugh that rang again.

"Oh, my eye!" says he, "has anyone got a crane to hoist in the Giant?" The lad told us to catch hold of him, and when Jack hesitated, says he:

"We've always been friends, Jack, and I want you to be one of the last to touch me!" So Jack laid hold of him by one side, and Old Land's End stepped out and took him by the other. The rest of us was, by this time, kicking off our shoes and pulling off our shirts, and getting our knives open in our teeth. The two men gave a great heave together and they sent the boy clean over the top of the stockade. We heard across the river a cheer from our boats, as we began to scramble. There was a pause within the fort for a few seconds, and then we saw the lad swarm up the bamboo flagstaff that swayed under him, and tear down the black flag. He pulled our own flag from his breast and hung it over the top of the post. And he waved his hand and cheered, and the cheer was echoed in thunder across the river. And then a shot fetched him down, and with a wild yell they all went for him, while the cheering from the boats came like a storm.

We never knew quite how we got over that stockade. To this day I can't even imagine how we done it! But when we leaped down, we saw something lying at the foot of the flagstaff all red, — and the kreeses was red, too! The devils had done their work! But it was their last, for we came at them with our cutlasses, — there was never a sound from the lips of any of us, — and we drove them like a hail-storm beats down standing corn! We didn't leave a living thing within the Red Stockade that day, and we wouldn't if there had been a million there!

It was a while before we heard the shouting again, for the boats was coming up the river, now that the fort was ours, and the men had other work for their breath than cheering.

Between us, we made a rare clearance of the pirates' nest that day. We destroyed every boat on the river, and the two ships that we was looking for, and one other that was careened. We tore down and burned every house, and jetty, and stockade in the place, and there was no quarter for them we caught. Some of them got away by a path they knew through the swamp where we couldn't follow them. The sun was getting low when we pulled back to the ship. It would have been a merry enough home-coming, despite our losses, — all but for one thing, and that was covered up with a Union Jack in the captain's own boat. Poor lad! when they lifted him on deck, and the men came round to look at him, his face was pale enough now, and, one and all, we felt that it was to make amends, as the captain stooped over and kissed him on the forehead.

"We'll bury him tomorrow," he said, "but in blue water, as becomes a gallant seaman."

At the dawn, next day, he lay on a grating, sewn in his hammock, with the shot at his feet, and the whole crew was mustered, and the chaplain read the service for the dead. Then he spoke a bit about him, — how he had done his duty, and was an example to all, — and he said how all loved and honored him. Then the men told off for the duty stood ready to slip the grating and let the gallant boy go plunging down to join the other heroes under the sea; but Old Land's End stepped out and touched his cap to the captain, and asked if he might say a word.

"Say on, my man!" said the captain, and he stood, with his cocked hat in his hand, whilst Old Land's End spoke:

"Mates! ye've heerd what the chaplain said. The boy done his duty, and died like the brave gentleman he was! And we wish he was here now. But, for all that, we can't be sorry for him, or for what he done, though it cost him his life. I had a lad once of my own, and I hoped for him what I never wanted for myself, — that he would win fame and honor, and become an admiral of the fleet, as others have done before. But, so help me God! I'd rather see him lying under the flag as we see that brave boy lie now, and know why he was there, than I'd see him in his epaulettes on the quarterdeck of the flagship! He died for his Queen and country, and for the honor of the flag! And what more would you have him do!"

*Death in the Wings**

"**W**hen I was apprenticed to theatrical carpentering my master was John Haliday, who was Master Machinist — we called men in his post 'Master Carpenter' in those days — of the old Victoria Theater, Hulme. It wasn't called Hulme; but that name will do. It would only stir up painful memories if I were to give the real name. I daresay some of you — not the Ladies (this with a gallant bow all round) — will remember the case of a Harlequin as was killed in an accident in the pantomime. We needn't mention names; Mortimer will do for a name to call him by — Henry Mortimer. The cause of it was never found out. But I knew it; and I've kept silence for so long that I may speak now without hurting anyone. They're all dead long ago that was interested in the death of Henry Mortimer or the man who wrought that death."

"Any of you who know of the case will remember what a handsome, dapper, well-built man Mortimer was. To my own mind he was the handsomest man I ever saw."

The Tragedian's low, grumbling whisper, "That's a large order," sounded a warning note. Hempitch, however, did not seem to hear it, but went on:

"Of course, I was only a boy then, and I hadn't seen any of you gentlemen — Yer very good health, Mr. Wellesley Dovercourt, sir, and cettera. I needn't tell you, Ladies, how well a harlequin's dress sets off a nice slim figure. No wonder that in these days of suffragettes, women wants to be harlequins as well as columbines. Though I hope they won't make the columbine a man's part!"

---

* Also published as "A Star Trap."

"Mortimer was the nimblest chap at the traps I ever see. He was so sure of hisself that he would have extra weight put on so that when the counter weights fell he'd shoot up five or six feet higher than anyone else could even try to. Moreover, he had a way of drawing up his legs when in the air — the way a frog does when he is swimming — that made his jump look ever so much higher."

"I think the girls were all in love with him, the way they used to stand in the wings when the time was comin' for his entrance. That wouldn't have mattered much, for girls are always falling in love with some man or other, but it made trouble, as it always does when the married ones take the same start. There were several of these that were always after him, more shame for them, with husbands of their own. That was dangerous enough, and hard to stand for a man who might mean to be decent in any way. But the real trial — and the real trouble, too — was none other than the young wife of my own master, and she was more than flesh and blood could stand. She had come into the panto, the season before, as a high-kicker — and she could! She could kick higher than girls that was more than a foot taller than her; for she was a wee bit of a thing and as pretty as pie; a gold-haired, blue-eyed, slim thing with much the figure of a boy, except for. . . and they saved her from any mistaken idea of that kind. Jack Haliday went crazy over her, and when the notice was up, and there was no young spark with plenty of oof coming along to do the proper thing by her, she married him. It was, when they was joined, what you Ladies call a marriage of convenience; but after a bit they two got on very well, and we all thought she was beginning to like the old man — for Jack was old enough to be her father, with a bit to spare. In the summer, when the house was closed, he took her to the Isle of Man; and when they came back he made no secret of it that he'd had the happiest time of his life. She looked quite happy, too, and treated him affectionate; and we all began to think that that marriage had not been a failure at any rate."

"Things began to change, however, when the panto, rehearsals began next year. Old Jack began to look unhappy, and didn't take no interest in his work. Loo — that was Mrs. Haliday's name — didn't seem over fond of him now, and

was generally impatient when he was by. Nobody said anything about this, however, to us men; but the married women
smiled and nodded their heads and whispered that perhaps
there were reasons. One day on the stage, when the harlequinade rehearsal was beginning, someone mentioned as
how perhaps Mrs. Haliday wouldn't be dancing that year, and
they smiled as if they was all in the secret. Then Mrs. Jack ups
and gives them Johnny-up-the-orchard for not minding their
own business and telling a pack of lies, and such like as you
Ladies like to express in your own ways when you get your
back hair down. The rest of us tried to soothe her all we could,
and she went off home."

"It wasn't long after that that she and Henry Mortimer left
together after rehearsal was over, he saying he'd leave her at
home. She didn't make no objections – I told you he was a
very handsome man."

"Well, from that on she never seemed to take her eyes from
him during every rehearsal, right up to the night of the last
rehearsal, which, of course, was full dress – 'Everybody and
Everything.'"

"Jack Haliday never seemed to notice anything that was
going on, like the rest of them did. True, his time was taken
up with his own work, for I'm telling you that a Master
Machinist hasn't got no loose time on his hands at the first
dress rehearsal of a panto. And, of course, none of the
company ever said a word or gave a look that would call his
attention to it. Men and women are queer beings. They will
be blind and deaf whilst danger is being run; and it's only
after the scandal is beyond repair that they begin to talk –
just the very time when most of all they should be silent."

"I saw all that went on, but I didn't understand it. I liked
Mortimer myself and admired him – like I did Mrs. Haliday,
too – and I thought he was a very fine fellow. I was only a
boy, you know, and Haliday's apprentice, so naturally I
wasn't looking for any trouble I could help, even if I'd seen
it coming. It was when I looked back afterwards at the whole
thing that I began to comprehend; so you will all understand
now, I hope, that what I tell you is the result of much
knowledge of what I saw and heard and was told of afterwards
– all morticed and clamped up by thinking."

"The panto, had been on about three weeks when one Saturday, between the shows, I heard two of our company talking. Both of them was among the extra girls that both sang and danced and had to make theirselves useful. I don't think either of them was better than she should be; they went out to too many champagne suppers with young men that had money to burn. That part doesn't matter in this affair — except that they was naturally enough jealous of women who was married — which was what they was aiming at — and what lived straighter than they did. Women of that kind like to see a good woman tumble down; it seems to make them all more even. Now real bad girls what have gone under altogether will try to save a decent one from following their road. That is, so long as they're young; for a bad one what is long in the tooth is the limit. They'll help anyone down hill — so long as they get anything out of it."

"Well — no offence, you Ladies, as has growed up! — these two girls was enjoyin' themselves over Mrs. Haliday and the mash she had set up on Mortimer. They didn't see that I was sitting on a stage box behind a built-out piece of the Prologue of the panto., which was set ready for night. They were both in love with Mortimer, who wouldn't look at either of them, so they was miaw'n cruel, like cats on the tiles. Says one:"

"'The Old Man seems worse than blind; he won't see.'"

"'Don't you be too sure of that,' says the other. 'He don't mean to take no chances. I think you must be blind, too, Kissie.' That was her name — on the bills anyhow, Kissie Mountpelier. 'Don't he make a point of taking her home hisself every night after the play. You should know, for you're in the hall yourself waiting for your young man till he comes from his club.'"

"'Wot-ho, you bally geeser,' says the other — which her language was mostly coarse — 'don't you know there's two ends to everything? The Old Man looks to one end only!' Then they began to snigger and whisper; and presently the other one says:"

"'Then he thinks harm can be only done when work is over!'"

"'Jest so,' she answers. 'Her and him knows that the old man has to be down long before the risin' of the rag; but she doesn't come in till the Vision of Venus dance after half time; and he not till the harlequinade!'"

"Then I quit. I didn't want to hear any more of that sort."

"All that week things went on as usual. Poor old Haliday wasn't well. He looked worried and had a devil of a temper. I had reason to know that, for what worried him was his work. He was always a hard worker, and the panto. season was a terror with him. He didn't ever seem to mind anything else outside his work. I thought at the time that that was how those two chattering girls made up their slanderous story; for, after all, a slander, no matter how false it may be, must have some sort of beginning. Something that seems, if there isn't something that is! But no matter how busy he might be, old Jack always made time to leave the wife at home."

"As the week went on he got more and more pale; and I began to think he was in for some sickness. He generally remained in the theater between the shows on Saturday; that is, he didn't go home, but took a high tea in the coffee shop close to the theater, so as to be handy in case there might be a hitch anywhere in the preparation for night. On that Saturday he went out as usual when the first scene was set, and the men were getting ready the packs for the rest of the scenes. By and bye there was some trouble – the usual Saturday kind – and I went off to tell him. When I went into the coffee shop I couldn't see him. I thought it best not to ask or to seem to take any notice, so I came back to the theater, and heard that the trouble had settled itself as usual, by the men who had been quarreling going off to have another drink. I hustled up those who remained, and we got things smoothed out in time for them all to have their tea. Then I had my own. I was just then beginning to feel the responsibility of my business, so I wasn't long over my food, but came back to look things over and see that all was right, especially the trap, for that was a thing Jack Haliday was most particular about. He would overlook a fault for anything else; but if it was along of a trap, the man had to go. He always told the men that that wasn't ordinary work; it was life or death."

"I had just got through my inspection when I saw old Jack coming in from the hall. There was no one about at that hour, and the stage was dark. But dark as it was I could see that the old man was ghastly pale. I didn't speak, for I wasn't near enough, and as he was moving very silently behind the scenes I thought that perhaps he wouldn't like anyone to notice that he had been away. I thought the best thing I could do would be to clear out of the way, so I went back and had another cup of tea."

"I came away a little before the men, who had nothing to think of except to be in their places when Haliday's whistle sounded. I went to report myself to my master, who was in his own little glass-partitioned den at the back of the carpenter's shop. He was there bent over his own bench, and was filing away at something so intently that he did not seem to hear me; so I cleared out. I tell you, Ladies and Gents., that from an apprentice point of view it is not wise to be too obtrusive when your master is attending to some private matter of his own!"

"When the 'get-ready' time came and the lights went up, there was Haliday as usual at his post. He looked very white and ill — so ill that the stage manager, when he came in, said to him that if he liked to go home and rest he would see that all his work would be attended to. He thanked him, and said that he thought he would be able to stay. 'I do feel a little weak and ill, sir,' he said. 'I felt just now for a few moments as if I was going to faint. But that's gone by already, and I'm sure I shall be able to get through the work before us all right.'"

"Then the doors was opened, and the Saturday night audience came rushing and tumbling in. The Victoria was a great Saturday night house. No matter what other nights might be, that was sure to be good. They used to say in the perfesh that the Victoria lived on it, and that the management was on holiday for the rest of the week. The actors knew it, and no matter how slack they might be from Monday to Friday they was all taut and trim then. There was no walking through and no fluffing on Saturday nights — or else they'd have had the bird."

"Mortimer was one of the most particular of the lot in this way. He never was slack at any time — indeed, slackness is not a harlequin's fault, for if there's slackness there's no harlequin, that's all. But Mortimer always put on an extra bit on the Saturday night. When he jumped up through the star trap he always went then a couple of feet higher. To do this we had always to put on a lot more weight. This he always saw to himself; for, mind you, it's no joke being driven up through the trap as if you was shot out of a gun. The points of the star had to be kept free, and the hinges at their bases must be well oiled, or else there can be a disaster at any time. Moreover, 'tis the duty of someone appointed for the purpose to see that all is clear upon the stage. I remember hearing that once at New York, many years ago now, a harlequin was killed by a 'grip' — as the Yankees call a carpenter — what outsiders here call a scene-shifter — walking over the trap just as the stroke had been given to let go the counter-weights. It wasn't much satisfaction to the widow to know that the 'grip' was killed too."

"That night Mrs. Haliday looked prettier than ever, and kicked even higher than I had ever seen her do. Then, when she got dressed for home, she came as usual and stood in the wings for the beginning of the harlequinade. Old Jack came across the stage and stood beside her; I saw him from the back follow up the sliding ground-row that closed in on the Realms of Delight. I couldn't help noticing that he still looked ghastly pale. He kept turning his eyes on the star trap. Seeing this, I naturally looked at it too, for I feared lest something might have gone wrong. I had seen that it was in good order, and that the joints were properly oiled when the stage was set for the evening show, and as it wasn't used all night for anything else I was reassured. Indeed, I thought I could see it shine a bit as the limelight caught the brass hinges. There was a spot light just above it on the bridge, which was intended to make a good show of harlequin and his big jump. The people used to howl with delight as he came rushing up through the trap and when in the air drew up his legs and spread them wide for an instant and then straightened them again as he came down — only bending his knees just as he touched the stage."

"When the signal was given the counter-weight worked properly. I knew, for the sound of it at that part was all right."

"But something was wrong. The trap didn't work smooth, and open at once as the harlequin's head touched it. There was a shock and a tearing sound, and the pieces of the star seemed torn about, and some of them were thrown about the stage. And in the middle of them came the colored and spangled figure that we knew."

"But somehow it didn't come up in the usual way. It was erect enough, but there was not the usual elasticity. The legs never moved; and when it went up a fair height — though nothing like usual — it seemed to topple over and fall on the stage on its side. The audience shrieked, and the people in the wings — actors and staff all the same — closed in, some of them in their stage clothes, others dressed for going home. But the man in the spangles lay quite still."

"The loudest shriek of all was from Mrs. Haliday; and she was the first to reach the spot where he — it — lay. Old Jack was close behind her, and caught her as she fell. I had just time to see that, for I made it my business to look after the pieces of the trap; there was plenty of people to look after the corpse. And the pit was by now crossing the orchestra and climbing up on the stage."

"I managed to get the bits together before the rush came. I noticed that there were deep scratches on some of them, but I didn't have time for more than a glance. I put a stage box over the hole lest anyone should put a foot through it. Such would mean a broken leg at least; and if one fell through, it might mean worse. Amongst other things I found a queer-looking piece of flat steel with some bent points on it. I knew it didn't belong to the trap; but it came from somewhere, so I put it in my pocket."

"By this time there was a crowd where Mortimer's body lay. That he was stone dead nobody could doubt. The very attitude was enough. He was all straggled about in queer positions; one of the legs was doubled under him with the toes sticking out in the wrong way. But let that suffice! It doesn't do to go into details of a dead body. . .I wish someone would give me a drop of punch."

"There was another crowd round Mrs. Haliday, who was lying a little on one side nearer the wings where her husband had carried her and laid her down. She, too, looked like a corpse; for she was as white as one and as still, and looked as cold. Old Jack was kneeling beside her, chafing her hands.

He was evidently frightened about her, for he, too, was deathly white. However, he kept his head, and called his men round him. He left his wife in care of Mrs. Homcroft, the Wardrobe Mistress, who had by this time hurried down. She was a capable woman, and knew how to act promptly. She got one of the men to lift Mrs. Haliday and carry her up to the wardrobe. I heard afterwards that when she got her there she turned out all the rest of them that followed up – the women as well as the men – and looked after her herself."

"I put the pieces of the broken trap on the top of the stage box, and told one of our chaps to mind them, and see that no one touched them, as they might be wanted. By this time the police who had been on duty in front had come round, and as they had at once telephoned to headquarters, more police kept coming in all the time. One of them took charge of the place where the broken trap was; and when he heard who put the box and the broken pieces there, sent for me. More of them took the body away to the property room, which was a large room with benches in it, and which could be locked up. Two of them stood at the door, and wouldn't let anyone go in without permission."

"The man who was in charge of the trap asked me if I had seen the accident. When I said I had, he asked me to describe it. I don't think he had much opinion of my powers of description, for he soon dropped that part of his questioning. Then he asked me to point out where I found the bits of the broken trap. I simply said:"

"'Lord bless you, sir, I couldn't tell. They was scattered all over the place. I had to pick them up between people's feet as they were rushing in from all sides.'"

"'All right, my boy,' he said, in quite a kindly way, for a policeman, 'I don't think they'll want to worry you. There are lots of men and women, I am told, who were standing by and saw the whole thing. They will be all subpoenaed.' I was a small-made lad in those days – I ain't a giant now! – and I suppose he thought it was no use having children for witnesses when they had plenty of grown-ups. Then he said something about me and an idiot asylum that was not kind – no, nor wise either, for I dried up and did not say another word."

"Gradually the public was got rid of. Some strolled off by degrees, going off to have a glass before the pubs closed, and talk it all over. The rest us and the police ballooned out. Then, when the police had taken charge of everything and put in men to stay all night, the coroner's officer came and took off the body to the city mortuary, where the police doctor made a post mortem. I was allowed to go home. I did so — and gladly — when I had seen the place settling down. Mr. Haliday took his wife home in a four-wheeler. It was perhaps just as well, for Mrs. Homcroft and some other kindly souls had poured so much whisky and brandy and rum and gin and beer and peppermint into her that I don't believe she could have walked if she had tried."

"When I was undressing myself something scratched my leg as I was taking off my trousers. I found it was the piece of flat steel which I had picked up on the stage. It was in the shape of a star fish, but the spikes of it were short. Some of the points were turned down, the rest were pulled out straight again. I stood with it in my hand wondering where it had come from and what it was for, but I couldn't remember anything in the whole theater that it could have belonged to. I looked at it closely again, and saw that the edges were all filed and quite bright. But that did not help me, so I put it on the table and thought I would take it with me in the morning; perhaps one of the chaps might know. I turned out the gas and went to bed — and to sleep."

"I must have begun to dream at once, and it was, naturally enough, all about the terrible thing that had occurred. But, like all dreams, it was a bit mixed. They were all mixed. Mortimer with his spangles flying up the trap, it breaking, and the pieces scattering round. Old Jack Haliday looking on at one side of the stage with his wife beside him — he as pale as death, and she looking prettier than ever. And then Mortimer coming down all crooked and falling on the stage, Mrs. Haliday shrieking, and her and Jack running forward, and me picking up the pieces of the broken trap from between people's legs, and finding the steel star with the bent points."

"I woke in a cold sweat, saying to myself as I sat up in bed in the dark:"

"'That's it!'"

"And then my head began to reel about so that I lay down again and began to think it all over. And it all seemed clear enough then. It was Mr. Haliday who made that star and put it over the star trap where the points joined! That was what Jack Haliday was filing at when I saw him at his bench; and he had done it because Mortimer and his wife had been making love to each other. Those girls were right, after all. Of course, the steel points had prevented the trap opening, and when Mortimer was driven up against it his neck was broken."

"But then came the horrible thought that if Jack did it, it was murder, and he would be hung. And, after all, it was his wife that the harlequin had made love to — and old Jack loved her very much indeed himself and had been good to her — and she was his wife. And that bit of steel would hang him if it should be known. But no one but me — and whoever made it, and put it on the trap — even knew of its existence — and Mr. Haliday was my master — and the man was dead — and he was a villain!"

"I was living then at Quarry Place; and in the old quarry was a pond so deep that the boys used to say that far down the water was boiling hot, it was so near Hell."

"I softly opened the window, and, there in the dark, threw the bit of steel as far as I could into the quarry."

"No one ever knew, for I have never spoken a word of it till this very minute. I was not called at the inquest. Everyone was in a hurry; the coroner and the jury and the police. Our governor was in a hurry too, because we wanted to go on as usual at night; and too much talk of the tragedy would hurt business. So nothing was known; and all went on as usual. Except that after that Mrs. Haliday didn't stand in the wings during the harlequinade, and she was as loving to her old husband as a woman can be. It was him she used to watch now; and always with a sort of respectful adoration. She knew, though no one else did, except her husband — and me."

When he finished there was a big spell of silence. The company had all been listening intently, so that there was no change except the cessation of Hempitch's voice. The eyes of all were now fixed on Mr. Wellesley Dovercourt. It was the role of the Tragedian to deal with such an occasion. He was quite alive to the privileges of his status, and spoke at once:

"H'm! Very excellent indeed! You will have to join the ranks of our profession, Mr. Master Machinist — the lower ranks, of course. A very thrilling narrative yours, and distinctly true. There may be some errors of detail, such as that Mrs. Haliday never flirted again. I . . . I knew John Haliday under, of course, his real name. But I shall preserve the secret you so judiciously suppressed. A very worthy person. He was stage carpenter at the Duke's Theater, Bolton, where I first dared histrionic triumphs in the year — ah H'm! I saw quite a good deal of Mrs. Haliday at that time. And you are wrong about her. Quite wrong! She was a most attractive little woman — very!"

The Wardrobe Mistress here whispered to the Second Old Woman:

"Well, ma'am, they all seem agoin' of it tonight. I think they must have ketched the infection from Mr. Bloze. There isn't a bally word of truth in all Hempitch has said. I was there when the accident occurred — for it was an accident when Jim Bungnose, the clown, was killed. For he was a clown, not a 'arlequin; an' there wasn't no lovemakin' with Mrs. 'Aliday. God 'elp the woman as would try to make love to Jim; which she was the Strong Woman in a Circus, and could put up her dooks like a man. Moreover, there wasn't no Mrs. 'Aliday. The carpenter at Grimsby, where it is he means, was Tom Elrington, as he was my first 'usband. And as to Mr. Dovercourt rememberin'! He's a cure, he is; an' the Limit!"

*T*he effect of the Master Machinist's story was so depressing that the M.C. tried to hurry things on; any change of sentiment would, he thought, be and advantage. So he bustled along:

"Now, Mr. Turner Smith, you are the next on the roster. It is a pity we have not an easel and a canvas and paint box here, or even some cartridge pager and charcoal, so that you might give us a touch of your art — what I may call a plastic diversion of the current of narrative genius which has been enlivening the snowy waste around us." The artistic audience applauded this flight of metaphor — all except the young man from Oxford, who contented himself by saying loudly, "Pip-pip!" He had heard something like it before at the Union.

In the Valley
of the Shadow

*T*he rubber-tired wheels jolt unevenly over the granite setts. Dimly I recognize the familiar grey streets and garden-centered squares.

We stop, and through the little crowd on the pavement I am carried indoors and up to the high-ceiling ward. Gently they lift me off the stretcher and put me in bed, and I say:

"What queer curtains you have! They have faces worked on the border. Are they those of your friends?"

The matron smiles, and I think what a quaint idea it is. Then suddenly it strikes me that I have said something foolish, but still the faces are there right enough. (Even when I got well I could sometimes see them in certain lights.)

One of the faces is familiar, and I am just going to ask how they know So-and-so, when I am left alone.

For hours and hours (it seems) no one comes near me. At first I am patient, but gradually a fierce anger seizes me. Did I submit to be brought here merely to die in solitude and in suffocating darkness? I will not stay in this place; far better to go back and die at home!

Suddenly I am borne in a winged machine up, up into the cool air. Far below and infinitesimally small lies the "New Town," half-hid beneath the fluffy smoke; yonder, clear and blue and glittering, is the Firth of Forth; and beyond the sunlit hills of Fife are the advance-guards of the Grampians. A moment only of sheer palpitating ecstasy, then a soul-shattering fall into the black abyss of oblivion. (I hold Mr. H. G.

Wells partially responsible for this little excursion.)

*I*t is light again, but what is that which prevents my seeing the window? A screen? What does that betoken?

A blackness of despair grips me. It is all over, then! No more mountaineering, no more pleasant holidays. This is the end of all my little ambitions. This is, in truth, the bitterness of death.

Presently a nurse comes with a cooling drink, and, making a tremendous effort to look unconcerned, I ask for the screen to be removed. She laughs and folds it up, when I see another screen opposite partially concealing a bed. So I have company. (This was a comparatively lucid interval.)

*W*hat a queer place to have texts! Right round the cornice of the room. And they are constantly changing too. "The Lord is my Shepherd —" "I will arise —" Really this is most irritating. I cannot finish any of them. If the letters would only stay still for a single moment!

But what is that below? It is a wide sandy beach with the blue sea beyond. On the top of a pole in the foreground is a — what is it? — yes, a man's head, of course. (It was really a hanging electric light which by some curious means I must have seen in an inverted position.)

"Sister, I am sure that could be worked up into a splendid story. Please give me some paper and my fountain pen. If I don't write it down now I shall forget it, just as has happened before when I have thought of things during the night." (As a matter of fact, when, I was convalescent I did want to write not only this particular tale, but a complete account of my visions. Of course, I was not permitted, and now, alas! it has gone to join that great company of magnificent — seeming but elusive ideas one has in dreams.)

"*H*onestly, Sister, I must go out for a few moments. The

man is in great danger, and I alone can save him. There is a desperate plot against his life. He lives quite close by in one of the two houses on each side of this."

Sister promises to see about this, and I lie back only half-satisfied.

Presently my bed begins noiselessly to move. It goes through the wall into the next house. Room after room is visited, but my doomed friend is not there. The other houses are then inspected in turn, with no result. I have a feeling that he is being spirited away just in front of me so as to be always in the next house. Sister is at the bottom of this trick, I am sure. (Here began that absurd hatred and suspicion of her which only left me with the delirium.)

"Oh, doctor, I am glad to see you! Really in a free country it is intolerable that a simple request like this cannot be granted me, and to save a man's life, too. You can see for yourself that I am quite sensible and very much in earnest. Try me."

The doctor asks what day of the week it is. I answer, Scots fashion:

"Oh, that's easy! If I am the man who came here on Monday, then it is Wednesday, but if I came on Thursday, then it's Saturday. If you will tell me which man I am, I will tell you what day it is."

Overcome by this logic, the doctor gives in, but suggests a compromise, to which I agree. It is that the four neighboring houses be brought in and placed before my bed, so that I can make sure of seeing and warning my friend in distress.

"No, I will not drink whisky. Surely you know perfectly well that I am a Mussulman and forbidden to drink spirits? You cannot wish me to violate the principles of my religion?"

Sister assures me that the draught is not whisky, and puts the glass to my lips.

In horror I dash it to the floor.

"Devil in human form, you tempt me to my destruction. Begone and let me die in the true faith." (Of course it was not whisky, but something of quite an opposite nature. Weeks later, on recounting this incident, I was reminded of having one day casually read a page or two of a novel in which a Mohammedan is tempted to drink wine. It made no impression whatever at the time, but it must have been stored up somewhere.)

Presently Sister returns with three other nurses and a fresh supply of the accursed stuff. All means are tried, from argument, in which they are signally worsted, to persuasion and gentle force.

Suddenly I resolve on flight, and actually reach the door of the room before being overpowered and brought back to bed. Then I am asked to put my finger in the dose and prove to myself that it is not whisky. In this suggestion I see Sister's malicious cunning, so I smell the wet finger, and triumphantly assert that it is whisky.

When they say it is twelve o'clock, and that I am keeping them all out of bed, I answer that they need not stay for me, and, anyway, what is that to the loss of my soul?

At length I am forced down, and the glass put to my clenched teeth. I pray inwardly for help in this dire extremity. Lo! a brilliant idea. I will pretend to be dead. I stiffen myself and hold my breath. (I can remember no further effort, but I was told afterwards the imitation was wonderful. Even the nurses grew alarmed, and the doctor was sent for. I have a dim recollection of his coming, and before I knew where I was he had injected something, which I thought was the whisky, into my arm.)

I sit up in bed, and glare at them all with concentrated hatred, then I fall back, heartbroken at my forced abjuration, sobbing, sobbing.

I am suffering for my sin. Sister is stabbing me in the Shoulder-blade with a red-hot dagger. (It was a fly-blister, and my skin is very sensitive.) I am aching all over.

Suddenly I am alone on a flat desert plain. I am sitting with my back against one of the stone pillars of a huge closed gateway reaching to the sky. In front of me is proceeding a cinematographic entertainment on a stupendous scale. (I cannot now remember much about it, but the series was long and of an appalling character. Below each picture was a placard stating the subject of the next one. I had the feeling that they were not pictures at all, but real events in the process of happening; further that by answering a question put to me by a mysterious voice I could bring the series to an end, but, though I knew the answer, it was quite beyond my power to give it. Immediately following my failure to reply, from somewhere behind me a full organ pealed forth and a choir of voices broke into a mocking ditty, which embodied the proper answer, and also words of scorn directed against myself. Till recently this ditty haunted me occasionally, but I have now, I am glad to say, forgotten both air and words. All I know is that it was like a quick chant, and quite unfamiliar to me. When the horrid song was over I fell into a state of self-condemnation mixed with helpless expectancy, which was so poignant as to move me still when I think of it.)

This picture is one of wars and earthquakes and burning mountains. Underneath it are the words "End of the World." I have a vision of the countless myriads of mankind kneeling in agony on the other side of the gate. A multitudinous murmur swells into an awful shriek for pity.

"Who am I, O God, that this burden is laid on me? Am I the keeper of that countless host? I cannot answer."

Even as I speak a shudder cleaves the air, a cataclysmal mirage comes into view, the organ booms and the impish choir begins its torturing refrain.

Underneath this picture there is no placard.

The dreadful music ceases, and the horrid scene before me works on in silence. It passes, and then there is neither light nor darkness. The desert disappears, the gateway is no more, the infinite host has gone like the dew of the morning, and I am left in presence of nothing.

The realization is frightful; my brain is whirling; relief must come; human nature cannot bear it. Ah, thank God, I am going mad — when from somewhere, but whence I know not, comes a light scornful laugh, a Satanic voice says, "Sold again!" the organ swells, the invisible choir sings anew, and the whole series of pictures begins again from the beginning. For a moment the tension is relaxed, "God's in His heaven" after all, when, like the clang of steel, the Voice utters the unanswerable question. Oh, God, I must — I shall speak. The answer, the answer is —

"What time is it, Russell?" (Russell was the male night-nurse, the necessity for whose presence the reader will by this time fully understand!)

"Half-past four, sir."

"Well, I must get up to catch the first train to Glasgow. It is a matter of life and death. Please give me my clothes."

Russell endeavors to soothe me with promises of going tomorrow, and so forth, all of which I see through with merciless clearness. In the end, as I threaten to alarm the whole household, I am wrapped up in blankets, carried to an easy chair before the fire, and a screen put behind me.

"You can't get a train, sir, before half-past six."

"Excuse me, there is a train at 5.55, and I am going to get it. By the way, are you sure Sister is not about? I thought I saw her round the corner of the screen. No? Then give me some soda and milk, and have you a cigarette anywhere?"

Russell naturally denied having cigarettes, whereupon, as he afterwards told me, I proceeded to curse him, his family, antecedents, and descendants together, with such copiousness and minuteness of diction that I spoke without stopping for an hour and a half! I fancy Mr. Kipling is responsible for at least the Indian meticulosity of my comminations. Anyhow, the effort having exhausted me, on Russell saying that I had now missed the train, and had better go back to bed to wait for the next, I sensibly agreed.

That was the climax, and on awaking some hours later from a peaceful sleep I found that the crisis was past, and that I was as sane again as usual. The first book I asked for was the Pilgrim's Progress, and as soon as I was permitted to read I turned to the account of Christian's passage through the Valley of the Shadow. I had felt before that Bunyan's demons were stage demons, his quagmires and pits merely simulacra, the accessories generally such as Drury Lane would laugh to scorn. Now I am sure of it. The real difficulty, of course, is to do it better.

The Secret of the Growing Gold

W HEN Margaret Delandre went to live at Brent's Rock the whole neighborhood awoke to the pleasure of an entirely new scandal. Scandals in connection with either the Delandre family or tie Brents of Brent's Rock, were not few; and if the secret history of the county had been written in full both names would have been found well represented. It is true that the status of each was so different that they might have belonged to different continents — or to different worlds for the matter of that — for hitherto their orbits had never crossed. The Brents were accorded by the whole section of the country a unique social dominance, and had ever held themselves as high above the yeoman class to which Margaret Delandre belonged, as a blue-blooded Spanish hidalgo outtops his peasant tenantry.

The Delandres had an ancient record and were proud of it in their way as the Brents were of theirs. But the family had never risen above yeomanry and although they had been once well-to-do in the good old times of foreign wars and protection, their fortunes had withered under the scorching of the free trade sun and the "piping times of peace." They had, as the elder members used to assert, "stuck to the land," with the result that they had taken root in it, body and soul. In fact, they, having chosen the life of vegetables, had flourished as vegetation does — blossomed and thrived in the good season and suffered in the bad. Their holding, Dander's Croft, seemed to have been worked out, and to be typical of the family which had inhabited it. The latter had declined generation after generation, sending out now and again some abortive shoot of unsatisfied energy in the shape of a soldier or sailor, who had worked his way to the minor grades of the services and had there stopped, cut short either from unheeding gallantry in action or from that destroying cause to men without breeding or youthful care — the recognition of a position above them which they feel unfitted to fill. So, little by little, the family dropped lower and lower, the men brooding and dissatisfied, and drinking themselves into the grave, the women drudging at home, or marrying beneath them — or worse. In process of time all disappeared, leaving only two in the Croft, Wykham Delandre and his sister Margaret. The man and woman seemed to have inherited in masculine and feminine form respectively the evil tendency of their race, sharing in common the principles, though manifesting them in different ways, of sullen passion, voluptuousness and recklessness.

The history of the Brents had been something similar, but showing the causes of decadence in their aristocratic and not their plebian forms. They, too, had sent their shoots to the wars; but their positions had been different and they had often attained honor — for without flaw they were gallant, and brave deeds were done by them before the selfish dissipation which marked them had sapped their vigor.

The present head of the family — if family it could now be called when one remained in the direct line — was Geoffrey Brent. He was almost a type of worn-out race, manifesting in some ways its most brilliant qualities, and in others its utter degradation. He might be fairly compared with some of those antique Italian nobles whom the painters have preserved to us with their courage, their unscrupulousness, their refinement of last and cruelty — the voluptuary actual with the fiend potential. He was certainly handsome, with that dark, aquiline, commanding beauty which women so generally recognize as dominant. With men he was distant and cold; but such a bearing never deters womankind. The inscrutable laws of sex have so arranged that even a timid woman is not afraid of a fierce and haughty man. And so it was that there was hardly a woman of any kind or degree, who lived within view of Brent's Rock, who did not cherish some form of secret admiration for the handsome wastrel. The category was a wide one, for Brent's Rock rose up steeply from the midst of a level region and for a circuit of a hundred miles it lay on the horizon, with its high old towers and steep roofs cutting the level edge of wood and hamlet, and far-scattered mansions.

So long as Geoffrey Brent confined his dissipations to London and Paris and Vienna — anywhere out of sight and sound of his home — opinion was silent. It is easy to listen to far-off echoes unmoved, and we can treat them with disbelief, or scorn, or disdain, or whatever attitude of coldness may suit our purpose. But when the scandal came close home it was another matter; and the feelings of independence and integrity which is in people of every community which is not utterly spoiled, asserted itself and demanded that condemnation should be expressed. Still there was a certain reticence in all, and no more notice was taken of the existing facts than was absolutely necessary. Margaret Delandre bore herself so fearlessly and so openly — she accepted her position as the justified companion of Geoffrey Brent so naturally that people came to believe that she was secretly married to him, and therefore thought it wiser to hold their tongues lest time should justify her and also make her an active enemy.

The one person who, by his interference, could have settled all doubts was debarred by circumstances from interfering in the matter. Wykham Delandre had quarreled with his sister — or perhaps it was that she had quarreled with him — and they were on terms not merely of armed neutrality but of bitter hatred. The quarrel had been antecedent to Margaret going to Brent's Rock. She and Wykham had almost come to blows. There had certainly been threats on one side and on the other; and in the end Wykham, overcome with passion, had ordered his sister to leave his house. She had risen straightaway, and, without waiting to pack up even her own personal belongings, had walked out of the house. On the threshold she had paused for a moment to hurl a bitter threat at Wykham that he would rue in shame and despair to the last hour of his life his act of that day. Some weeks had since passed; and it was understood in the neighborhood that Margaret had gone to London, when she suddenly appeared driving out with Geoffrey Brent, and the entire neighborhood knew before nightfall that she had taken up her abode at the Rock. It was no subject of surprise that Brent had come back unexpectedly, for such was his usual custom. Even his own servants never knew when to expect him, for there was a private door, of which he alone had the key, by which he sometimes entered without anyone in the house being aware of his coming. This was his usual method of appearing after a long absence.

Wykham Delandre was furious at the news. He vowed vengeance — and to keep his mind level with his passion drank deeper than ever. He tried several times to see his sister, but she contemptuously refused to meet him. He tried to have an interview with Brent and was refused by him also. Then he tried to stop him in the road, but without avail, for Geoffrey was not a man to be stopped against his will. Several actual encounters took place between the two men, and many more were threatened and avoided. At last Wykham Delandre settled down to a morose, vengeful acceptance of the situation.

Neither Margaret nor Geoffrey was of a pacific temperament, and it was not long before there began to be quarrels between them. One thing would lead to another, and wine flowed freely at Brent's Rock. Now and again the quarrels would assume a bitter aspect, and threats would be exchanged in uncompromising language that fairly awed the listening servants. But such quarrels generally ended where domestic altercations do, in reconciliation, and in a mutual respect for the fighting qualities proportionate to their manifestation. Fighting for its own sake is found by a certain class of persons, all the world over, to be a matter of absorbing interest, and there is no reason to believe that domestic conditions minimize its potency. Geoffrey and Margaret made occasional absences from Brent's Rock, and on each of these occasions Wykham Delandre also absented himself; but as he generally heard of the absence too late to be of any service, he returned; home each time in a more bitter and discontented frame of mind than before.

At last there came a time when the absence from Brent's Rock became longer than before. Only a few days earlier there had been a quarrel, exceeding in bitterness anything which had gone before; but this, too, had been made up, an a trip on the Continent had been mentioned before the servants. After a few days Wykham Delandre also went away, and it was some weeks before he returned. It was noticed that he was full of some new importance — satisfaction, exaltation — they hardly knew how to call it. He went straightaway to Brent's Rock, and demanded to see Geoffrey Brent, and on being told that he had not yet returned, said, with a grim decision which the servants noted:

"I shall come again. My news is solid — it can wait!" and turned away. Week after week went by, and month after month; and then there came a rumor, certified later on, that an accident had occurred in the Zermatt valley. Whilst crossing a dangerous pass the carriage containing an English lady and the driver had fallen over a precipice, the gentleman of the party, Mr. Geoffrey Brent, having been fortunately saved as he had been walking up the hill to ease the horses. He gave information, and search was made. The broken rail, the excoriated roadway, the marks where the horses had struggled on the decline before finally pitching over into the torrent — all told the sad tale. It was a wet season, and there had been much snow in the winter, so that the river was swollen beyond its usual volume, and the eddies of the stream were packed with ice. All search was made, and finally the wreck of the carriage and the body of one horse were found in an eddy of the river. Later on the body of the driver was found on the sandy, torrent-swept waste near Täsch; but the body of the lady, like that of the other horse, had quite disappeared, and was — what was left of it by that time — whirling amongst the eddies of the Rhone on its way down to the Lake of Geneva.

Wykham Delandre made all the enquiries possible, but could not find any trace of the missing woman. He found, however, in the books of the various hotels the name of "Mr. and Mrs. Geoffrey Brent." And he had a stone erected at Zermatt to his sister's memory, under her married name, and a tablet put up in the church at Bretten, the parish in which both Brent's Rock and Dander's Croft were situated.

There was a lapse of nearly a year, after the excitement of the matter had worn away, and the whole neighborhood had gone on its accustomed way. Brent was still absent, and Delandre more drunken, more morose, and more revengeful than before.

Then there was a new excitement. Brent's Rock was being made ready for a new mistress. It was officially announced by Geoffrey himself in a letter to the Vicar, that he had been married some months before to an Italian lady, and that they were then on their way home. Then a small army of workmen invaded the house; and hammer and plane sounded, and a general air of size and paint pervaded the atmosphere. One wing of the old house, the south, was entirely re-done; and then the great body of the workmen departed, leaving only materials for the doing of the old hall when Geoffrey Brent should have returned, for he had directed that the decoration was only to be done under his own eyes: He had brought with him accurate drawings of a hall in the house of his bride's father, for he wished to reproduce for her the place to which she had been accustomed. As the molding had all to be redone, some scaffolding poles and boards were brought in and laid on one side of the great hall, and also a great wooden tank or box for mixing the lime, which was laid in bags beside it.

When the new mistress of Brent's Rock arrived the bells of the church rang out, and there was a general jubilation. She was a beautiful creature, full of the poetry and fire and passion of the South; and the few English words which she had learned were spoken in such a sweet and pretty broken way that she won the hearts of the people almost as much by the music of her voice as by the melting beauty of her dark eyes.

Geoffrey Brent seemed more happy than he had ever before appeared; but there was a dark, anxious look on his face that was new to those who knew him of old, and he started at times as though at some noise that was unheard by others.

And so months passed and the whisper grew that at last Brent's Rock was to have an heir. Geoffrey was very tender to his wife, and the new bond between them seemed to soften him. He took more interest in his tenants and their needs than he had ever done; and works of charity on his part as well as on his sweet young wife's were not lacking. He seemed to have set all his hopes on the child that was coming, and as he looked deeper into the future the dark shadow that had come over his face seemed to die gradually away.

All the time Wykham Delandre nursed his revenge. Deep in his heart had grown up a purpose of vengeance which only waited an opportunity to crystallize and take a definite shape His vague idea was somehow centered in the wife of Brent, for he knew that he could strike him best through those he loved, and the coming time seemed to hold in its womb the opportunity for which he longed. One night he sat alone in the living room of his house. It had once been a handsome room in its way, but time and neglect had done their work and it was now little better than a ruin, without dignity or picturesqueness of any kind. He had been drinking heavily for some time and was more than half stupefied. He thought he heard a noise as of someone at the door and looked up. Then he called half savagely to come in; but there was no response. With a muttered blasphemy he renewed his potations. Presently he forgot all around him, sank into a daze, but suddenly awoke to see standing before him someone or something like a battered, ghostly edition of his sister. For a few moments there came upon him a sort of fear. The woman before him, with distorted features and burning eyes seemed hardly human, and the only thing that seemed a reality of his sister, as she had been, was her wealth of golden hair, and this was now streaked with grey. She eyed her brother with a long, cold stare; and he, too, as he looked and began to realize the actuality of her presence, found the hatred of her which he had had, once again surging up in his heart. All the brooding passion of the past year seemed to find a voice at once as he asked her:

"Why are you here? You're dead and buried."

"I am here, Wykham Delandre, for no love of you, but because I hate another even more than I do you!" A great passion blazed in her eyes.

"Him?" he asked, in so fierce a whisper that even the woman was for an instant startled till she regained her calm.

"Yes, him!" she answered. "But make no mistake, my revenge is my own; and I merely use you to help me to it." Wykham asked suddenly:

"Did he marry you?"

The woman's distorted face broadened out in a ghastly attempt at a smile. It was a hideous mockery, for the broken features and seamed scars took strange shapes and strange colors, and queer lines of white showed out as the straining muscles pressed on the old cicatrices.

"So you would like to know! It would please your pride to feel that you sister was truly married! Well, you shall not know. That was my revenge on you, and I do not mean to change it by a hair's breadth. I have come here tonight simply to let you know that I am alive, so that if any violence be done me where I am going there may be a witness."

"Where are you going?" demanded her brother.

"That is my affair! and I have not the least intention of letting you know!" Wykham stood up, but the drink was on him and he reeled and fell. As he lay on the floor he announced his intention of following his sister; and with an outburst of splenetic humor told her that he would follow her through the darkness by the light of her hair, and of her beauty. At this she turned on him, and said that there were others beside him that would rue her hair and her beauty too. "As he will," she hissed; "for the hair remains though the beauty be gone. When he withdrew the lynch-pin and sent us over the precipice into the torrent, he had little thought of my beauty. Perhaps his beauty would be scarred like mine were he whirled, as I was, among the rocks of the Visp, and frozen on the ice pack in the drift of the river. But let him beware! His time is coming!" and with a fierce gesture she flung open the door and passed out into the night.

*L*ater on that night, Mrs. Brent, who was but half-asleep, became suddenly awake and spoke to her husband:

"Geoffrey, was not that the click of a lock somewhere below our window?"

But Geoffrey — though she thought that he, too, had started at the noise — seemed sound asleep, and breathed heavily. Again Mrs. Brent dozed; but this time awoke to the fact that her husband had arisen and was partially dressed. He was deadly pale, and when the light of the lamp which he had in his hand fell on his face, she was frightened at the look in his eyes.

"What is it, Geoffrey? What dost thou?" she asked.

"Hush! little one," he answered, in a strange, hoarse voice. "Go to sleep. I am restless, and wish to finish some work I left undone."

"Bring it here, my husband," she said; "I am lonely and I fear when thou art away."

For reply he merely kissed her and went out, closing the door behind him. She lay awake for awhile, and then nature asserted itself, and she slept.

Suddenly she started broad awake with the memory in her ears of a smothered cry from somewhere not far off. She jumped up and ran to the door and listened, but there was no sound. She grew alarmed for her husband, and called out "Geoffrey! Geoffrey!"

After a few moments the door of the great hall opened, and Geoffrey appeared at it, but without his lamp.

"Hush!" he said, in a sort of whisper, and his voice was harsh and stern. "Hush! Get to bed! I am working, and must not be disturbed. Go to sleep, and do not wake the house!"

With a chill in her heart — for the harshness of her husband's voice was new to her — she crept back to bed and lay there trembling, too frightened to cry, and listened to every sound. There was a long pause of silence, and then the sound of some iron implement striking muffled blows! Then there came a clang of a heavy stone falling, followed by a muffled curse. Then a dragging sound, and then more noise of stone on stone. She lay all the while in an agony of fear, and her heart beat dreadfully. She heard a curious sort of scraping sound; and then there was silence. Presently the door opened gently, and Geoffrey appeared. His wife pretended to be asleep; but through her eyelashes she saw him wash from his hands something white that looked like lime.

In the morning he made no allusion to the previous night, and she was afraid to ask any question.

From that day there seemed some shadow over Geoffrey Brent. He neither ate nor slept as he had been accustomed, and his former habit of turning suddenly as though someone were speaking from behind him revived. The old hall seemed to have some kind of fascination for him. He used to go there many times in the day, but grew impatient if anyone, even his wife, entered it. When the builder's foreman came to inquire about continuing his work Geoffrey was out driving; the man went into the hall, and when Geoffrey returned the servant told him of his arrival and where he was. With a frightful oath he pushed the servant aside and hurried up to the old hall. The workman met him almost at the door; and as Geoffrey burst into the room he ran against him. The man apologized:

"Beg pardon, sir, but I was just going out to make some inquiries. I directed twelve sacks of lime to be sent here, but I see there are only ten."

"Damn the ten sacks and the twelve too!" was the ungracious and incomprehensible rejoinder.

The workman looked surprised, and tried to turn the conversation.

"I see, sir, there is a little matter which our people must have done; but the governor will of course see it set right at his own cost."

"What do you mean?"

"That 'ere 'arth-stone, sir: Some idiot must have put a scaffold pole on it and cracked it right down the middle, and it's thick enough you'd think to stand hanythink." Geoffrey was silent for quite a minute, and then said in a constrained voice and with much gentler manner:

"Tell your people that I am not going on with the work in the hall at present. I want to leave it as it is for a while longer."

"All right sir. I'll send up a few of our chaps to take away these poles and lime bags and tidy the place up a bit."

"No! No!" said Geoffrey, "leave them where they are. I shall send and tell you when you are to get on with the work." So the foreman went away, and his comment to his master was:

"I'd send in the bill, sir, for the work already done. 'Pears to me that money's a little shaky in that quarter."

Once or twice Delandre tried to stop Brent on the road, and, at last, finding that he could not attain his object rode after the carriage, calling out:

"What has become of my sister, your wife?" Geoffrey lashed his horses into a gallop, and the other, seeing from his white face and from his wife's collapse almost into a faint that his object was attained, rode away with a scowl and a laugh.

That night when Geoffrey went into the hall he passed over to the great fireplace, and all at once started back with a smothered cry. Then with an effort he pulled himself together and went away, returning with a light. He bent down over the broken hearth-stone to see if the moonlight falling through the storied window had in any way deceived him. Then with a groan of anguish he sank to his knees.

There, sure enough, through the crack in the broken stone were protruding a multitude of threads of golden hair, just tinged with grey!

He was disturbed by a noise at the door, and looking round, saw his wife standing in the doorway. In the desperation of the moment he took action to prevent discovery, and lighting a match at the lamp, stooped down and burned away the hair that rose through the broken stone. Then rising as nonchalantly as he could, he pretended surprise at seeing his wife beside him.

For the next week he lived in an agony; for, whether by accident or design, he could not find himself alone in the hall for any length of time. At each visit the hair had grown afresh through the crack, and he had to watch it carefully lest his terrible secret should be discovered. He tried to find a receptacle for the body of the murdered woman outside the house, but someone always interrupted him; and once, when he was coming out of the private doorway, he was met by his wife, who began to question him about it, and manifested surprise that she should not have before noticed the key which he now reluctantly showed her. Geoffrey dearly and passionately loved his wife, so that any possibility of her discovering his dread secrets, or even of doubting him, filled him with anguish; and after a couple of days had passed, he could not help coming to the conclusion that, at least, she suspected something.

That very evening she came into the hall after her drive and found him there sitting moodily by the deserted fireplace. She spoke to him directly.

"Geoffrey, I have been spoken to by that fellow Delandre, and he says horrible things. He tells to me that a week ago his sister returned to this house, the wreck and ruin of her former self, with only her golden hair as of old, and announced some fell intention. He asked me where she is — and oh, Geoffrey, she is dead, she is dead! So how can she have returned? Oh! I am in dread, and I know not where to turn!"

For answer, Geoffrey burst into a torrent of blasphemy which made her shudder. He cursed Delandre and his sister and all their kind, and in especial he hurled curse after curse on her golden hair.

"Oh, hush! hush!" she said, and was then silent, for she feared her husband when she saw the evil effect of his humor. Geoffrey in the torrent of his anger stood up and moved away from the hearth; but suddenly stopped as he saw a new look of terror in his wife's eyes. He followed their glance, and then he, too, shuddered — for there on the broken hearth-stone lay a golden streak as the point of the hair rose through the crack.

"Look, look!" she shrieked. "Is it some ghost of the dead! Come away — come away!" and seizing her husband by the wrist with the frenzy of madness, she pulled him from the room.

That night she was in a raging fever. The doctor of the district attended her at once, and special aid was telegraphed for to London. Geoffrey was in despair, and in his anguish at the danger to his young wife almost forgot his own crime and its consequences. In the evening the doctor had to leave to attend to others; but he left Geoffrey in charge of his wife. His last words were:

"Remember, you must humor her till I come in the morning, or till some other doctor has her case in hand. What you have to dread is another attack of emotion. See that she is kept warm. Nothing more can be done."

Late in the evening, when the rest of the household had retired, Geoffrey's wife got up from her bed and called to her husband.

"Come!" she said. "Come to the old hall! I know where the gold comes from! I want to see it grow!"

Geoffrey would fain have stopped her, but he feared for her life or reason on the one hand, and lest in a paroxysm she should shriek out her terrible suspicion, and seeing that it was useless to try to prevent her, wrapped a warm rug around her and went with her to the old hall. When they entered, she turned and shut the door and locked it.

"We want no strangers amongst us three tonight!" she whispered with a wan smile.

"We three! nay we are but two," said Geoffrey with a shudder; he feared to say more.

"Sit here," said his wife as she put out the light. "Sit here by the hearth and watch the gold growing. The silver moonlight is jealous! See, it steals along the floor towards the gold — our gold!" Geoffrey looked with growing horror, and saw that during the hours that had passed the golden hair had protruded further through the broken hearth-stone. He tried to hide it by placing his feet over the broken place; and his wife, drawing her chair beside him, leant over and laid her head on his shoulder.

"Now do not stir, dear," she said; "let us sit still and watch. We shall find the secret of the growing gold!" He passed his arm round her and sat silent; and as the moonlight stole along the floor she sank to sleep.

He feared to wake her; and so sat silent and miserable as the hours stole away.

Before his horror-struck eyes the golden hair from the broken stone grew and grew; and as it increased, so his heart got colder and colder, till at last he had not power to stir, and sat with his eyes full of terror watching his doom.

*I*n the morning when the London doctor came, neither Geoffrey nor his wife could be found. Search was made in all the rooms, but without avail. As a last resource the great door of the old hall was broken open, and those who entered saw a grim and sorry sight.

There by the deserted hearth Geoffrey Brent and his young wife sat cold and white and dead. Her face was peaceful, and her eyes were closed in sleep; but his face was a sight that made all who saw shudder, for there was on it a look of unutterable horror. The eyes were open and stared glassily at his feet, which were twined with tresses of golden hair, streaked with grey, which came through the broken hearth-stone.

The Chain of Destiny
I. A Warning

*I*t was so late in the evening when I arrived at Scarp that I had but little opportunity of observing the external appearance of the house; but, as far as I could judge in the dim twilight, it was a very stately edifice of seemingly great age, built of white stone. When I passed the porch, however, I could observe its internal beauties much more closely, for a large wood fire burned in the hall and all the rooms and passages were lighted. The hall was almost baronial in its size, and opened on to a staircase of dark oak so wide and so generous in its slope that a carriage might almost have been driven up it. The rooms were large and lofty, with their walls, like those of the staircase, paneled with oak black from age. This somber material would have made the house intensely gloomy but for the enormous width and height of both rooms and passages. As it was, the effect was a homely combination of size and warmth. The windows were set in deep embrasures, and, on the ground story, reached from quite level with the floor to almost the ceiling. The fireplaces were quite in the old style, large and surrounded with massive oak carvings, representing on each some scene from Biblical history, and at the side of each fireplace rose a pair of massive carved iron firedogs. It was altogether just such a house as would have delighted the heart of Washington Irving or Nathaniel Hawthorne.

The house had been lately restored; but in effecting the restoration comfort had not been forgotten, and any modern

improvement which tended to increase the homelike appearance of the rooms had been added. The old diamond-paned
casements, which had remained probably from the Elizabe-
than age, had given place to more useful plate glass; and, in
like manner, many other changes had taken place. But so
judiciously had every change been effected that nothing of
the new clashed with the old, but the harmony of all the parts
seemed complete.

I thought it no wonder that Mrs. Trevor had fallen in love
with Scarp the first time she had seen it. Mrs. Trevor's liking
the place was tantamount to her husband's buying it, for he
was so wealthy that he could get almost anything money
could purchase. He was himself a man of good taste, but still
he felt his inferiority to his wife in this respect so much that
he never dreamt of differing in opinion from her on any
matter of choice or judgment. Mrs. Trevor had, without
exception, the best taste of anyone whom I ever knew, and,
strange to say, her taste was not confined to any branch of
art. She did not write, or paint, or sing; but still her judgment
in writing, painting, or music, was unquestioned by her
friends. It seemed as if nature had denied to her the power
of execution in any separate branch of art, in order to make
her perfect in her appreciation of what was beautiful and true
in all. She was perfect in the art of harmonizing — the art of
everyday life. Her husband used to say, with a far-fetched joke,
that her star must have been in the House of Libra, because
everything which she said and did showed such a nicety of
balance.

Mr. and Mrs. Trevor were the most model couple I ever
knew — they really seemed not twain, but one. They appeared
to have adopted something of the French idea of man and
wife — that they should not be the less like friends because
they were linked together by indissoluble bonds — that they
should share their pleasures as well as their sorrows. The
former outbalanced the latter, for both husband and wife
were of that happy temperament which can take pleasure
from everything, and find consolation even in the chastening
rod of affliction.

Still, through their web of peaceful happiness ran a thread
of care. One that cropped up in strange places, and disap-

peared again, but which left a quiet tone over the whole fabric — they had no child.

"They had their share of sorrow, for when time was ripe
  The still affection of the heart became an outward
      breathing type,
  That into stillness passed again,
  But left a want unknown before."

There was something simple and holy in their patient endurance of their lonely life — for lonely a house must ever be without children to those who love truly. Theirs was not the eager, disappointed longing of those whose union had proved fruitless. It was the simple, patient, hopeless resignation of those who find that a common sorrow draws them more closely together than many common joys. I myself could note the warmth of their hearts and their strong philoprogenitive feeling in their manner towards me.

From the time when I lay sick in college when Mrs. Trevor appeared to my fever-dimmed eyes like an angel of mercy, I felt myself growing in their hearts. Who can imagine my gratitude to the lady who, merely because she heard of my sickness and desolation from a college friend, came and nursed me night and day till the fever left me. When I was sufficiently strong to be moved she had me brought away to the country, where good air, care, and attention soon made me stronger than ever. From that time I became a constant visitor at the Trevors' house; and as month after month rolled by I felt that I was growing in their affections. For four summers I spent my long vacation in their house, and each year I could feel Mr. Trevor's shake of the hand grow heartier, and his wife's kiss on my forehead — for so she always saluted me — grow more tender and motherly.

Their liking for me had now grown so much that in their heart of hearts — and it was a sanctum common to them both — they secretly loved me as a son. Their love was returned manifold by the lonely boy, whose devotion to the kindest friends of his youth and his trouble had increased with his growth into manhood. Even in my own heart I was ashamed to confess how I loved them both — how I worshipped Mrs.

Trevor as I adored the mother whom I had lost so young, and whose eyes shone sometimes even then upon me, like stars, in my sleep.

It is strange how timorous we are when our affections are concerned. Merely because I had never told her how I loved her as a mother, because she had never told me how she loved me as a son, I used sometimes to think of her with a sort of lurking suspicion that I was trusting too much to my imagination. Sometimes even I would try to avoid thinking of her altogether, till my yearning would grow too strong to be repelled, and then I would think of her long and silently, and would love her more and more. My life was so lonely that I clung to her as the only thing I had to love. Of course I loved her husband, too, but I never thought about him in the same way; for men are less demonstrative about their affections to each other, and even acknowledge them to themselves less.

Mrs. Trevor was an excellent hostess. She always let her guests see that they were welcome, and, unless in the case of casual visitors, that they were expected. She was, as may be imagined, very popular with all classes; but what is more rare, she was equally popular with both sexes. To be popular with her own sex is the touchstone of a woman's worth. To the houses of the peasantry she came, they said, like an angel, and brought comfort wherever she came. She knew the proper way to deal with the poor; she always helped them materially, but never offended their feelings in so doing. Young people all adored her.

My curiosity had been aroused as to the sort of place Scarp was; for, in order to give me a surprise, they would not tell me anything about it, but said that I must wait and judge it for myself. I had looked forward to my visit with both expectation and curiosity.

When I entered the hall, Mrs. Trevor came out to welcome me and kissed me on the forehead, after her usual manner. Several of the old servants came near, smiling and bowing, and wishing welcome to "Master Frank." I shook hands with several of them, whilst their mistress looked on with a pleased smile.

As we went into a snug parlor, where a table was laid out with the materials for a comfortable supper, Mrs. Trevor said to me:

"I am glad you came so soon, Frank. We have no one here at present, so you will be quite alone with us for a few days; and you will be quite alone with me this evening, for Charley is gone to a dinner-party at Westholm."

I told her that I was glad that there was no one else at Scarp, for that I would rather be with her and her husband than anyone else in the world. She smiled as she said:

"Frank, if anyone else said that, I would put it down as a mere compliment; but I know you always speak the truth. It is all very well to be alone with an old couple like Charley and me for two or three days; but just you wait till Thursday, and you will look on the intervening days as quite wasted."

"Why?" I inquired.

"Because, Frank, there is a girl coming to stay with me then, with whom I intend you to fall in love."

I answered jocosely:

"Oh, thank you, Mrs. Trevor, very much for your kind intentions — but suppose for a moment that they should be impracticable. 'One man may lead a horse to the pond's brink.' 'The best laid schemes o' mice an' men.' Eh?"

"Frank, don't be silly. I do not want to make you fall in love against your inclination; but I hope and I believe that you will."

"Well, I'm sure I hope you won't be disappointed; but I never yet heard a person praised that I did not experience a disappointment when I came to know him or her."

"Frank, did I praise anyone?"

"Well, I am vain enough to think that your saying that you knew I would fall in love with her was a sort of indirect praise."

"Dear, me, Frank, how modest you have grown. 'A sort of indirect praise!' Your humility is quite touching."

"May I ask who the lady is, as I am supposed to be an interested party?"

"I do not know that I ought to tell you on account of your having expressed any doubt as to her merits. Besides, I might weaken the effect of the introduction. If I stimulate your curiosity it will be a point in my favor."

"Oh, very well; I suppose I must only wait?"

"Ah, well, Frank, I will tell you. It is not fair to keep you waiting. She is a Miss Fothering."

"Fothering? Fothering? I think I know that name. I remember hearing it somewhere, a long time ago, if I do not mistake. Where does she come from?"

"Her father is a clergyman in Norfolk, but he belongs to the Warwickshire family. I met her at Winthrop, Sir Harry Blount's place, a few months ago, and took a great liking for her, which she returned, and so we became fast friends. I made her promise to pay me a visit this summer, so she and her sister are coming here on Thursday to stay for some time."

"And, may I be bold enough to inquire what she is like?"

"You may inquire if you like, Frank; but you won't get an answer. I shall not try to describe her. You must wait and judge for yourself."

"Wait," said I, "three whole days? How can I do that? Do, tell me."

She remained firm to her determination. I tried several times in the course of the evening to find out something more about Miss Fothering, for my curiosity was roused; but all the answer I could get on the subject was — "Wait, Frank; wait, and judge for yourself."

When I was bidding her good night, Mrs. Trevor said to me —

"By-the-bye, Frank, you will have to give up the room which you will sleep in tonight, after tomorrow. I will have such a full house that I cannot let you have a doubled-bedded room all to yourself; so I will give that room to the Miss Fotherings, and move you up to the second floor. I just want you to see the room, as it has a romantic look about it, and has all the old furniture that was in it when we came here. There are several pictures in it worth looking at."

My bedroom was a large chamber — immense for a bed-room — with two windows opening level with the floor, like those of the parlors and drawing rooms. The furniture was old-fashioned, but not old enough to be curious, and on the walls hung many pictures — portraits — the house was full of portraits — and landscapes. I just glanced at these, intending to examine them in the morning, and went to bed. There was a fire in the room, and I lay awake for some time looking dreamily at the shadows of the furniture flitting over the walls and ceiling as the flames of the wood fire leaped and fell, and the red embers dropped whitening on the hearth. I tried to give the rein to my thoughts, but they kept constantly to the one subject — the mysterious Miss Fothering, with whom I was to fall in love. I was sure that I had heard her name somewhere, and I had at times lazy recollections of a child's face. At such times I would start awake from my growing drowsiness, but before I could collect my scattered thoughts the idea had eluded me. I could remember neither when nor where I had heard the name, nor could I recall even the expression of the child's face. It must have been long, long ago, when I was young. When I was young my mother was alive. My mother — mother — mother. I found myself half awakening, and repeating the word over and over again. At last I fell asleep.

I thought that I awoke suddenly to that peculiar feeling which we sometimes have on starting from sleep, as if some one had been speaking in the room, and the voice is still echoing through it. All was quite silent, and the fire had gone out. I looked out of the window that lay straight opposite the foot of the bed, and observed a light outside, which gradually grew brighter till the room was almost as light as by day. The window looked like a picture in the framework formed by the cornice over the foot of the bed, and the massive pillars shrouded in curtains which supported it.

With the new accession of light I looked round the room, but nothing was changed. All was as before, except that some of the objects of furniture and ornament were shown in stronger relief than hitherto. Amongst these, those most in relief were the other bed, which was placed across the room, and an old picture that hung on the wall at its foot. As the bed was merely the counterpart of the one in which I lay, my attention became fixed on the picture. I observed it closely and with great interest. It seemed old, and was the portrait of a young girl, whose face, though kindly and merry, bore signs of thought and a capacity for deep feeling — almost for passion. At some moments, as I looked at it, it called up before my mind a vision of Shakespeare's Beatrice, and once I thought of Beatrice Cenci. But this was probably caused by the association of ideas suggested by the similarity of names.

The light in the room continued to grow even brighter, so I looked again out of the window to seek its source, and saw there a lovely sight. It seemed as if there were grouped without the window three lovely children, who seemed to float in mid-air. The light seemed to spring from a point far behind them, and by their side was something dark and shadowy, which served to set off their radiance.

The children seemed to be smiling in upon something in the room, and, following their glances, I saw that their eyes rested upon the other bed. There, strange to say, the head which I had lately seen in the picture rested upon the pillow. I looked at the wall, but the frame was empty, the picture was gone. Then I looked at the bed again, and saw the young girl asleep, with the expression of her face constantly changing, as though she were dreaming.

As I was observing her, a sudden look of terror spread over her face, and she sat up like a sleep-walker, with her eyes wide open, staring out of the window.

Again turning to the window, my gaze became fixed, for a great and weird change had taken place. The figures were still there, but their features and expressions had become woefully different. Instead of the happy innocent look of childhood was one of malignity. With the change the children had grown old, and now three hags, decrepit and deformed, like typical witches, were before me.

But a thousand times worse than this transformation was the change in the dark mass that was near them. From a cloud, misty and undefined, it became a sort of shadow with a form. This gradually, as I looked, grew darker and fuller, till at length it made me shudder. There stood before me the phantom of the Fiend.

There was a long period of dead silence, in which I could hear the beating of my heart; but at length the phantom spoke to the others. His words seemed to issue from his lips mechanically, and without expression – "Tomorrow, and tomorrow, and tomorrow. The fairest and the best." He looked so awful that the question arose in my mind – "Would I dare to face him without the window – would anyone dare to go amongst those fiends?" A harsh, strident, diabolical laugh from without seemed to answer my unasked question in the negative.

But as well as the laugh I heard another sound — the tones of a sweet sad voice in despair coming across the room.

"Oh, alone, alone! is there no human thing near me? No hope — no hope. I shall go mad — or die."

The last words were spoken with a gasp.

I tried to jump out of bed, but could not stir, my limbs were bound in sleep. The young girl's head fell suddenly back upon the pillow, and the limp-hanging jaw and wide-open, purposeless mouth spoke but too plainly of what had happened.

Again I heard from without the fierce, diabolical laughter, which swelled louder and louder, till at last it grew so strong that in very horror I shook aside my sleep and sat up in bed. listened and heard a knocking at the door, but in another moment I became more awake, and knew that the sound came from the hall. It was, no doubt, Mr. Trevor returning from his party.

The hall-door was opened and shut, and then came a subdued sound of tramping and voices, but this soon died away, and there was silence throughout the house.

I lay awake for long thinking, and looking across the room at the picture and at the empty bed; for the moon now shone brightly, and the night was rendered still brighter by occasional flashes of summer lightning. At times the silence was broken by an owl screeching outside.

As I lay awake, pondering, I was very much troubled by what I had seen; but at length, putting several things together, I came to the conclusion that I had had a dream of a kind that might have been expected. The lightning, the knocking at the hall-door, the screeching of the owl, the empty bed, and the face in the picture, when grouped together, supplied materials for the main facts of the vision. The rest was, of course, the offspring of pure fancy, and the natural consequence of the component elements mentioned acting with each other in the mind.

I got up and looked out of the window, but saw nothing but the broad belt of moonlight glittering on the bosom of the lake, which extended miles and miles away, till its farther shore was lost in the night haze, and the green sward, dotted with shrubs and tall grasses, which lay between the lake and the house.

The vision had utterly faded. However, the dream — for so, I suppose, I should call it — was very powerful, and I slept no more till the sunlight was streaming broadly in at the window, and then I fell into a doze.

II. More Links

*L*ate in the morning I was awakened by Parks, Mr. Trevor's man, who always used to attend on me when I visited my friends. He brought me hot water and the local news; and, chatting with him, I forgot for a time my alarm of the night.

Parks was staid and elderly, and a type of a class now rapidly disappearing — the class of old family servants who are as proud of their hereditary loyalty to their masters, as those masters are of name and rank. Like all old servants he had a great loving for all sorts of traditions. He believed them, and feared them, and had the most profound reverence for anything which had a story.

I asked him if he knew anything of the legendary history of Scarp. He answered with an air of doubt and hesitation, as of one carefully delivering an opinion which was still incomplete.

"Well, you see, Master Frank, that Scarp is so old that it must have any number of legends; but it is so long since it was inhabited that no one in the village remembers them. The place seems to have become in a kind of way forgotten, and died out of people's thoughts, and so I am very much afraid, sir, that all the genuine history is lost."

"What do you mean by the genuine history?" I inquired.

"Well, sir, I mean the true tradition, and not the inventions of the village folk. I heard the sexton tell some stories, but I am quite sure that they were not true, for I could see, Master

Frank, that he did not believe them himself, but was only trying to frighten us."

"And could you not hear of any story that appeared to you to be true?"

"No, sir, and I tried very hard. You see, Master Frank, that there is a sort of club held every week in the tavern down in the village, composed of very respectable men, sir — very respectable men, indeed — and they asked me to be their chairman. I spoke to the master about it, and he gave me leave to accept their proposal. I accepted it as they made a point of it; and from my position I have of course a fine opportunity of making inquiries. It was at the club, sir, that I was, last night, so that I was not here to attend on you, which I hope that you will excuse."

Parks's air of mingled pride and condescension, as he made the announcement of the club, was very fine, and the effect was heightened by the confiding frankness with which he spoke. I asked him if he could find no clue to any of the legends which must have existed about such an old place. He answered with a very slight reluctance —

"Well, sir, there was one woman in the village who was awfully old and doting, and she evidently knew something about Scarp, for when she heard the name she mumbled out something about 'awful stories,' and 'times of horror,' and such like things, but I couldn't make her understand what it was I wanted to know, or keep her up to the point."

"And have you tried often, Parks? Why do you not try again?"

"She is dead, sir!"

I had felt inclined to laugh at Parks when he was telling me of the old woman. The way in which he gloated over the words "awful stories," and "times of horror," was beyond the power of description; it should have been heard and seen to have been properly appreciated. His voice became deep and mysterious, and he almost smacked his lips at the thought of so much pabulum for nightmares. But when he calmly told me that the woman was dead, a sense of blankness, mingled with awe, came upon me. Here, the last link between myself and the mysterious past was broken, never to be mended. All the rich stores of legend and tradition that had arisen from strange conjunctures of circumstances, and from the belief and imagination of long lines of villagers, loyal to their suzerain lord, were lost forever. I felt quite sad and disappointed; and no attempt was made either by Parks or myself to continue the conversation. Mr. Trevor came presently into my room, and having greeted each other warmly we went together to breakfast.

At breakfast Mrs. Trevor asked me what I thought of the girl's portrait in my bedroom. We had often had discussions as to characters in faces for we were both physiognomists, and she asked the question as if she were really curious to hear my opinion. I told her that I had only seen it for a short time, and so would rather not attempt to give a final opinion without a more careful study; but from what I had seen of it I had been favorably impressed.

"Well, Frank, after breakfast go and look at it again carefully, and then tell me exactly what you think about it."

After breakfast I did as directed and returned to the breakfast room, where Mrs. Trevor was still sitting.

"Well, Frank, what is your opinion — mind, correctly. I want it for a particular reason."

I told her what I thought of the girl's character; which, if there be any truth in physiognomy, must have been a very fine one.

"Then you like the face?"

I answered —

"It is a great pity that we have none such nowadays. They seem to have died out with Sir Joshua and Greuze. If I could meet such a girl as I believe the prototype of that portrait to have been I would never be happy till I had made her my wife."

To my intense astonishment my hostess jumped up and clapped her hands. I asked her why she did it, and she laughed as she replied in a mocking tone imitating my own voice —

"But suppose for a moment that your kind intentions should be frustrated. 'One man may lead a horse to the pond's brink.' 'The best laid schemes o' mice an' men.' Eh?"

"Well," said I, "there may be some point in the observation. I suppose there must be since you have made it. But for my part I don't see it."

"Oh, I forgot to tell you, Frank, that that portrait might have been painted for Diana Fothering."

I felt a blush stealing over my face. She observed it and took my hand between hers as we sat down on the sofa, and said to me tenderly —

"Frank, my dear boy, I intend to jest with you no more on the subject. I have a conviction that you will like Diana, which has been strengthened by your admiration for her portrait, and from what I know of human nature I am sure that she will like you. Charley and I both wish to see you married, and we would not think of a wife for you who was not in every way eligible. I have never in my life met a girl like Di; and if you and she fancy each other it will be Charley's pleasure and my own to enable you to marry — as far as means are concerned. Now, don't speak. You must know perfectly well how much we both love you. We have always regarded you as our son, and we intend to treat you as our only child when it pleases God to separate us. There now, think the matter over, after you have seen Diana. But, mind me, unless you love each other well and truly, we would far rather not see you married. At all events, whatever may happen you have our best wishes and prayers for your happiness. God bless you, Frank, my dear, dear boy."

There were tears in her eyes as she spoke. When she had finished she leaned over, drew down my head and kissed my forehead very, very tenderly, and then got up softly and left the room. I felt inclined to cry myself. Her words to me were tender, and sensible, and womanly, but I cannot attempt to describe the infinite tenderness and gentleness of her voice and manner. I prayed for every blessing on her in my secret heart, and the swelling of my throat did not prevent my prayers finding voice. There may have been women in the world like Mrs. Trevor, but if there had been I had never met any of them, except herself.

As may be imagined, I was most anxious to see Miss Fothering, and or the remainder of the day she was constantly in my thoughts. That evening a letter came from the younger Miss Fothering apologizing for her not being able to keep her promise with reference to her visit, on account of the unexpected arrival of her aunt, with whom she was obliged to go to Paris for some months. That night I slept in my new room, and had neither dream nor vision. I awoke in the morning half ashamed of having ever paid any attention to such a silly circumstance as a strange dream in my first night in an old house.

After breakfast next morning, as I was going along the corridor, I saw the door of my old bedroom open, and went in to have another look at the portrait. Whilst I was looking at it I began to wonder how it could be that it was so like Miss Fothering as Mrs. Trevor said it was. The more I thought of this the more it puzzled me, till suddenly the dream came back — the face in the picture, and the figure in the bed, the phantoms out in the night, and the ominous words — "The fairest and the best." As I thought of these things all the possibilities of the lost legends of the old house thronged so quickly into my mind that I began to feel a buzzing in my ears and my head began to swim, so that I was obliged to sit down.

"Could it be possible," I asked myself, "that some old curse hangs over the race that once dwelt within these walls, and can she be of that race? Such things have been before now!"

The idea was a terrible one for me, for it made to me a reality that which I had come to look upon as merely the dream of a distempered imagination. If the thought had come to me in the darkness and stillness of the night it would have been awful. How happy I was that it had come by daylight, when the sun was shining brightly, and the air was cheerful with the trilling of the song birds, and the lively, strident cawing from the old rookery.

I stayed in the room for some little time longer, thinking over the scene, and, as is natural, when I had got over the remnants of my fear, my reason began to question the genuineness — vraisemblance of the dream. I began to look for the internal evidence of the untruth to facts; but, after thinking earnestly for some time the only fact that seemed to me of any importance was the confirmatory one of the younger Miss Fothering's apology. In the dream the frightened girl had been alone, and the mere fact of two girls coming on a visit had seemed a sort of disproof of its truth. But, just as if things were conspiring to force on the truth of the dream, one of the sisters was not to come, and the other was she who resembled the portrait whose prototype I had seen sleeping in a vision. I could hardly imagine that I had only dreamt.

I determined to ask Mrs. Trevor if she could explain in any way Miss Fothering's resemblance to the portrait, and so went at once to seek her.

I found her in the large drawing room alone, and, after a few casual remarks, I broached the subject on which I had come to seek for information. She had not said anything further to me about marrying since our conversation on the previous day, but when I mentioned Miss Fothering's name I could see a glad look on her face which gave me great pleasure. She made none of those vulgar commonplace remarks which many women find it necessary to make when talking to a man about a girl for whom he is supposed to have an affection, but by her manner she put me entirely at my ease, as I sat fidgeting on the sofa, pulling purposelessly the woolly tufts of an antimacassar, painfully conscious that my cheeks were red, and my voice slightly forced and unnatural.

She merely said, "Of course, Frank, I am ready if you want to talk about Miss Fothering, or any other subject." She then put a marker in her book and laid it aside, and, folding her arms, looked at me with a grave, kind, expectant smile.

I asked her if she knew anything about the family history of Miss Fothering. She answered —

"Not further than I have already told you. Her father's is a fine old family, although reduced in circumstances."

"Has it ever been connected with any family in this county? With the former owners of Scarp, for instance?"

"Not that I know of. Why do you ask?"

"I want to find out how she comes to be so like that portrait."

"I never thought of that. It may be that there was some remote connection between her family and the Kirks who formerly owned Scarp. I will ask her when she comes. Or stay. Let us go and look if there is any old book or tree in the library that will throw a light upon the subject. We have rather a good library now, Frank, for we have all our own books, and all those which belonged to the Scarp library also. They are in great disorder, for we have been waiting till you came to arrange them, for we knew that you delighted in such work."

"There is nothing I should enjoy more than arranging all these splendid books. What a magnificent library. It is almost a pity to keep it in a private house."

We proceeded to look for some of those old books of family history which are occasionally to be found in old county houses. The library of Scarp, I saw, was very valuable, and as we prosecuted our search I came across many splendid and rare volumes which I determined to examine at my leisure, for I had come to Scarp for a long visit.

We searched first in the old folio shelves, and, after some few disappointments, found at length a large volume, magnificently printed and bound, which contained views and plans of the house, illuminations of the armorial bearings of the family of Kirk, and all the families with whom it was connected, and having the history of all these families carefully set forth. It was called on the title-page "The Book of Kirk," and was full of anecdotes and legends, and contained a large stock of family tradition. As this was exactly the book which we required, we searched no further, but, having carefully dusted the volume, bore it to Mrs. Trevor's boudoir where we could look over it quite undisturbed.

On looking in the index, we found the name of Fothering mentioned, and on turning to the page specified, found the arms of Kirk quartered on those of Fothering. From the text we learned that one of the daughters of Kirk had, in the year 1573, married the brother of Fothering against the united wills of her father and brother, and that after a bitter feud of some ten or twelve years, the latter, then master of Scarp, had met the brother of Fothering in a duel and had killed him. Upon receiving the news Fothering had sworn a great oath to revenge his brother, invoking the most fearful curses upon himself and his race if he should fail to cut off the hand that had slain his brother, and to nail it over the gate of Fothering. The feud then became so bitter that Kirk seems to have gone quite mad on the subject. When he heard of Fothering's oath he knew that he had but little chance of escape, since his enemy was his master at every weapon; so he determined upon a mode of revenge which, although costing him his own life, he fondly hoped would accomplish the eternal destruction of his brother-in-law through his violated oath. He sent Fothering a letter cursing him and his race, and praying for the consummation of his own curse invoked in case of failure. He concluded his missive by a prayer for the complete destruction, soul, mind, and body, of the first Fothering who should enter the gate of Scarp, who he hoped would be the fairest and best of the race. Having dispatched this letter he cut off his right hand and threw it into the center of a roaring fire, which he had made for the purpose. When it was entirely consumed he threw himself upon his sword, and so died.

A cold shiver went through me when I read the words "fairest and best." All my dream came back in a moment, and I seemed to hear in my ears again the echo of the fiendish laughter. I looked up at Mrs. Trevor, and saw that she had become very grave. Her face had a half-frightened look, as if some wild thought had struck her. I was more frightened than ever, for nothing increases our alarms so much as the sympathy of others with regard to them; however, I tried to conceal my fear. We sat silent for some minutes, and then Mrs. Trevor rose up saying:

"Come with me, and let us look at the portrait."

I remember her saying the and not that portrait, as if some concealed thought of it had been occupying her mind. The same dread had assailed her from a coincidence as had grown in me from a vision. Surely — surely I had good grounds for fear!

We went to the bedroom and stood before the picture, which seemed to gaze upon us with an expression which reflected our own fears. My companion said to me in slightly excited tones: "Frank, lift down the picture till we see its back." I did so, and we found written in strange old writing on the grimy canvas a name and a date, which, after a great deal of trouble, we made out to be "Margaret Kirk, 1572." It was the name of the lady in the book.

Mrs. Trevor turned round and faced me slowly, with a look of horror on her face.

"Frank, I don't like this at all. There is something very strange here."

I had it on my tongue to tell her my dream, but was ashamed to do so. Besides, I feared that it might frighten her too much, as she was already alarmed.

I continued to look at the picture as a relief from my embarrassment, and was struck with the excessive griminess of the back in comparison to the freshness of the front. I mentioned my difficulty to my companion, who thought for a moment, and then suddenly said —

"I see how it is. It has been turned with its face to the wall."

I said no word but hung up the picture again; and we went back to the boudoir.

On the way I began to think that my fears were too wildly improbable to bear to be spoken about. It was so hard to believe in the horrors of darkness when the sunlight was falling brightly around me. The same idea seemed to have struck Mrs. Trevor, for she said, when we entered the room:

"Frank, it strikes me that we are both rather silly to let our imaginations carry us away so. The story is merely a tradition, and we know how report distorts even the most innocent facts. It is true that the Fothering family was formerly connected with the Kirks, and that the picture is that of the Miss Kirk who married against her father's will; it is likely that he quarreled with her for so doing, and had her picture turned to the wall — a common trick of angry fathers at all times — but that is all. There can be nothing beyond that. Let us not think anymore upon the subject, as it is one likely to lead us into absurdities. However, the picture is a really beautiful one — independent of its being such a likeness of Diana, and I will have it placed in the dining room."

The change was effected that afternoon, but she did not again allude to the subject. She appeared, when talking to me, to be a little constrained in manner — a very unusual thing with her, and seemed to fear that I would renew the forbidden topic. I think that she did not wish to let her imagination lead her astray, and was distrustful of herself. However, the feeling of constraint wore off before night — but she did not renew the subject.

I slept well that night, without dreams of any kind; and next morning — the third tomorrow promised in the dream — when I came down to breakfast, I was told that I would see

Miss Fothering before that evening.

I could not help blushing, and stammered out some commonplace remark, and then glancing up, feeling very sheepish, I saw my hostess looking at me with her kindly smile intensified. She said:

"Do you know, Frank, I felt quite frightened yesterday when we were looking at the picture; but I have been thinking the matter over since, and have come to the conclusion that my folly was perfectly unfounded. I am sure you agree with me. In fact, I look now upon our fright as a good joke, and will tell it to Diana when she arrives."

Once again I was about to tell my dream; but again was restrained by shame. I knew, of course, that Mrs. Trevor would not laugh at me or even think little of me for my fears, for she was too well-bred, and kind-hearted, and sympathetic to do anything of the kind, and, besides, the fear was one which we had shared in common.

But how could I confess my fright at what might appear to others to be a ridiculous dream, when she had conquered the fear that had been common to us both, and which had arisen from a really strange conjuncture of facts. She appeared to look on the matter so lightly that I could not do otherwise. And I did it honestly for the time.

III. The Third Tomorrow

*I*n the afternoon I was out in the garden lying in the shadow of an immense beech, when I saw Mrs. Trevor approaching. I had been reading Shelley's "Stanzas Written in Dejection," and my heart was full of melancholy and a vague yearning after human sympathy. I had thought of Mrs. Trevor's love for me, but even that did not seem sufficient. I wanted the love of some one more nearly of my own level, some equal spirit, for I looked on her, of course, as I would have regarded my mother. Somehow my thoughts kept returning to Miss

Fothering till I could almost see her before me in my memory of the portrait. I had begun to ask myself the question: "Are you in love?" when I heard the voice of my hostess as she drew near.

"Ha! Frank, I thought I would find you here. I want you to come to my boudoir."

"What for?" I inquired, as I rose from the grass and picked up my volume of Shelley.

"Di has come ever so long ago; and I want to introduce you and have a chat before dinner," said she, as we went towards the house.

"But won't you let me change my dress? I am not in correct costume for the afternoon."

I felt somewhat afraid of the unknown beauty when the introduction was imminent. Perhaps it was because I had come to believe too firmly in Mrs. Trevor's prediction.

"Nonsense, Frank, just as if any woman worth thinking about cares how a man is dressed."

We entered the boudoir and found a young lady seated by a window that overlooked the croquet-ground. She turned round as we came in, so Mrs. Trevor introduced us, and we were soon engaged in a lively conversation. I observed her, as may be supposed, with more than curiosity, and shortly found that she was worth looking at. She was very beautiful, and her beauty lay not only in her features but in her expression. At first her appearance did not seem to me so perfect as it afterwards did, on account of her wonderful resemblance to the portrait with whose beauty I was already acquainted. But it was not long before I came to experience the difference between the portrait and the reality. No matter how well it may be painted a picture falls far short of its prototype. There is something in a real face which cannot exist on canvas — some difference far greater than that contained in the contrast between the one expression, however beautiful of the picture, and the moving features and varying expression of the reality. There is something living and lovable in a real face that no art can represent.

When we had been talking for a while in the usual conventional style, Mrs. Trevor said, "Di, my love, I want to tell you of a discovery Frank and I have made. You must know that

I always call Mr. Stanford, Frank — he is more like my own son than my friend, and that I am very fond of him."

She then put her arms round Miss Fothering's waist, as they sat on the sofa together, and kissed her, and then, turning towards me, said, "I don't approve of kissing girls in the presence of gentlemen, but you know that Frank is not supposed to be here. This is my sanctum, and who invades it must take the consequences. But I must tell you about the discovery."

She then proceeded to tell the legend, and about her finding the name of Margaret Kirk on the back of the picture.

Miss Fothering laughed gleefully as she heard the story, and then said, suddenly,

"Oh, I had forgotten to tell you, dear Mrs. Trevor, that I had such a fright the other day. I thought I was going to be prevented coming here. Aunt Deborah came to us last week for a few days, and when she heard that I was about to go on a visit to Scarp she seemed quite frightened, and went straight off to papa and asked him to forbid me to go. Papa asked her why she made the request, so she told a long family legend about any of us coming to Scarp — just the same story that you have been telling me. She said she was sure that some misfortune would happen if I came; so you see that the tradition exists in our branch of the family too. Oh, you can't fancy the scene there was between papa and Aunt Deborah. I must laugh whenever I think of it, although I did not laugh then, for I was greatly afraid that aunty would prevent me coming. Papa got very grave, and aunty thought she had carried her point when he said, in his dear, old, pompous manner,

"'Deborah, Diana has promised to pay Mrs. Trevor, of Scarp, a visit, and, of course, must keep her engagement. And if it were for no other reason than the one you have just alleged, I would strain a point of convenience to have her go to Scarp. I have always educated my children in such a manner that they ought not to be influenced by such vain superstitions; and with my will their practice shall never be at variance with the precepts which I have instilled into them.'

"Poor aunty was quite overcome. She seemed almost speechless for a time at the thought that her wishes had been neglected, for you know that Aunt Deborah's wishes are commands to all our family."

Mrs. Trevor said —

"I hope Mrs. Howard was not offended?"

"Oh, no. Papa talked to her seriously, and at length — with a great deal of difficulty I must say — succeeded in convincing her that her fears were groundless — at least, he forced her to confess that such things as she was afraid of could not be."

I thought of the couplet —

"A man convinced against his will
Is of the same opinion still,"

but said nothing.

Miss Fothering finished her story by saying —

"Aunty ended by hoping that I might enjoy myself, which I am sure, my dear Mrs. Trevor, that I will do."

"I hope you will, my love."

I had been struck during the above conversation by the mention of Mrs. Howard. I was trying to think of where I had heard the name, Deborah Howard, when suddenly it all came back to me. Mrs. Howard had been Miss Fothering, and was an old friend of my mother's. It was thus that I had been accustomed to her name when I was a child. I remembered now that once she had brought a nice little girl, almost a baby, with her to visit. The child was her niece, and it was thus that I now accounted for my half-recollection of the name and the circumstance on the first night of my arrival at Scarp. The thought of my dream here recalled me to Mrs. Trevor's object in bringing Miss Fothering to her boudoir, so I said to the latter —

"Do you believe these legends?"

"Indeed I do not, Mr. Stanford; I do not believe in anything half so silly."

"Then you do not believe in ghosts or visions?"

"Most certainly not."

How could I tell my dream to a girl who had such profound disbelief? And yet I felt something whispering to me that I ought to tell it to her. It was, no doubt, foolish of me to have this fear of a dream, but I could not help it. I was just going to risk being laughed at, and unburden my mind, when Mrs. Trevor started up, after looking at her watch, saying —

"Dear me, I never thought it was so late. I must go and see if any others have come. It will not do for me to neglect my guests."

We all left the boudoir, and as we did so the gong sounded for dressing for dinner, and so we each sought our rooms.

When I came down to the drawing room I found assembled a number of persons who had arrived during the course of the afternoon. I was introduced to them all, and chatted with them till dinner was announced. I was given Miss Fothering to take into dinner, and when it was over I found that we had improved our acquaintance very much. She was a delightful girl, and as I looked at her I thought with a glow of pleasure of Mrs. Trevor's prediction. Occasionally I saw our hostess observing us, and as she saw us chatting pleasantly together as though we enjoyed it a more than happy look came into her face. It was one of her most fascinating points that in the midst of gaiety, while she never neglected anyone, she specially remembered her particular friends. No matter what position she might be placed in she would still remember that there were some persons who would treasure up her recognition at such moments.

After dinner, as I did not feel inclined to enter the drawing room with the other gentlemen, I strolled out into the garden by myself, and thought over things in general, and Miss Fothering in particular. The subject was such a pleasant one that I quite lost myself in it, and strayed off farther than I had intended. Suddenly I remembered myself and looked around. I was far away from the house, and in the midst of a dark, gloomy walk between old yew trees. I could not see through them on either side on account of their thickness, and as the walk was curved I could see but a short distance either before or behind me. I looked up and saw a yellowish, luminous sky with heavy clouds passing sluggishly across it. The moon had not yet risen, and the general gloom reminded me forcibly of some of the weird pictures which William Blake so loved to paint. There was a sort of vague melancholy and ghostliness in the place that made me shiver, and I hurried on.

At length the walk opened and I came out on a large sloping lawn, dotted here and there with yew trees and tufts of pampas grass of immense height, whose stalks were crowned with large flowers. To the right lay the house, grim and gigantic in the gloom, and to the left the lake which stretched away so far that it was lost in the evening shadow. The lawn sloped from the terrace round the house down to the water's edge, and was only broken by the walk which continued to run on round the house in a wide sweep.

As I came near the house a light appeared in one of the windows which lay before me, and as I looked into the room I saw that it was the chamber of my dream.

Unconsciously I approached nearer and ascended the terrace from the top of which I could see across the deep trench which surrounded the house, and looked earnestly into the room. I shivered as I looked. My spirits had been damped by the gloom and desolation of the yew walk, and now the dream and all the subsequent revelations came before my mind with such vividness that the horror of the thing again seized me, but more forcibly than before. I looked at the sleeping arrangements, and groaned as I saw that the bed where the dying woman had seemed to lie was alone prepared, while the other bed, that in which I had slept, had its curtains drawn all round. This was but another link in the chain of doom. Whilst I stood looking, the servant who was in the room came and pulled down one of the blinds, but, as she was about to do the same with the other, Miss Fothering entered the room, and, seeing what she was about, evidently gave her contrary directions, for she let go the window string, and then went and pulled up again the blind which she had let down. Having done so she followed her mistress out of the room. So wrapped up was I in all that took place with reference to that chamber, that it never even struck me that I was guilty of any impropriety in watching what took place.

I stayed there for some little time longer purposeless and terrified. The horror grew so great to me as I thought of the events of the last few days, that I determined to tell Miss Fothering of my dream, in order that she might not be frightened in case she should see anything like it, or at least that she might be prepared for anything that might happen.

As soon as I had come to this determination the inevitable question "when?" presented itself. The means of making the communication was a subject most disagreeable to contemplate, but as I had made up my mind to do it, I thought that there was no time like the present. Accordingly I was determined to seek the drawing room, where I knew I should find Miss Fothering and Mrs. Trevor, for, of course, I had determined to take the latter into our confidence. As I was really afraid to go through the awful yew walk again, I completed the half circle of the house and entered the backdoor, from which I easily found my way to the drawing room.

When I entered Mrs. Trevor, who was sitting near the door, said to me, "Good gracious, Frank, where have you been to make you look so pale? One would think you had seen a ghost!"

I answered that I had been strolling in the garden, but made no other remark, as I did not wish to say anything about my dream before the persons to whom she was talking, as they were strangers to me. I waited for some time for an opportunity of speaking to her alone, but her duties, as hostess, kept her so constantly occupied that I waited in vain. Accordingly I determined to tell Miss Fothering at all events, at once, and then to tell Mrs. Trevor as soon as an opportunity for doing so presented itself.

With a good deal of difficulty — for I did not wish to do anything marked — I succeeded in getting Miss Fothering away from the persons by whom she was surrounded, and took her to one of the embrasures, under the pretence of looking out at the night view. Here we were quite removed from observation, as the heavy window curtains completely covered the recess, and almost isolated us from the rest of the company as perfectly as if we were in a separate chamber. I proceeded at once to broach the subject for which I had sought the interview; for I feared lest contact with the lively company of the drawing room would do away with my present fears, and so breakdown the only barrier that stood between her and Fate.

"Miss Fothering, do you ever dream?"

"Oh, yes, often. But I generally find that my dreams are most ridiculous."

"How so?"

"Well, you see, that no matter whether they are good or bad they appear real and coherent whilst I am dreaming them; but when I wake I find them unreal and incoherent, when I remember them at all. They are, in fact, mere disconnected nonsense."

"Are you fond of dreams?"

"Of course I am. I delight in them, for whether they are sense or gibberish when you wake, they are real whilst you are asleep."

"Do you believe in dreams?"

"Indeed, Mr. Stanford, I do not."

"Do you like hearing them told?"

"I do, very much, when they are worth telling. Have you been dreaming anything? If you have, do tell it to me."

"I will be glad to do so. It is about a dream which I had that concerns you, that I came here to tell you."

"About me. Oh, how nice. Do, go on."

I told her all my dream, after calling her attention to our conversation in the boudoir as a means of introducing the subject. I did not attempt to heighten the effect in any way or to draw any inferences. I tried to suppress my own emotion and merely to let the facts speak for themselves. She listened with great eagerness, but, as far as I could see, without a particle of either fear or belief in the dream as a warning. When I had finished she laughed a quiet, soft laugh, and said —

"That is delicious. And was I really the girl that you saw afraid of ghosts? If papa heard of such a thing as that even in a dream what a lecture he would give me! I wish I could dream anything like that."

"Take care," said I, "you might find it too awful. It might indeed prove the fulfilling of the ban which we saw in the legend in the old book, and which you heard from your aunt."

She laughed musically again, and shook her head at me wisely and warningly.

"Oh, pray do not talk nonsense and try to frighten me — for I warn you that you will not succeed."

"I assure you on my honor, Miss Fothering, that I was never more in earnest in my whole life."

"Do you not think that we had better go into the room?" said she, after a few moment's pause.

"Stay just a moment, I entreat you," said I. "What I say is true. I am really in earnest."

"Oh, pray forgive me if what I said led you to believe that I doubted your word. It was merely your inference which I disagreed with. I thought you had been jesting to try and frighten me."

"Miss Fothering, I would not presume to take such a liberty. But I am glad that you trust me. May I venture to ask you a favor? Will you promise me one thing?"

Her answer was characteristic —

"No. What is it?"

"That you will not be frightened at anything which may take place tonight?"

She laughed softly again.

"I do not intend to be. But is that all?"

"Yes, Miss Fothering, that is all; but I want to be assured that you will not be alarmed — that you will be prepared for anything which may happen. I have a horrid foreboding of evil — some evil that I dread to think of — and it will be a great comfort to me if you will do one thing."

"Oh, nonsense. Oh, well, if you really wish it I will tell you if I will do it when I hear what it is."

Her levity was all gone when she saw how terribly in earnest I was. She looked at me boldly and fearlessly, but with a tender, half-pitying glance as if conscious of the possession of strength superior to mine. Her fearlessness was in her free, independent attitude, but her pity was in her eyes. I went on —

"Miss Fothering, the worst part of my dream was seeing the look of agony on the face of the girl when she looked round and found herself alone. Will you take some token and keep it with you till morning to remind you, in case anything should happen, that you are not alone — that there is one thinking of you, and one human intelligence awake for you, though all the rest of the world should be asleep or dead?"

In my excitement I spoke with fervor, for the possibility of her enduring the horror which had assailed me seemed to be growing more and more each instant. At times since that awful night I had disbelieved the existence of the warning, but when I thought of it by night I could not but believe, for the very air in the darkness seemed to be peopled by phantoms to my fevered imagination. My belief had been perfected tonight by the horror of the yew walk, and all the somber, ghostly thoughts that had arisen amid its gloom.

There was a short pause. Miss Fothering leaned on the edge of the window, looking out at the dark, moonless sky. At length she turned and said to me, with some hesitation, "But really, Mr. Stanford, I do not like doing anything from fear of supernatural things, or from a belief in them. What you want me to do is so simple a thing in itself that I would not hesitate a moment to do it, but that papa has always taught me to believe that such occurrences as you seem to dread are quite impossible, and I know that he would be very much displeased if any act of mine showed a belief in them."

"Miss Fothering, I honestly think that there is not a man living who would wish less than I would to see you or anyone else disobeying a father either in word or spirit, and more particularly when that father is a clergyman; but I entreat you to gratify me on this one point. It cannot do you any harm; and I assure you that if you do not I will be inexpressibly miserable. I have endured the greatest tortures of suspense for the last three days, and tonight I feel a nervous horror of which words can give you no conception. I know that I have not the smallest right to make the request, and no reason for doing it except that I was fortunate, or unfortunate, enough to get the warning. I apologize most sincerely for the great liberty which I have taken, but believe me that I act with the best intentions."

My excitement was so great that my knees were trembling, and the large drops of perspiration rolling down my face.

There was a long pause, and I had almost made up my mind for a refusal of my request when my companion spoke again.

"Mr. Stanford, on that plea alone I will grant your request. I can see that for some reason which I cannot quite comprehend you are deeply moved; and that I may be the means of saving pain to anyone, I will do what you ask. Just please to state what you wish me to do."

I thought from her manner that she was offended with me; however I explained my purpose:

"I want you to keep about you, when you go to bed, some token which will remind you in an instant of what has passed between us, so that you may not feel lonely or frightened — no matter what may happen."

"I will do it. What shall I take?"

She had her handkerchief in her hand as she spoke. So I put my hand upon it and blessed it in the name of the Father, Son, and Holy Ghost. I did this to fix its existence in her memory by awing her slightly about it. "This," said I, "shall be a token that you are not alone." My object in blessing the handkerchief was fully achieved, for she did seem somewhat awed, but still she thanked me with a sweet smile. "I feel that you act from your heart," said she, "and my heart thanks you." She gave me her hand as she spoke, in an honest, straightforward manner, with more the independence of a man than the timorousness of a woman. As I grasped it I felt the blood rushing to my face, but before I let it go an impulse seized me and I bent down and touched it with my lips. She drew it quickly away, and said more coldly than she had yet spoken: "I did not mean you to do that."

"Believe me I did not mean to take a liberty — it was merely the natural expression of my gratitude. I feel as if you had done me some great personal service. You do not know how much lighter my heart is now than it was an hour ago, or you would forgive me for having so offended."

As I made my apologetic excuse, I looked at her wistfully. She returned my glance fearlessly, but with a bright, forgiving smile. She then shook her head slightly, as if to banish the subject.

There was a short pause, and then she said:

"I am glad to be of any service to you; but if there be any possibility of what you fear happening it is I who will be benefited. But mind, I will depend upon you not to say a word of this to anybody. I am afraid that we are both very foolish."

"No, no, Miss Fothering. I may be foolish, but you are acting nobly in doing what seems to you to be foolish in order that you may save me from pain. But may I not even tell Mrs. Trevor?"

"No, not even her. I should be ashamed of myself if I thought that anyone except ourselves knew about it."

"You may depend upon me. I will keep it secret if you wish."

"Do so, until morning at all events. Mind, if I laugh at you then I will expect you to join in my laugh."

"I will," said I. "I will be only too glad to be able to laugh at it." And we joined the rest of the company.

When I retired to my bedroom that night I was too much excited to sleep — even had my promise not forbidden me to do so. I paced up and down the room for some time, thinking and doubting. I could not believe completely in what I expected to happen, and yet my heart was filled with a vague dread. I thought over the events of the evening — particularly my stroll after dinner through that awful yew walk and my looking into the bedroom where I had dreamed. From these my thoughts wandered to the deep embrasure of the window where I had given Miss Fothering the token. I could hardly realize that whole interview as a fact. I knew that it had taken place, but that was all. It was so strange to recall a scene that, now that it was enacted, seemed half comedy and half tragedy, and to remember that it was played in this practical nineteenth century, in secret, within earshot of a room full of people, and only hidden from them by a curtain, I felt myself blushing, half from excitement, half from shame, when I thought of it. But then my thoughts turned to the way in which Miss Fothering had acceded to my request, strange as it was; and as I thought of her my blundering shame changed to a deeper glow of hope. I remembered Mrs. Trevor's prediction — "from what I know of human nature I think that she will like you" — and as I did so I felt how dear to me Miss Fothering was already becoming. But my joy was turned to anger on thinking what she might be called on to endure; and the thought of her suffering pain or fright caused me greater distress than any suffered myself. Again my thoughts flew back to the time of my own fright and my dream, with all the subsequent revelations concerning it, rushed across my mind. I felt again the feeling of extreme terror — as if something was about to happen — as if the tragedy was approaching its climax. Naturally I thought of the time of night and so I looked at my watch. It was within a few minutes of one o'clock. I remembered that the clock had struck twelve after Mr. Trevor had come home on the night of my dream. There was a large clock at Scarp which tolled the hours so loudly that for a long way round the estate the country people all regulated their affairs by it. The next few minutes passed so slowly that each moment seemed an age.

I was standing, with my watch in my hand, counting the moments when suddenly a light came into the room that made the candle on the table appear quite dim, and my shadow was reflected on the wall by some brilliant light which streamed in through the window. My heart for an instant ceased to beat, and then the blood rushed so violently to my temples that my eyes grew dim and my brain began to reel. However, I shortly became more composed, and then went to the window expecting to see my dream again repeated.

The light was there as formerly, but there were no figures of children, or witches, or fiends. The moon had just risen, and I could see its reflection upon the far end of the lake. I turned my head in trembling expectation to the ground below where I had seen the children and the hags, but saw merely the dark yew trees and tall crested pampas tufts gently moving in the night wind. The light caught the edges of the flowers of the grass, and made them most conspicuous.

As I looked a sudden thought flashed like a flame of fire through my brain. I saw in one second of time all the folly of my wild fancies. The moonlight and its reflection on the water shining into the room was the light of my dream, or phantasm as I now understood it to be. Those three tufts of pampas grass clumped together were in turn the fair young children and the withered leaves and the dark foliage of the yew beside them gave substance to the semblance of the fiend. For the rest, the empty bed and the face of the picture, my half recollection of the name of Fothering, and the long-forgotten legend of the curse. Oh, fool! fool that I had been! How I had been the victim of circumstances, and of my own wild imagination! Then came the bitter reflection of the agony of mind which Miss Fothering might be compelled to suffer. Might not the recital of my dream, and my strange request regarding the token, combined with the natural causes of night and scene, produce the very effect which I so dreaded? It was only at that bitter, bitter moment that I realized how foolish I had been. But what was my anguish of mind to hers? For an instant I conceived the idea of rousing Mrs. Trevor and telling her all the facts of the case so that she might go to Miss Fothering and tell her not to be alarmed. But I had no time to act upon my thought. As I was hastening to the door the clock struck one and a moment later I heard from the room below me a sharp scream — a cry of surprise rather than fear. Miss Fothering had no doubt been awakened by the striking of the clock, and had seen outside the window the very figures which I had described to her.

I rushed madly down the stairs and arrived at the door of her bedroom, which was directly under the one which I now occupied. As I was about to rush in I was instinctively restrained from so doing by the thoughts of propriety; and so for a few moments I stood silent, trembling, with my hand upon the door-handle.

Within I heard a voice — her voice — exclaiming, in tones of stupefied surprise —

"Has it come then? Am I alone?" She then continued joyously, "No, I am not alone. His token! Oh, thank God for that. Thank God for that."

Through my heart at her words came a rush of wild delight. I felt my bosom swell and the tears of gladness spring to my eyes. In that moment I knew that I had strength and courage to face the world, alone, for her sake. But before my hopes had well time to manifest themselves they were destroyed, for again the voice came wailing from the room of blank despair that made me cold from head to foot.

"Ah-h-h! still there? Oh! God, preserve my reason. Oh! for some human thing near me." Then her voice changed slightly to a tone of entreaty: "You will not leave me alone? Your token. Remember your token. Help me. Help me now." Then her voice became more wild, and rose to an inarticulate, wailing scream of horror.

As I heard that agonized cry, I realized the idea that it was madness to delay — that I had hesitated too long already — I must cast aside the shackles of conventionality if I wished to repair my fatal error. Nothing could save her from some serious injury — perhaps madness — perhaps death; save a shock which would break the spell which was over her from fear and her excited imagination. I flung open the door and rushed in, shouting loudly:

"Courage, courage. You are not alone. I am here. Remember the token."

She grasped the handkerchief instinctively, but she hardly comprehended my words, and did not seem to heed my presence. She was sitting up in bed, her face being distorted with terror, and was gazing out upon the scene. I heard from without the hooting of an owl as it flew across the border of the lake. She heard it also, and screamed —

"The laugh, too! Oh, there is no hope. Even he will not dare to go amongst them."

Then she gave vent to a scream, so wild, so appalling that, as I heard it, I trembled, and the hair on the back of my head bristled up. Throughout the house I could hear screams of affright, and the ringing of bells, and the banging of doors, and the rush of hurried feet; but the poor sufferer comprehended not these sounds; she still continued gazing out of the window awaiting the consummation of the dream.

I saw that the time for action and self-sacrifice was come. There was but one way now to repair my fatal error. To burst through the window and try by the shock to wake her from her trance of fear.

I said no word but rushed across the room and hurled myself, back foremost, against the massive plate glass. As I turned I saw Mrs. Trevor rushing into the room, her face wild with excitement. She was calling out —

"Diana, Diana, what is it?"

The glass crashed and shivered into a thousand pieces, and I could feel its sharp edges cutting me like so many knives. But I heeded not the pain, for above the rushing of feet and crashing of glass and the shouting both within and without the room I heard her voice ring forth in a joyous, fervent cry, "Saved. He has dared," as she sank down in the arms of Mrs. Trevor, who had thrown herself upon the bed.

Then I felt a mighty shock, and all the universe seemed filled with sparks of fire that whirled around me with light-ning speed, till I seemed to be in the center of a world of flame, and then came in my ears the rushing of a mighty wind, swelling ever louder, and then came a blackness over all things and a deadness of sound as if all the earth had passed away, and I remembered no more.

IV. Afterwards

When I next became conscious I was lying in bed in a dark room. I wondered what this was for, and tried to look around me, but could hardly stir my head. I attempted to speak, but my voice was without power — it was like a whisper from another world. The effort to speak made me feel faint, and again I felt a darkness gathering round me.

I became gradually conscious of something cool on my forehead. I wondered what it was. All sorts of things I conjectured, but could not fix my mind on any of them. I lay thus for some time, and at length opened my eyes and saw my mother bending over me — it was her hand which was so deliciously cool on my brow. I felt amazed somehow. I expected to see her; and yet I was surprised, for I had not seen her for a long time — a long, long time. I knew that she was dead — could I be dead, too? I looked at her again more carefully, and as I looked, the old features died away, but the expression remained the same. And then the dear, well-known face of Mrs. Trevor grew slowly before me. She smiled as she saw the look of recognition in my eyes, and, bending down, kissed me very tenderly. As she drew back her head something warm fell on my face. I wondered what this could be, and after thinking for a long time, to do which I closed my eyes, I came to the conclusion that it was a tear. After some more thinking I opened my eyes to see why she was crying; but she was gone, and I could see that although the window-blinds were pulled up the room was almost dark. I felt much more awake and much stronger than I had been before, and tried to call Mrs. Trevor. A woman got up from a chair behind the bed-curtains and went to the door, said something, and came back and settled my pillows.

"Where is Mrs. Trevor?" I asked, feebly. "She was here just now."

The woman smiled at me cheerfully, and answered:

"She will be here in a moment. Dear heart! but she will be glad to see you so strong and sensible."

After a few minutes she came into the room, and, bending over me, asked me how I felt. I said that I was all right – and then a thought struck me, so I asked,

"What was the matter with me?"

I was told that I had been ill, very ill, but that I was now much better. Something, I know not what, suddenly recalled to my memory all the scene of the bedroom, and the fright which my folly had caused, and I grew quite dizzy with the rush of blood to my head. But Mrs. Trevor's arm supported me, and after a time the faintness passed away, and my memory was completely restored. I started violently from the arm that held me up, and called out:

"Is she all right? I heard her say, 'saved.' Is she all right?"

"Hush, dear boy, hush – she is all right. Do not excite yourself."

"Are you deceiving me?" I inquired. "Tell me all – I can bear it. Is she well or no?"

"She has been very ill, but she is now getting strong and well, thank God."

I began to cry, half from weakness and half from joy, and Mrs. Trevor seeing this, and knowing with the sweet instinct of womanhood that I would rather be alone, quickly left the room, after making a sign to the nurse, who sank again to her old place behind the bed-curtain.

I thought for long; and all the time from my first coming to Scarp to the moment of unconsciousness after I sprung through the window came back to me as in a dream. Gradually the room became darker and darker, and my thoughts began to give semblance to the objects around me, till at length the visible world passed away from my wearied eyes, and in my dreams I continued to think of all that had been. I have a hazy recollection of taking some food and then relapsing into sleep; but remember no more distinctly until I woke fully in the morning and found Mrs. Trevor again in the room. She came over to my bedside, and sitting down said gaily —

"Ah, Frank, you look bright and strong this morning, dear boy. You will soon be well now I trust."

Her cool deft fingers settled my pillow and brushed back the hair from my forehead. I took her hand and kissed it, and the doing so made me very happy. By-and-by I asked her how was Miss Fothering.

"Better, much better this morning. She has been asking after you ever since she has been able; and today when I told her how much better you were she brightened up at once."

I felt a flush painfully strong rushing over my face as she spoke, but she went on —

"She has asked me to let her see you as soon as both of you are able. She wants to thank you for your conduct on that awful night. But there, I won't tell any more tales — let her tell you what she likes herself."

"To thank me — me — for what? For having brought her to the verge of madness or perhaps death through my silly fears and imagination. Oh, Mrs. Trevor, I know that you never mock anyone — but to me that sounds like mockery."

She leaned over me as she sat on my bedside and said, oh, so sweetly, yet so firmly that a sense of the truth of her words came at once upon me —

"If I had a son I would wish him to think as you have thought, and to act as you have acted. I would pray for it night and day and if he suffered as you have done, I would lean over him as I lean over you now and feel glad, as I feel now, that he had thought and acted as a true — hearted man should think and act. I would rejoice that God had given me such a son; and if he should die — as I feared at first that you should — I would be a prouder and happier woman kneeling by his dead body than I would in clasping a different son, living, in my arms.

Oh, how my weak fluttering heart did beat as she spoke. With pity for her blighted maternal instincts, with gladness that a true-hearted woman had approved of my conduct toward a woman whom I loved, and with joy for the deep love for myself. There was no mistaking the honesty of her words — her face was perfectly radiant as she spoke them.

I put up my arms — it took all my strength to do it — round her neck, and whispered softly in her ear one word, "mother."

She did not expect it, for it seemed to startle her; but her arms tightened around me convulsively. I could feel a perfect rain of tears falling on my upturned face as I looked into her eyes, full of love and long-sought joy. As I looked I felt stronger and better; my sympathy for her joy did much to restore my strength.

For some little time she was silent, and then she spoke as if to herself — "God has given me a son at last. I thank thee, O Father; forgive me if I have at any time repined. The son I prayed for might have been different from what I would wish. Thou doest best in all things."

For some time after this she stayed quite silent, still supporting me in her arms. I felt inexpressibly happy. There was an atmosphere of love around me, for which I had longed all my life. The love of a mother, for which I had pined since my orphan childhood, I had got at last, and the love of a woman to become far dearer to me than a mother I felt was close at hand.

At length I began to feel tired, and Mrs. Trevor laid me back on my pillow. It pleased me inexpressibly to observe her kind motherly manner with me now. The ice between us had at last been broken, we had declared our mutual love, and the white-haired woman was as happy in the declaration as the young man.

The next day I felt a shade stronger, and a similar improvement was manifested on the next. Mrs. Trevor always attended me herself, and her good reports of Miss Fothering's progress helped to cheer me not a little. And so the days wore on, and many passed away before I was allowed to rise from bed.

One day Mrs. Trevor came into the room in a state of suppressed delight. By this time I had been allowed to sit up a little while each day, and was beginning to get strong, or rather less weak, for I was still very helpless.

"Frank, the doctor says that you may be moved into

another room tomorrow for a change, and that you may see Di."

As may be supposed I was anxious to see Miss Fothering. Whilst I had been able to think during my illness, I had thought about her all day long, and sometimes all night long. I had been in love with her even before that fatal night. My heart told me that secret whilst I was waiting to hear the clock strike, and saw all my folly about the dream; but now I not only loved the woman but I almost worshipped my own bright ideal which was merged in her. The constant series of kind messages that passed between us tended not a little to increase my attachment, and now I eagerly looked forward to a meeting with her face to face.

I awoke earlier than usual next morning, and grew rather feverish as the time for our interview approached. However, I soon cooled down upon a vague threat being held out, that if I did not become more composed I must defer my visit.

The expected time at length arrived, and I was wheeled in my chair into Mrs. Trevor's boudoir. As I entered the door I looked eagerly round and saw, seated in another chair near one of the windows, a girl, who, turning her head round languidly, disclosed the features of Miss Fothering. She was very pale and ethereal looking, and seemed extremely delicate; but in my opinion this only heightened her natural beauty. As she caught sight of me a beautiful blush rushed over her poor, pale face, and even tinged her alabaster forehead. This passed quickly, and she became calm again, and paler than before. My chair was wheeled over to her, and Mrs. Trevor said, as she bent over and kissed her, after soothing the pillow in her chair —

"Di, my love, I have brought Frank to see you. You may talk together for a little while; but, mind, the doctor's orders are very strict, and if either of you excite yourselves about anything I must forbid you to meet again until you are both much stronger."

She said the last words as she was leaving the room.

I felt red and pale, hot and cold by turns. I looked at Miss Fothering and faltered. However, in a moment or two I summoned up courage to address her.

"Miss Fothering, I hope you forgive me for the pain and

danger I caused you by that foolish fear of mine. I assure you that nothing I ever did" —

Here she interrupted me.

"Mr. Stanford, I beg you will not talk like that. I must thank you for the care you thought me worthy of. I will not say how proud I feel of it, and for the generous courage and wisdom you displayed in rescuing me from the terror of that awful scene."

She grew pale, even paler than she had been before, as she spoke the last words, and trembled all over. I feared for her, and said as cheerfully as I could:

"Don't be alarmed. Do calm yourself. That is all over now and past. Don't let its horror disturb you ever again."

My speaking, although it calmed her somewhat, was not sufficient to banish her fear, and, seeing that she was really excited, I called to Mrs. Trevor, who came in from the next room and talked to us for a little while. She gradually did away with Miss Fothering's fear by her pleasant cheery conversation. She, poor girl, had received a sad shock, and the thought that I had been the cause of it gave me great anguish. After a little quiet chat, however, I grew more cheerful, but presently feeling faintish, was wheeled back to my own room and put to bed.

For many long days I continued very weak, and hardly made any advance. I saw Miss Fothering every day, and each day I loved her more and more. She got stronger as the days advanced, and after a few weeks was comparatively in good health, but still I continued weak. Her illness had been merely the result of the fright she had sustained on that unhappy night; but mine was the nervous prostration consequent on the long period of anxiety between the dream and its seeming fulfillment, united with the physical weakness resulting from my wounds caused by jumping through the window. During all this time of weakness Mrs. Trevor was, indeed, a mother to me. She watched me day and night, and as far as a woman could, made my life a dream of happiness. But the crowning glory of that time was the thought that sometimes forced itself upon me — that Diana cared for me. She continued to remain at Scarp by Mrs. Trevor's request, as her father had gone to the Continent for the winter, and with my adopted mother she shared the attendance on me. Day after day her care for my every want grew greater, till I came to fancy her like a guardian angel keeping watch over me. With the peculiar delicate sense that accompanies extreme physical prostration I could see that the growth of her pity kept pace with the growth of her strength. My love kept pace with both. I often wondered if it could be sympathy and not pity that so forestalled my wants and wishes; or if it could be love that answered in her heart when mine beat for her. She only showed pity and tenderness in her acts and words, but still I hoped and longed for something more.

Those days of my long-continued weakness were to me sweet, sweet days. I used to watch her for hours as she sat opposite to me reading or working, and my eyes would fill with tears as I thought how hard it would be to die and leave her behind me. So strong was the flame of my love that I believed, in spite of my religious teaching, that, should I die, I would leave the better part of my being behind me. I used to think in a vague imaginative way, that was no less powerful because it was undefined, of what speeches I would make to her — if I were well. How I would talk to her in nobler language than that in which I would now allow my thoughts to mould themselves. How, as I talked, my passion, and honesty, and purity would make me so eloquent that she would love to hear me speak. How I would wander with her through the sunny-gladed woods that stretched away before me through the open window, and sit by her feet on a mossy bank beside some purling brook that rippled gaily over the stones, gazing into the depths of her eyes, where my future life was pictured in one long sheen of light. How I would whisper in her ear sweet words that would make me tremble to speak them, and her tremble to hear. How she would bend to me and show me her love by letting me tell her mine without reproof. And then would come, like the shadow of a sudden rain-cloud over an April landscape, the bitter, bitter thought that all this longing was but a dream, and that when the time had come when such things might have been, I would, most likely, be sleeping under the green turf. And she might, perhaps, be weeping in the silence of her chamber sad, sad tears for her blighted love and for me. Then my thoughts

would become less selfish, and I would try to imagine the
bitter blow of my death — if she loved me — for I knew that
a woman loves not by the value of what she loves, but by the
strength of her affection and admiration for her own ideal,
which she thinks she sees bodied forth in some man. But
these thoughts had always the proviso that the dreams of
happiness were prophetic. Alas! I had altogether lost faith in
dreams. Still, I could not but feel that even if I had never
frightened Miss Fothering by telling my vision, she might,
nevertheless, have been terrified by the effect of the moonlight upon the flowers of the pampas tufts, and that, under
Providence, I was the instrument of saving her from a shock
even greater than that which she did experience, for help
might not have come to her so soon. This thought always
gave me hope. Whenever I thought of her sorrow for my
death, I would find my eyes filled with a sudden rush of tears
which would shut out from my waking vision the object of
my thoughts and fears. Then she would come over to me and
place her cool hand on my forehead, and whisper sweet words
of comfort and hope in my ears. As I would feel her warm
breath upon my cheek and wafting my hair from my brow,
I would lose all sense of pain and sorrow and care, and live
only in the brightness of the present. At such times I would
cry silently from very happiness, for I was sadly weak, and
even trifling things touched me deeply. Many a stray memory
of some tender word heard or some gentle deed done, or of
some sorrow or distress, would set me thinking for hours and
stir all the tender feelings of my nature.

Slowly — very slowly — I began to get stronger, but for many
days more I was almost completely helpless. With returning
strength came the strengthening of my passion — for passion
my love for Diana had become. She had been so woven into
my thoughts that my love for her was a part of my being, and
I felt that away from her my future life would be but a bare
existence and no more. But strange to say, with increasing
strength and passion came increasing diffidence. I felt in her
presence so bashful and timorous that I hardly dared to look
at her, and could not speak save to answer an occasional
question. I had ceased to dream entirely, for such daydreams
as I used to have seemed now wild and almost sacrilegious to

my sur-excited imagination. But when she was not looking
at me I would be happy in merely seeing her or hearing her
speak. I could tell the moment she left the house or entered
it, and her footfall was the music sweetest to my ears — except
her voice. Sometimes she would catch sight of my bashful
looks at her, and then, at my conscious blushing, a bright
smile would flit over her face. It was sweet and womanly, but
sometimes I would think that it was no more than her pity
finding expression. She was always in my thoughts and these
doubts and fears constantly assailed me, so that I could feel
that the brooding over the subject — a matter which I was
powerless to prevent — was doing me an injury; perhaps
seriously retarding my recovery.

One day I felt very sad. There had a bitter sense of loneliness come over me which was unusual. It was a good sign of
returning health, for it was like the waking from a dream to
a world of fact, with all its troubles and cares. There was a
sense of coldness and loneliness in the world, and I felt that
I had lost something without gaining anything in return — I
had, in fact, lost somewhat of my sense of dependence, which
is a consequence of prostration, but had not yet regained my
strength. I sat opposite a window itself in shade, but looking
over a garden that in the summer had been bright with
flowers, and sweet with their odors, but which, now, was lit
up only in patches by the quiet mellow gleams of the autumn
sun, and brightened by a few stray flowers that had survived
the first frosts.

As I sat I could not help thinking of what my future would
be. I felt that I was getting strong, and the possibilities of my
life seemed very real to me. How I longed for courage to ask
Diana to be my wife! Any certainty would be better than the
suspense I now constantly endured. I had but little hope that
she would accept me, for she seemed to care less for me now
than in the early days of my illness. As I grew stronger she
seemed to hold somewhat aloof from me; and as my fears
and doubts grew more and more, I could hardly bear to think
of my joy should she accept me, or of my despair should she
refuse. Either emotion seemed too great to be borne.

Today when she entered the room my fears were vastly
increased. She seemed much stronger than usual, for a glow,

as of health, ruddied her cheeks, and she seemed so lovely that I could not conceive that such a woman would ever condescend to be my wife. There was an unusual constraint in her manner as she came and spoke to me, and flitted round me, doing in her own graceful way all the thousand little offices that only a woman's hand can do for an invalid. She turned to me two or three times, as if she was about to speak; but turned away again, each time silent, and with a blush. I could see that her heart was beating violently. At length she spoke.

"Frank."

Oh! what a wild throb went through me as I heard my name from her lips for the first time. The blood rushed to my head, so that for a moment I was quite faint. Her cool hand on my forehead revived me.

"Frank, will you let me speak to you for a few minutes as honestly as I would wish to speak, and as freely?"

"Go on."

"You will promise me not to think me unwomanly or forward, for indeed I act from the best motives — promise me?"

This was said slowly with much hesitation, and a convulsive heaving of the chest.

"I promise."

"We can see that you are not getting as strong as you ought, and the doctor says that there is some idea too much in your mind — that you brood over it, and that it is retarding your recovery. Mrs. Trevor and I have been talking about it. We have been comparing notes, and I think we have found out what your idea is. Now, Frank, you must not pale and red like that, or I will have to leave off."

"I will be calm — indeed, I will. Go on."

"We both thought that it might do you good to talk to you freely, and we want to know if our idea is correct. Mrs. Trevor thought it better that I should speak to you than she should."

"What is the idea?"

Hitherto, although she had manifested considerable emotion, her voice had been full and clear, but she answered this last question very faintly, and with much hesitation.

"You are attached to me, and you are afraid I — I don't love you."

Here her voice was checked by a rush of tears, and she turned her head away.

"Diana," said I, "dear Diana," and I held out my arms with what strength I had.

The color rushed over her face and neck, and then she turned, and with a convulsive sigh laid her head upon my shoulder. One weak arm fell round her waist, and my other hand rested on her head. I said nothing. I could not speak, but I felt the beating of her heart against mine, and thought that if I died then I must be happy forever, if there be memory in the other world.

For a long, long, blissful time she kept her place, and gradually our hearts ceased to beat so violently, and we became calm.

Such was the confession of our love. No plighted faith, no passionate vows, but the silence and the thrill of sympathy through our hearts were sweeter than words could be.

Diana raised her head and looked fearlessly but appealingly into my eyes as she asked me –

"Oh, Frank, did I do right to speak? Could it have been better if I had waited?"

She saw my wishes in my eyes, and bent down her head to me. I kissed her on the forehead and fervently prayed, "Thank God that all was as it has been. May He bless my own darling wife forever and ever."

"Amen," said a sweet, tender voice.

We both looked up without shame, for we knew the tones of my second mother. Her face, streaming with tears of joy, was lit up by a sudden ray of sunlight through the casement.

www.ingramcontent.com/pod-product-compliance
Lightning Source LLC
Chambersburg PA
CBHW032146020726
47496CB00003B/739